"What will people think about Cottonwood's most eligible bachelor tromping around the wilderness with someone like me?"

"I don't know, that I'm a lucky guy?" he answered. Why did she have such a dim view of herself? As far as he could tell, Kenna was a rare gem that dazzled, but everyone in this town seemed to be blind to that. But not him. "On second thought, how about dinner?"

She wanted to say yes, he could feel it, but something held her back. Was it him?

Kenna swallowed, and her eyes watered, which was the opposite reaction he'd been going for. He started to apologize, but she stopped him. "No, it's not you. It's me. Can I be honest with you?"

"Of course."

"It's embarrassing to admit, but it seems I have some unhealthy patterns, which I'm trying to change, but I can't do that if I keep falling into the same rut."

"May I ask what that rut is?" he asked, intrigued by her honesty and a little wary. He was trying to stop making the same mistakes, too.

"Falling in love with the wrong people."

Dear Reader,

I had such a wonderful time writing Kenna and Lucas's story. It was a change for me to write a character with a sweet soul like Kenna, but I truly enjoyed her soft strength in the face of terrible adversity. Strength comes in many forms and sometimes it's not found in brawn but in the spirit. My heart goes out to every person who has found their strength through terrible circumstances and come out the other side, safe and ready to heal.

No one is perfect, but Lucas came pretty close.

Hearing from readers is a special joy. You can always find me on social media or you can always email me.

Facebook: Facebook.com/kim.vanmeter.37

Email: alexandria2772@hotmail.com

Happy reading!

Kimberly

HER K-9 PROTECTOR

Kimberly Van Meter

HARLEQUIN®

ROMANTIC SUSPENSE™

Recycling programs
for this product may
not exist in your area.

ISBN-13: 978-1-335-73833-2

Her K-9 Protector

Copyright © 2023 by Kimberly Sheetz

For questions and comments about the quality of this book,
please contact us at CustomerService@Harlequin.com.

Harlequin Enterprises ULC
22 Adelaide St. West, 41st Floor
Toronto, Ontario M5H 4E3, Canada
www.Harlequin.com

Printed in U.S.A.

Kimberly Van Meter wrote her first book at sixteen and finally achieved publication in December 2006. She has written for the Harlequin Superromance, Blaze and Romantic Suspense lines. She and her husband of thirty years have three children, two cats, and always a houseful of friends, family and fun.

Books by Kimberly Van Meter

Harlequin Romantic Suspense

Big Sky Justice

Danger in Big Sky Country
Her K-9 Protector

The Coltons of Kansas

Colton's Amnesia Target

Military Precision Heroes

Soldier for Hire
Soldier Protector

The Sniper
The Agent's Surrender
Moving Target
Deep Cover
The Killer You Know

Visit the Author Profile page at Harlequin.com for more titles.

Chapter 1

"Kenna, can you put Noble and Officer Merritt into Room Two?"

Without looking, Kenna Griffin finished filing and rose with a ready smile—only to stop short at the man waiting in the lobby with the impeccably trained German shepherd. Noble didn't react to anything but his partner's cues, despite a yapping poodle and a skittish cocker spaniel.

And his partner stole Kenna's breath.

Kenna vaguely remembered something her sister had mentioned over dinner about the new K-9 officer hired through an extension grant that saved the program from being axed. Still, she hadn't mentioned the man being good-looking as hell.

Not too tall but tall enough, a solid build that tapered to lean hips and a full head of dark hair that looked as if given half the chance, it would spring into a riot of stubborn curls—Officer Merritt was eye candy to a female population with a sweet tooth.

Which, for Kenna, was a big red flag flapping in front of her.

Although a tough pill to swallow, Kenna had finally accepted the bitter truth about her internal compass—when it came to picking good guys, the damn thing was broken.

And she'd made a vow to herself that men were out of the picture until she could get herself figured out. She owed that much to her son, Ty, who'd been through the wringer right alongside her, and she was determined to make better choices.

Especially after the last guy. An involuntary shudder passed through Kenna. *You're safe. He can't find you. Stay focused. Everything is fine.*

"Kenna?" Isabel's inquiry punctured Kenna's stall. She recovered with an even brighter smile, even if it was more fake than a three-dollar bill. She'd only just gotten this job at the veterinary office. She wasn't about to blow it over something as stupid as a momentary glitch in her hormonal brain.

"Sorry, yes, absolutely," she said, motioning to the officer and his K-9 partner, "if you'll follow me."

Once inside the exam room, she pulled the chart to take notes for Dr. Mallory. "And what brings you here today?"

"I think Noble might've tweaked his paw running after a perp the other night. He seems to be favoring it a bit. I wanted to get him checked out, just to be sure."

Kenna, always a sucker for an animal in need, softened at the mention of a perceived injury. "Poor guy. Did he catch his suspect?"

"He did," Officer Merritt answered with pride, his

brown eyes lighting up as his mouth curved in a grin. "The perp will likely think twice about trying to outrun a working police dog like Noble. His teeth are as fast as his feet."

Kenna forgot and smiled with genuine delight but cocked her head, recalling, "I thought it wasn't PC to have dogs biting people anymore, even if they're criminals."

"There are two kinds of K-9 training—bite and bark. The dogs trained to bite will apprehend the suspect with their teeth on an arm or a leg. The bark dog is trained to alert the officer of the location of the perp without contact. Noble is a bite dog. Much more effective, if you ask me, but yeah, some departments are reluctant to take on the liability of a bite-trained K-9 and opt for the bark."

Kenna wished someone had sicced their police dog on her ex the last time he put her in the hospital. *Stop it. Don't go there. Let the past die.* "Well, he's beautiful, and I hope his paw is okay. The doctor will be in shortly."

But before she could leave, the officer said, "I'm new to town, so I haven't met everyone yet. What's your name?"

No personal details. The knee-jerk reaction was part of her new playbook, but he worked with her sister at the police station, and they were bound to run into each other again when the town was impossibly small. "Kenna Griffin," she answered, knowing it wouldn't take long for the light of recognition to dawn.

"Griffin? Any relation to Detective Luna Griffin?" he asked.

"She's my older sister," Kenna confirmed with a short smile, taking that as her cue to exit gracefully, but he was too quick.

"Like I said, I'm new to town. Lucas Merritt," he said with a good-natured grin that seemed too wholesome for someone like her. If he only knew the skeletons in her closet, he might not be so eager to get to know her. "Originally from Kansas, but don't hold that against me. I'm already loving Montana."

"Welcome to Cottonwood," she murmured with a short smile, relieved as Dr. Mallory rounded the corner so she could make a quick exit. But she added, "Nice to meet you," and then practically ran back to the front desk.

Isabel, her coworker, finished checking in a tabby cat with a torn ear and a sour disposition, then turned to Kenna, eager to gossip and trade notes about the newest Cottonwood resident.

"It isn't every day a man like that walks into town. I could drown in those eyes," Isabel said with a sigh. "Mmm, men like him are a reminder that God does, in fact, have favorites."

"I didn't notice," Kenna lied with an airy smile, returning to her filing even as her heart pounded against her rib cage. "He's probably married, though."

Please be married.

"He's not," Isabel returned with a certainty that spoke of research behind the scenes. "Lucas Merritt became Cottonwood's most eligible bachelor the minute he stepped into town. I wish he were a little bit taller, though. Then he'd be almost perfect."

Kenna frowned. "He's tall," she said. "I mean, he seems tall enough."

Isabel mentally sized Lucas up from memory. "Hmm, I'd say probably about five-ten. I like guys who are at least six foot."

Kenna paused, glancing over at Isabel with mild confusion. "You're barely five foot two. Why would you want someone so much taller than you?"

Isabel shivered with a slight grin. "Just feels more masculine when they're towering over you. Not that I don't enjoy a short king. I'm just saying, if I'm looking to settle down, I want my future baby daddy to have some height to pass on to the kids."

Isabel was younger than Kenna, and conversations like this were a stark reminder of that age gap. Life had taught Kenna that a man's height didn't make him a good person. "Well, sounds like a permanent crick in the neck when they're too tall," she said, eager to change the subject. "I'm going to do a quick check on the spayed pit mix. Watch the front for me?"

"I could check the pit if you want," Isabel offered, gesturing toward exam room two, but that was exactly why Kenna didn't want to be around. Let Isabel drool over Cottonwood's newest eligible bachelor. Kenna didn't want anything to do with a man like him.

Or any man, for that matter.

It was safer that way.

Lucas Merritt listened with half an ear to Dr. Mallory as she examined Noble's paw, a bit too distracted by the exotic woman who'd nearly blown him over at first glance. Common sense told him getting hooked by the first beautiful woman he saw in his new environment was a bad idea. He'd put it into his head that he'd stay single for a year while he got his bearings in his new town. Seemed like a solid plan at the time, but how was he supposed to hold himself to that plan when a woman like Kenna Griffin waltzed into his life? Those high cheekbones were sharp enough to cut glass, but those dark eyes were like those of a doe, wild and untamed yet gentle.

She had the kind of face men in history books went to war over.

He wasn't the poetic type, but the flutters in his gut weren't from the burrito he'd eaten earlier. The last time he'd felt this kind of jolt, he'd fallen head over heels for the devil's concubine, who'd nearly destroyed his life. Not a great endorsement for the flutters, which was why he'd made the plan to stay single until the dust settled on his move. He'd spent a long time reading up on repeating patterns and whatnot, and he was determined to avoid that trap like a bad haircut.

Besides, he didn't leave all that behind in Kansas only to play the sequel in Montana.

Fresh starts required discipline.

And yet, he wanted to know more about the brunette with the shy smile.

Dr. Mallory interrupted his thoughts with her decision. "I think Noble is fine, but we should do an X-ray to be sure." She jotted down her notes with quick efficiency. "The department has set up an account for Noble, so we can get started if you're available."

"Yes, ma'am," he said, dragging his attention back to the moment. "I thought maybe he bruised his pad or something, but I didn't want to take any chances."

"Better to be safe than sorry," Dr. Mallory agreed with a nod, moving to click a temporary leash onto Noble's collar. "It'll be a few minutes. You can wait in the lobby if you want."

"Yep," he said, eager to talk to Kenna again, but he saw Kenna was gone as he exited the room. His enthusiasm dimmed, but the strawberry blonde smiled his way as if knowing immediately that Kenna had caught his eye and she was eager to share information.

"She's checking on another patient," the woman said with a quick grin, "but she should be back in a few minutes. I'm Isabel Donahue. So, you're the new K-9 officer. What do you think of Cottonwood so far?"

"Beautiful town," he answered, trying not to appear preoccupied with Kenna returning. "And the people are friendly." Isabel gave off a *real* friendly vibe, but even though she was cute as a button, no fireworks went off in his head as they had with Kenna.

"Some are," she acknowledged with a wink, "but then, it's not hard being sweet to someone as cute as you."

He felt the heat crawl up his cheeks at the bold compliment. "I don't know about that, but I'm happy to be here. The department has been real accommodating." He paused a minute, wondering if he ought to leave well enough alone, but he couldn't quite help himself and asked anyway. "So, uh, your coworker, Kenna—is she, um, single?"

"Good gravy, there's not a hint of shyness in you, is there? Most guys beat around the bush before getting to the real point of their interest. Kinda refreshing to meet someone who knows what they want."

"I'm just curious, is all. Nothing serious."

"Nothing wrong with being a little curious," Isabel said. "But one thing you should know right off the bat with Kenna is she's a single mom, so she's not really looking for anything new, from what I can tell. But to be honest, Kenna is kinda private, so it's hard to really know. I only just met her a few weeks ago when she started here at the office. I guess she grew up here in Cottonwood, though."

Single mom—definitely on his red flag checklist—but applied to Kenna, he wasn't as put off as he thought he would be. He acknowledged that information with a short nod. "Copy that."

"I, however, am single as a Pringle and definitely no one's mom," Isabel supplied with a flirty grin. "I'd be happy to show you around town, introduce you to a few people, if you want."

Not gonna touch that with a ten-foot pole. Isabel looked like a fun time, but fun times turned into nightmares when things didn't go their way, and drama was the last thing he wanted to court in his new town.

"I appreciate the offer," he said, not wanting to hurt Isabel's feelings. Meaningless hookups weren't his style, and he wasn't about to start now, but there was more to his plan to stay single than just an aversion to hookups. His last emotional ride had been enough to turn a man celibate, and he was determined to shake off the residue of that life. Hell, he didn't know how or when he'd be ready to trust another human being with his heart after Becca, so no sense in dragging someone along for a ride that ended up nowhere. Better to keep to himself than hurt feelings because his head was all messed up, but he wouldn't be rude, either. He smiled, adding, "When I get settled, maybe I'll do that."

"I hope you do." She grabbed a business card and scribbled her number on the back. "That's my cell. If you find yourself all alone, bored and ready to have some fun, call me."

He pocketed the card, even though he knew he wouldn't call. "You got it."

Before Isabel could say more, Dr. Mallory returned with good news, unsnapping Noble's leash. "Noble is just fine. Picture of health. I think you were right on the money—he's got a little bit of a bruised paw, but a few days of rest and he should be right as rain."

Noble dutifully returned to Lucas's side, looking at him with that alert gaze, ready for his following command. Relieved, Lucas said, "Thank you, Dr. Mallory. Good to hear." He resisted the urge to linger, hoping that Kenna might reappear. "I appreciate you squeezing us in today."

"Of course. We're happy to accommodate our newest Cottonwood officer," Dr. Mallory said with a wink and indulgent smile directed at Noble before leaving to see her next patient.

Still no Kenna. Where'd she go? The moon?

No, this was a good thing—a reminder that the last thing he needed was to get involved with a single mom who was skittish as hell.

Usually, they had their reasons.

And their reasons were all sorts of trouble he didn't need.

Chapter 2

"*You're mine. When you going to get that simple fact through that thick skull of yours?*"

Kenna awoke with a cry, clapping her hand over her mouth on instinct so no more sound escaped. Her heart thundered like a wild thing against her chest as she took a minute to orient herself. She gulped down the golf ball–size lump lodged in her throat, realizing she was home, far away from him and safe.

The familiar silhouette of her childhood room soothed the panic terrorizing her heart even as darkness blanketed around her. She reached for her cell phone charging on the nightstand and drew a deep breath as the dim screen light chased away the inky dark.

Before Leon, she'd never been afraid of the dark. Now, the shadows felt menacing, as if he somehow lurked and waited for his opportunity to slit her throat when she let her guard down.

She smoothed the flyaways from her face with trembling fingers. Her head throbbed with phantom pain as if his fingers were still clutched in her hair, yanking it free from the root. How had she ever thought he was anything but a monster? How had she been so stupid? So blind? She'd naively ignored the red flags, and it'd landed her in the hospital.

"Is this seat taken?"

The memory of that first encounter at the bar was a moment she'd wished she could take back a million times.

She rubbed at the tender scar at the back of her skull where a hairline fracture was still healing from when he threw her across the room and she'd smashed her head into a marble statue.

"Can I say you are the most captivating creature I've ever laid eyes upon?"

A shudder coursed through her, her skin crawling at the memory. Tears of rage and helplessness threatened, but she sniffed them back. *Don't live in the past. It's finally over. He won't find me. We're safe.*

But nothing felt safe anymore. Kenna drew the blanket closer to her neck, like she had as a kid—as if a handmade quilt could protect her from the real monsters of the world.

Running home had been her only option, but not even this old house, where all her happy childhood memories were created, had protected any of them from the evil bastard who'd invaded their home and killed her father a few months ago.

It was hard to stop playing that night over and over again in her head, a hellish movie clip that fit seamlessly in the nightmare she'd been living before running back to Cottonwood.

Never in a million years would she have guessed that her sweet father would've been shot and killed in her childhood home. Home had always been a sanctuary. And now? Everything felt wrong. Even if her father had lived, the burden of her secret contaminated everything.

She couldn't bear for her sisters to know the truth. Oh God, the disappointment—and the possible judgment—was enough to cripple her for life.

Nope, that's why I'll take this secret to the grave. End of story.

Crap. No chance for more sleep. Wide-awake, she threw the blankets free and padded quietly to the kitchen. It was too early for the house to be up, but Kenna wasn't falling back asleep, and she couldn't stand the noise in her head. *Perfect time for cinnamon cream-cheese muffins.* After putting on a pot of coffee, she started pulling the ingredients for Ty's favorite.

Baking was her feel-good place. When nothing made sense, a recipe for something sweet and delicious made everything right again, even if it was only temporary. The tantalizing aroma of something in the oven reminded her of Nancy, her sweet adoptive mother, who always had a kind word for everyone and did her best to provide a good life for three little girls who weren't her own but whom she loved as if they were. Nancy and Bill had adopted Kenna and her sisters when they were small after their biological parents were killed in an explosion on the Macawi Reservation. As the middle sister, she was too little then to remember much about life with her biological parents, but her older sister, Luna, remembered more, and from what she'd shared, life had been hard. Poverty was an unwelcome presence on the reservation but well-known and hard to escape.

But even as much as Nancy had loved them, Kenna

couldn't shake the sadness that always lurked in the back of her heart, a lingering black cloud that hovered no matter where she went, threatening to chase away her happiness with the sudden appearance of rain.

Her sisters, Luna and Sayeh, had recently discovered disturbing details from their early childhood that only deepened her confusion about a past she didn't quite remember but made her wonder if untangling the knots might help her heal.

Luna loved pushing the therapy angle, as if the answer to all their problems could be found in a therapist's office, but Kenna preferred to keep her hurts private.

It wasn't that she didn't believe that healing the past was the key to building a better future, but the idea of sharing her deepest shame with anyone made her want to crawl into a cave and die.

She wanted to change her terrible track record with relationships. The last one was enough to scare her away from men forever, but she wanted Ty to know what it was like to have at least one decent father figure in his life.

But how could she possibly trust someone enough to let that happen? The circular problem didn't have an answer.

Kenna couldn't bear the thought that her son was permanently damaged from all the bullshit she'd dragged him through.

And now, he had the additional trauma of watching his grandfather die right in front of him.

Hell, if she was struggling with how to heal from that, how could she expect her son to figure out how to do it?

It felt hopeless.

The obvious answer—according to Luna—was that

Ty might benefit from therapy, but how could she let her son talk to a therapist when he might inadvertently reveal what'd happened in Kentucky? A therapist was a mandatory reporter—they'd be obligated to take Ty from her.

Fear raced through her veins at the thought of losing her son.

No, it was better that they handle this together, on their own. All they needed was time to heal, to start fresh.

She was sure of it. The scent of warm cinnamon wafted through the kitchen, bathing her senses in security and assuring her that everything would eventually be okay.

Because how could anything be wrong when it smelled this good?

A smile found her as the timer went off.

Her sister Luna appeared, dressed for the day even though the dawn had only crested the horizon. She closed her eyes with a nostalgic inhale. "Reminds me of Mom," she said, going for the coffeepot and pouring a mug. "I'd forgotten how much you love to bake. A skill set I definitely didn't inherit, but I'm glad one of us did."

"Mom's cinnamon cream-cheese muffins are Ty's favorite," Kenna murmured from above her coffee mug. "I thought it might be good to start the day off with something sweet."

"No complaints from me," Luna said, reaching for a hot muffin, adding as she sat at the table, "I heard you met our newest officer, Lucas."

His name set off warning butterflies, but Kenna shrugged as if unaffected. "Oh yeah, he brought in his dog, Noble. What a beautiful dog. It's nice that the department got the grant. Everyone loves a K-9 officer."

"Definitely. It's a three-year grant, which means there's no guarantees that the grant will be extended after the end of the term, but I guess we'll cross that bridge when we come to it."

"What happens if the grant expires and the department can't afford to take on the expense?" she asked.

"Then the program will be dissolved and either Lucas will be absorbed into a regular position or he'll be let go," Luna explained, sipping her coffee. "But that's a long ways off, and a lot can happen between now and then."

The realization that Lucas's position could be relatively short-term made her relax. She didn't have to worry about developing feelings for someone who wouldn't be around. Somehow that made her attraction to him less threatening. She was not looking to act on her attraction, but it helped ease her anxiety.

"He seems nice," she said, leaving it at that.

"I was planning to introduce you two but seems fate took care of that for me."

"Why?" she asked, the word coming out slightly sharp.

Luna shrugged. "Because you're around the same age and he's an actual good guy. I like him. After everything you've been through, I thought a good man might be a refreshing change."

Kenna tried not to bristle. She didn't need her sister reminding her at every turn how bad her compass was when it came to men. "Well, I'm not interested in dating right now. I've got my hands full restarting my life from scratch," she said, going to pull the muffins from the tin and placing them on a serving platter, because she needed to do something. "Besides, the last thing Ty needs is me dating."

"Actually, I'm glad you brought up Ty," Luna admitted, pursing her lips. "I know you don't want to talk about it, but I think Ty really needs some help right now."

"He's fine."

"He's not."

"I think I know what my son needs," Kenna said quietly. "I hate to point out the obvious, but you're not a mother. Forgive me if I'm not keen to take advice from someone who's never done the job."

"Okay, fair point, but *I* hate to point out the obvious—you haven't really done a bang-up job yourself."

She didn't want to fight this early, not after that hellish nightmare. Throttling down the urge to spit back in defense, Kenna forced herself to calm down and try a different approach. "I appreciate what you're saying, but I'm trying to change everything. The last thing I need is a distraction, okay?"

That seemed to make sense to Luna. Nodding, she accepted Kenna's answer. "Well," she said, wiping her hands and finishing her coffee, "I gotta run. If you change your mind, let me know. I think he likes you."

And then Luna was out the door.

No, she told herself. *No butterflies allowed.*

Kenna had learned the hard way that no such thing as a nice guy existed. Eventually, they all wanted something, and when you couldn't—or wouldn't—deliver, they dropped the mask and revealed the monster.

"It wasn't me!"

The kid twisting in his grip was a slippery thing, scowling as if Lucas was the devil when he'd been caught red-handed with the spray paint in his hand. "Settle down and stop wiggling like a worm on a hook. I saw you with the paint, okay?"

The boy, wiry with a mop of dark blond hair, tried yanking himself free and running, but Lucas knew a thing or two about angry young boys with a chip on their shoulder and anticipated the move. "Look, if you're not going to listen, we'll do this hard way," he said, grabbing his zip ties to subdue the kid quickly. He radioed dispatch for backup, because he couldn't transport the kid with Noble in the back seat. "Might as well chill out a minute while we're waiting for your ride, kid, because you're not going nowhere."

"You're arresting me?" the kid asked incredulously. "Do you know who my aunt is?"

"Should I?"

"If you like your job," the kid shot back smugly. "My aunt is Detective Luna Griffin, and she'll have you fired for arresting me like this when I didn't do nothing."

"The wall with your artwork might disagree," Lucas said dryly, but his mind was working fast. This brat's aunt was Luna Griffin. Did that mean his mom was Kenna Griffin? He rubbed at his forehead, hoping against hope that Luna had another sister who was a single mom and this little delinquent wasn't Kenna's. "School just started. Why aren't you in class? What's your name?"

"I'm not supposed to talk to strangers," the kid shot back with a short smirk.

"Yeah. That's a good rule. There's also a great rule about not defacing public property, but you breezed past that one, so it seems you like to pick and choose what you follow. Your mom gonna be cool with your little art project?"

At the mention of his mom, a flicker of guilt passed over the boy's features, but he rebounded quickly with a shrug. "She'll get over it. She always does."

"What does that mean?"

"It means I want a lawyer."

"Jeez, kid, you've seen too many movies." Lucas resisted the urge to laugh. The boy was all piss and vinegar. Reminded him of someone from a long time ago. "You know, I'm going to find out your name sooner or later, but it's faster if you tell me. End the suspense." But the kid wasn't interested in making Lucas's life any easier. He sighed. "Fine. Have it your way. Your ride will be here in a few minutes, anyway. We can sit here in uncomfortable silence while we wait."

"You could just let me go," the kid suggested, as if that were the best option. "I mean, the paperwork is probably a pain in the ass, right? Especially when it's just a misdemeanor offense and I'm just going to get probation because the system is overloaded. Why don't you do us both a favor and forget it happened?"

"Real slick, kid, but that's not how these things work," he said. "You did the crime, I caught you doing the crime, paperwork is part of the job and it'll be up to a judge to figure out how you'll do the time."

"Whatever."

"So, just curious, is a life of crime your highest aspiration or is this just a phase?"

"What are you talking about?"

"Just wondering if you're planning to escalate your criminal activity or if this is your ceiling."

"That's a weird, stupid question."

"Not so weird or stupid." He gestured to Noble, waiting patiently in the squad car. "You see that dog? That's Noble. He's my partner. He likes to chew on criminals.

Just wondering if you've ever had seventy-five-pounds of pure muscle use your femur for a chew toy. It hurts. A lot. That's what he did to the last criminal that thought he was smarter—and faster—than my partner. News flash, he wasn't, and the nasty bite on the perp's leg is evidence of his stupid choice. So, I'll ask again, you plan on escalating or is this your ceiling of criminal activity?"

But the kid didn't get a chance to answer. Wes Standford rolled up on the scene and immediately frowned when he saw the kid. "Aww, c'mon Ty, what are you doing now?" he asked, disappointed. "Your mom's gonna be so worried."

"Ty? That's his name?"

"Yeah, Tyler Anthony Griffin, age ten, just moved to Cottonwood from Kentucky with his mom, and this is the second time he's been picked up for acting stupid."

"That's my personal information! You can't just share that stuff without my consent," Ty shouted above Wes, glaring like the mutinous little hellion he appeared to be. *Poor Kenna.* Kids like Ty were a great advertisement for birth control.

Lucas ignored Ty's barking. "Second time, huh?" He shot the kid a derisive look. "Seems he's not big on learning his lesson. Is he mentally challenged or something?"

"Hey!"

Lucas smothered the grin, knowing he'd hit a nerve with the smart-mouthed kid. He knew how kids like him operated, how their brains worked. His little brother had been an excellent teacher.

Wes sighed with chagrin, admitting, "Naw, we didn't write him up the first time. Seemed like the wrong thing to do, seeing as he just lost his grandpa and everything." Wes helped Ty into the squad car and closed the door securely behind him. "But looks like this time he's going to have to go into the books. What a shame. I know it's hard to imagine it right now, but he's a good kid. Just a little lost at the moment."

Lucas had only just met Wes, but he could see the guy had a good, kind heart. Maybe even a little too soft for a career in law enforcement, but that was for Wes to figure out.

He ought to leave it alone, but curiosity got the better of him. "What happened to his grandpa?"

"I shouldn't say but it's all in the report, so I guess I'm not doing anything outside the lines. His grandpa was murdered right in front of him."

"Murdered?" Lucas repeated, surprised. "What happened?"

"It was terrible. An intruder broke into the Griffin house and held them all at gunpoint. The situation escalated and Bill, a retired officer, got shot trying to save his family. The only saving grace was that he died almost instantly. Anyway, we've all been trying to be a little understanding, you know? But… I don't know, maybe the kid needs to get his hand slapped before he'll learn. See you back at the station."

Lucas watched as Wes drove off with the troubled young Griffin. *Not your problem. Let it go.* But there was a time he'd been that pissed-off kid, punishing the world for the hurts he'd acquired through no fault of his own, and it took someone else caring to put him on the right path. Hell, he and his brother were a hot mess for a long time until he got himself straight, but his brother never climbed out.

He winced at the familiar pain that never failed to

punch him in the gut every time he let thoughts of Brock knock on his memory.

Can't save everyone.

When would he learn that every broken person that crossed his path wasn't his responsibility to fix?

Ty Griffin was going to have to figure things out without his help.

Good luck, kid.

Chapter 3

Kenna hurried into the police station, shocked that Ty had been picked up for vandalism. There had to be a mistake. Ty wasn't a vandalizer. He was the kid who always went out of his way to pick up any bits of trash he found. The son she'd raised would never willfully deface public property. What was happening to her sweet boy? He'd gone from gentle and caring to sulky and rude in weeks, with each week getting progressively worse than the last.

Tears burned beneath her lids as panic threatened to steal her ability to remain calm. *C'mon, Ty, work with me!*

Another officer brought Kenna into the interrogation room, where Luna was trying to talk with Ty, but he wasn't cooperating, and her frustration started to show.

"Buddy, you understand what you did was wrong, right?" Luna said, peering at her nephew with confusion as Kenna walked in. That early-morning conversation about Kenna not doing a *bang-up job* as a mother came back to slap Kenna. This situation wasn't exactly a point in Kenna's parenting column.

Kenna shifted her gaze away from Luna and to Ty, only to gasp when she saw Ty in restraints, like he was about to go on a murder spree and a danger to everyone around him.

She gestured emphatically. "Do you really think that's necessary? He's not a flight risk, for God's sake. He's just a kid."

"Yeah, I'm just a kid," Ty agreed, looking to Kenna to rescue him. "Mom, these really hurt."

Her heart contracted, and she had to swallow the immediate lump in her throat. "Luna? Please."

But Luna wasn't moved. "It's procedure," Luna replied, as if it couldn't be helped, when Kenna knew damn well that wasn't true. Luna was proving a point, and Kenna didn't appreciate it.

"This is going too far," Kenna warned in a brittle tone. "What are you trying to do? Scar him for life? Don't you think he's been through enough? He's your goddamn nephew, for crying out loud, and you know exactly what he's been through. A little compassion wouldn't be out of line."

Luna knew Kenna was referring to the recent horrific death of their father, but Luna didn't budge. Sometimes Kenna wondered if her older sister had a stone heart.

"He was caught red-handed defacing public property. I can't keep giving him special treatment," Luna said in a low tone. "Everyone has been really understanding up to this point, Kenna. We have to charge him."

"Charge him?" Kenna was appalled. "He's a ten-year-old boy."

"Yeah, a boy who's determined to self-destruct. There have to be consequences."

"I'll ground him," Kenna said, trying to negotiate. "I'll pay for the damage—"

"*He* needs to pay for the damage, not you," a voice cut in behind her. She whirled on her heel, ready to shred whoever dared to give her parenting advice, and stopped short when she saw Lucas Merritt. He gestured to her sullen child. "Trust me when I say he's not going to learn unless you make him face a real consequence for his actions. Make him pay for the damage."

"A ten-year-old can't get a job, genius," Ty muttered.

"Tyler! Enough out of you," Kenna snapped, privately mortified by Ty's attitude. Would it kill him to show even a little remorse? It seemed he purposely was trying to make it harder for her to help him. But Ty did have a point. "He doesn't have any money. What am I supposed to do? Put him on a chain gang?"

"Nothing so dramatic, but mowing lawns never hurt anyone, and it builds character," Lucas answered. "Sometimes a good sweat is the best way to work out some personal demons."

"He has school," Kenna said, looking to Luna for help, but her sister seemed to agree with Lucas. *Of course she did.* Luna was going to push the therapy angle again, no doubt. Her son didn't need therapy—he needed time to figure stuff out. She maintained stubbornly, "School needs to be his priority."

"I agree, but seeing as I caught him defacing public property while *not at school where he should've been*, it's easy to see where his priorities are right now."

Frustration burned in her, because she couldn't argue

the point. *Damn it, Ty.* She looked to Luna, but her sister was already excusing herself. "This is Lucas's case, so I'll leave you to it. It's best I stay out of it, anyway, so no one can claim a conflict of interest."

Kenna glared at her retreating sister's backside before returning to Lucas. If Luna thought this conversation was over, she had another think coming, but Kenna wasn't going to argue about personal issues in front of a stranger. She returned to Lucas, asking stiffly, "Okay, so what happens next?"

When Ty realized his aunt really wasn't going to bail him out, his demeanor changed. He looked to Kenna with apprehension. "Mom, am I going to jail?" The tiny tremor in his voice was her undoing. Ty tried to put a brave face on the situation, but he was scared. She recognized the signs, and it made her shake with fury.

"Of course not," she assured Ty, looking to Lucas. "Can I speak to you privately, please?"

Lucas nodded and gestured for her to follow. They exited the room, and Kenna launched into Lucas. "Have you no empathy? My son has been through hell and back. He needs compassion, not punishment. I'm sure you've heard by now that my father was killed a few months ago and that Ty saw it all. You can't imagine what that's done to him. Normally, he's a really sweet kid, but he's going through something, and I don't want to make it worse by punishing him when what he really needs is kindness."

"He is going through something—something that won't magically get better if he doesn't learn the lesson now," Lucas said, disregarding her plea. Kenna recoiled. How had she thought he was handsome? As with most men, he was cold and cruel when it suited him—a lesson the universe seemed happy to pound into her head at every turn. "The court will likely order therapy—"

"No!"

He narrowed his gaze at her vehement reaction, and she cursed herself for being so damn transparent with her emotions. She swallowed, stammering, "I—I don't trust court-appointed therapists. I haven't had the best experiences, and I don't want my son to go through the same."

His gaze softened. "I understand, but the court has a protocol for first-time juvenile offenders, and it includes therapy, probation and community service. But the upside is kids usually respond well to intervention at this age."

No! No! No! No one understood their situation or what they'd been through. Tears burned beneath her eyelids. She couldn't save Ty from this situation, and it felt like her fault for failing him again. She nodded numbly, holding back her tears with everything she had. She refused to let Lucas see her cry. "Can I talk to my son, please?" she asked, holding a stiff upper lip.

"Sure," he said. "I'll wait out here."

"Thank you."

Lucas opened the door and closed it behind her. Ty looked so small and young in that metal chair, restrained like a feral animal, locked in a gray box of a room. How had they come to this? She sat opposite her son to explain what was going to happen. "Ty, you broke the law, and they have to charge you."

"But Mom, I didn't do anything!"

Kenna looked at Ty with distress, so disappointed. "Ty, c'mon buddy, you were caught red-handed. The spray paint was in your hand."

"I swear to you, I didn't! That cop is lying!"

Tears burned beneath her eyes again. Her son was

lying to her face. They'd always been so close. It'd always been Kenna and Ty against the world, and now her world was crumbling because Ty was turning into a kid she didn't know. She swallowed the lump in her throat and tried again. "Buddy, here's the deal. As a first-time offender, you're likely going to get court-ordered therapy, probation and community service, but if you keep doing stuff like this, the consequences will escalate. Do you understand what that means?"

Ty shook his head, his eyes brimming with angry tears. "So you believe that cop over me?"

"Tyler Anthony, I would never, but you're lying right now," Kenna said, her heart breaking. "Just admit that you were caught vandalizing the building wall and let's work to put this behind us."

"Whatever."

She wasn't getting anywhere. Ty was angry and hurt. They'd have to try and deal with his feelings about the situation later.

The door opened, and Lucas returned. She acknowledged him, asking, "When can he be released?"

"I need a few minutes to get his statement and charge him, and then I can release him into your custody."

Another officer appeared and took her to the room behind the interrogation room so she could watch but not interfere.

Never in a million years would she ever imagine that she'd be watching her son from behind a pane of two-way glass in a police station.

Congrats, Kenna, you've completely failed at being a parent.

Lucas saw the anguish in Kenna's eyes at her son's attitude. She seemed bewildered and genuinely lost at her son's behavior. Pain without an outlet curdled good kids—it was fixable if you soon caught the rot, but could she do what was necessary to really help turn things around? Lucas wasn't made of stone; he didn't like to see any kid go sour, but he also knew some people didn't have what it took to change. He didn't know Kenna or her kid, but a part of him wanted things to work out for them.

Don't get involved, a voice warned, but something tugged at him, whispering not to turn away. It was probably the worst advice he'd ever gotten from that little voice in his head, but the pull was too strong to ignore.

Lucas sighed, snipping the zip ties free. Ty rubbed at his reddened wrists with a scowl toward Lucas hard enough to feel in his gut. Then, pulling the paperwork free, he started the formal process. "Okay, start at the beginning. Don't waste time lying about anything. Neither of us wants to spend more time than we need to on paperwork. Plus, your mom looks like she's about to cry her eyes out. Let's not make this harder on her than it needs to be."

"Oh, now you care about my mom?" Ty said with enough acid to burn through concrete. His gaze was older than a ten-year-old boy's should be. Damn, what had this kid been through? "That's how it starts. They all want to help at first, but that changes real quick."

"They who?" Lucas eyed the boy. "Your mom have a bad boyfriend or something?"

Ty refused to answer at first, as if ingrained loyalty to his mom buttoned his lip, but then he spat, "Yeah, something like that."

"Is he still around?" Lucas asked carefully.

"No."

That was something of a relief. "Is he your dad?"

"Hell no," Ty answered with a curled lip. "I ain't got

no dad—and I don't need one," he added pointedly, as if he thought Lucas was angling for the gig, which he was not.

"Glad we got that sorted. Back to the vandalism. Where'd you get the spray paint?"

"My grandpa's garage."

Something clicked. Sometimes when people acted out from grief, it took odd forms. "You miss your grandpa?"

Ty shrugged as if he didn't care, but his eyes welled up.

That was grief without an outlet, but there was something else in there, too. *Something deeper.* "I didn't know your grandpa, but word around the station was that he was a real good guy. I'm sorry he died the way he did."

Ty sniffed, accepting Lucas's condolences without a caustic quip, which was a good sign.

"Were you close?"

"Yeah, I guess. He was teaching me to drive a stick shift. He didn't get the chance to finish."

Lucas's heart contracted at the raw sorrow in that simple statement. This poor kid was twisting in on himself, and no one could see how dangerously close to imploding he was. His pain didn't excuse breaking the law, but sometimes things weren't so easily black-and-white, which was something he knew too well.

"Can your mom finish teaching you?"

He growled, "I don't want my mom to teach me."

Anger.

The kid is pissed at his mom for something but feels guilty, too. "Okay, let's put that aside for a minute. Why were you vandalizing the building with your grandpa's spray paint?"

He shrugged. "Seemed more fun than going to school. This town is stupid anyway."

"You liked Kentucky better?"

At the mention of his former home, Ty stiffened. "No, I didn't say that. I just said this place was stupid."

"When bad things happen, we tend to blame the place we're in for the situation, but places aren't bad," Lucas said. "Places are just places."

"Yeah, well, I hate it here."

"Does your mom know how you feel?"

"It wouldn't matter. We don't have nowhere else to go. Mom says we're only safe if—"

Lucas stilled, holding his breath, waiting, but Ty realized his mistake and quickly buttoned up. He tried pushing the boy a little bit. "If your mom's in trouble…"

"It's nothing. We're fine," Ty said quickly, his eyes darting. "Look, I'm sorry I messed up the wall. Can we be done now?"

"A few more questions," he assured Ty, his thoughts circling that one tiny admission. "Are there any other acts of vandalism you're responsible for that we should know about?"

Ty shook his head, and Lucas believed him.

"Okay, I'm going to go out on a limb and trust you're being honest, but if I find out you're lying to me…"

"I swear I'm not."

Lucas nodded, finishing his notes. "I'll get your mom," he said. As he rose, he shared a bit of advice. "Do yourself a favor and stay out of trouble. You only get so many chances to screw up and learn. If you don't learn, the lessons are only going to get harder. Understand?"

"Why do you care?"

Great question. "Let's just say I've been where you're at, and I know what happens when you don't appreciate second chances—and beneath that smart mouth and bad attitude might be a decent kid, but we'll see."

Ty nodded, looking like the scared little kid he was instead of the burgeoning bad seed he'd tried to be when they met.

Maybe that was a good sign.

But he sensed the kid was hiding something bigger than his grief.

And that's what gave him a bad feeling.

Chapter 4

Lucas picked up the phone without checking the caller ID, which was a mistake he realized seconds into the call.

"Lucas?"

Swearing beneath his breath, he resisted the urge to hang up, change his number—and his identity, for that matter—and instead answered with a terse "Becca."

"Don't sound so happy to hear from me," she said with wounded reproach. "It's bad enough the way we left things."

Left, as in no looking back, which made the sound of her voice on the other line the last thing he wanted.

"What do you want?" he asked, cutting straight to the point.

"Maybe you don't feel the same, but I'm so happy to hear your voice again. I thought after our last conversation, you were serious about all that stuff you said and it broke my freaking heart, you know?"

"I did mean what I said," he answered without feeling. No, that's not accurate—when it came to Becca, there was a whole lot of feeling, but none of it good and all of it complicated. He'd left Kansas—and Becca—for a reason, and he didn't much like that one of the two had chased him down. "Spit it out, then. What do you want?"

"Lucas, why are you doing this? Please, you can't mean that. You loved me once, remember? We were all so close. It was me, you and Brock against the world," she said with a sniff as if her heart were truly breaking in half, but Lucas didn't have anything remaining in the tank for Becca. "We used to be so close, and then you up and left. How am I supposed to take that? I mean, what would Brock think about what you're doing? Have you thought about that for once? He loved you. Really loved—we both did. And now you're abandoning me when I need someone the most. That's cold, Lucas. Real cold."

He wasn't going to be lectured by Becca on responsibility. Not when she played fast and loose with the rules when it suited her. "I didn't abandon you, Becca. I tried to help you," he started but realized this was exactly what she wanted—to put him in a defensive position—and stopped. "If you called to try and make me feel bad for finally putting me first, you're wasting your breath. I'm done with Kansas, the past and you."

"Just like that?"

"That's what happens when you squeeze every last drop out of someone and give nothing in return," he said. "You're toxic, Becca. Getting away from you was the smartest thing I ever did. I only wish my brother had figured that out before he died."

"Screw you," she shot back, her breath catching as

if Lucas had slapped her face. It was true, they'd all been close at one time, but bad decisions and circumstances had corroded that connection until nothing but a frayed, torn-up mess remained. "That was a nasty thing to say. I loved your brother, and don't you dare try to say I didn't."

"You loved drugs more."

"I made mistakes," Becca admitted, but she clung to her usual defense. "Brock wasn't perfect, either."

"Brock is dead. He's earned the right to peace."

"And what about me? Don't I deserve to know happiness? To finally know peace?"

"Becca, you're so messed up in the head, you wouldn't know what to do with peace if it came with instructions," he said, the nape of his neck starting to prickle. "But you know what? Not my problem. Figure out your life but leave me the hell alone."

"So that's it?"

"Pretty much."

He should've hung up, but some part of him refused to be that cruel, even though Becca had been a poison between him and his brother up until the day Brock died. It was hard to remember a time when the three of them had been thick as thieves, but then, kids who grew up in hard situations often forged connections with those who understood their pain.

Becca's home life had been as ugly as his and Brock's—worse, even—because even though Lucas and Brock's dad was a mean, abusive drunk, he'd never touched them sexually. That much couldn't be said for Becca's old man.

Lucas drew a deep breath, trying to rein in his growing temper. It was just like Becca to ignore his boundaries and chase after him when he'd plainly ended their connection to one another when he left Kansas.

"How'd you get my number?" he asked.

"Does it matter?"

"Hell yes, it matters," he growled. "If I'd wanted you to have my new number, I would've given it to you."

"I got it from your buddy Ryan," she answered sullenly. "Told him I lost it when you left."

Lucas swore under his breath, even though he couldn't blame Ryan when he hadn't told his friend not to share any information with Becca. Especially when everyone from his old life knew his connection to Becca had always been complicated.

"I know you're mad—"

"You think?" he returned caustically. "What was your first clue?"

"Look, I'm sorry, but when you left, it got me to thinking, and I realized that maybe I need a fresh start, too."

He didn't believe that for a second, but he had to ask. "Yeah? How so? You mean, like you actually might want to get clean this time?"

"I'm trying, Lucas," Becca said quietly. "But it's hard without any support. Brock is gone, and now you're gone, too. You know I don't have no one else in my life who cares about me."

Lucas fought the tug on his heartstrings. He was too damn soft sometimes. Especially when it came to Becca.

Becca had been his Achilles' heel for too long. There'd been a time when he'd thought he was in love with her, but then, they'd been kids with an us-against-the-world attitude until he'd gotten his shit straight. However, Becca and Brock had stayed the course—

right into the ground. Not to mention, Becca had always been in love with Brock, even if she'd strung Lucas along a few times, especially after Brock died.

The thing was, Becca was the reason his relationships ultimately failed and why he knew he'd never get his own fresh start if she was around.

After Brock overdosed, he'd felt honor-bound to help Becca find her way to sobriety, but Becca had a way of twisting help into a mess of unintended consequences that'd nearly ruined his life and career. That's when he'd known, either leave Kansas—and the past behind—or get stuck in a pattern that ultimately destroyed everything he'd built.

"How are you trying to get clean, Becca?" he asked. "Tell me what's different?"

"Why is it always an interrogation with you? Can't you be supportive? I don't need another parole officer, okay?"

"Why'd you call, then?"

"Because I didn't know who else to call," she admitted.

"Are you using again?"

"No," Becca answered sharply, sounding offended. "Why is that your go-to question for every problem in my life?"

"Because you're an addict," he returned with a sigh. "And you've fought every attempt at getting sober. Why wouldn't it be my go-to question?"

"That's unfair," Becca said. "I've been trying this time. I know you don't believe me, but your leaving put things into perspective. I know I should've been more grateful for your help, but I was too messed up to see that. What do you want me to say, Lucas? That I'm sorry? Hell yeah, I'm sorry, but I still need your help.

C'mon, please don't abandon me when I need you the most. I'm asking for you to remember what we once meant to each other and help me."

She needed money. He could feel it in his bones. Becca was predictable in her patterns, too. It'd been the same pattern with Brock until the day he died, aspirating on his own vomit on a cold bathroom floor in a shitty roadside motel with Becca passed out in the other room.

But Lucas had left Kansas for a reason. He couldn't keep repeating the same shit or he'd never get out of the cycle.

"I can't help you anymore, Becca," he said quietly, fighting against the guilt that inevitably rose up to choke him. "I've done all I can, and now it's your time to stand on your own."

"What would Brock say to that?"

"I don't know. My brother was an addict, too," he admitted, wincing at the pain that simple admission caused. "And he died for that addiction. Are you willing to die for yours?"

"I'm trying not to," she answered with a tremble in her voice that cut at him. "That's what I've been trying to say. I'm ready to change."

He wanted to believe her, but Becca was a master manipulator and he'd heard it all before.

Lucas could sense the storm building in the tense silence on the other end. Usually this was when Becca started crying or having a meltdown. It could go either way, and he was tired of the game. Whatever Becca had going on, was no longer his concern. He was seconds away from clicking off when she said, "There's a treatment facility with an opening. I need your help with the intake paperwork. Can you do that?"

She wasn't asking for money, he realized with a start. Was Becca truly turning a corner? That tiny sliver of hope was his undoing. He knew he ought to wish her the best and let her figure things out on her own, but a part of him wished Brock had come to him with the same plea. It'd been two years since Brock died, and Lucas felt the loss of his little brother every day. Becca, as much as he needed to cut ties, was still a part of him in ways that he couldn't quite seem to cut. He lost his emotional footing long enough to say, "I can't do much from here, but I can put you in contact with someone at my old precinct who handles addiction recovery services." He tacked on quickly, "It's the best I can do."

"Okay," she accepted with a sniff, seeming grateful. "I appreciate your help. I know I've done a lot to ruin trust between us, but I'm serious this time. I want to change. I want to get better."

The earnest sincerity in her voice played with his head. Becca was good at making people dance to her tune. He couldn't be sure if Becca was legit or not but hoped so for her sake. When you played fast and loose with fate, eventually it got your number. As much as Lucas had issues with Becca, he didn't want her to die. "Got a pen and paper?" he said, hoping for the best. When she was ready, he rattled off the name and number of the contact. "If you're serious about this, don't sit on the impulse. Make the call as soon as I hang up, okay?"

"Okay," she agreed, swallowing. "Are you really not coming back to Kansas?"

"No, I'm not."

"Was it me? Did I chase you away?" she asked.

The answer was complicated. Yes, in part, but not completely. The ghosts in Kansas were just too many to fight daily, and with the added burden of Becca's constant care suffocating him, he hadn't been able to keep his head above water. He'd done everything he could for his little brother, only to have Brock end up on the slab, and Becca seemed determined to follow his brother to the grave.

It was more than he could handle.

But it wasn't all Becca's fault, and he wouldn't put that on her—not when she seemed ready to actually try to get better this time.

"No," he finally answered. "I needed a fresh start for a lot of reasons."

"So, where'd you end up?" she asked, fishing for information.

"Far enough away," he said, not giving up his location. "Take care, Becca."

Thankfully, she took the hint and accepted his answer. "Yeah, you, too."

She clicked off, and he breathed a sigh of relief, his hands shaking from holding the phone too hard. The anxiety Becca created with only her voice on the other end solidified his conviction that leaving his home state had been the right choice.

Some might call what he'd done running away, but he called it saving himself.

Because a drowning person will drag under the person trying to rescue them.

And that's 100 percent what Becca had been doing to him.

Kenna had to find a way to reach Ty. The demoralizing realization that her son was falling into a pit of darkness because of situations she'd put him through was enough to cripple her with depression, but she had to figure out how to fix things.

Time to pick herself by her bootstraps, right? At least that was something she was familiar with, and the steps were usually the same.

"I was thinking, maybe I could pick up where Grandpa left off with your driving lessons. You interested in taking the old truck out for a spin?" she asked, holding her breath and forcing a bright, hopeful smile. "Could be fun."

"Not really," Ty answered without looking up from his comic book. "When can I have my phone back?"

"We talked about this," she reminded Ty. "In light of the most recent situation, you're grounded from your electronics."

"That's stupid."

"Buddy, I hate to be the bearer of bad news, but actions have consequences," she said. "From this point forward, we need to get back on track. You have court next week. We don't want to do anything that might work against us. Let's focus on staying positive, okay?"

"Whatever." Ty tossed the comic to the end table and rose to leave the room, but Kenna stopped him with a frown. "What?" he asked, annoyed.

"Ty," she implored. "Don't shut me out, please. Talk to me."

"What do you want to talk about, Mother?"

Mother? She drew back, stung. Who was this angry changeling? And where did her sweet boy go? "Um, well, we could talk about what you're feeling. I'm here to listen if you need to get something off your chest. I miss Grandpa, too."

He smirked, as if she'd said something inane. Shame curled in her cheeks. She wanted to cry but held back her tears. Couldn't they catch a freaking break? Why was the universe determined to crush every bit of happiness in their lives?

"I guess shit happens," Ty said, shrugging.

"Tyler," she admonished, hating how he was becoming a potty mouth. "Don't talk like that. You don't have to pretend that you're not hurting. We're all hurting over what happened, but Grandpa would've wanted us to move forward. He would be devastated at how you've been acting."

"Well, I guess it's a good thing he's not around, then," Ty quipped, not giving an inch. "Is that all?"

She was afraid to ask, but maybe she had to. "Ty," she ventured, "you know you're all that matters to me in this world, right? I would do anything to protect you." She lowered her voice. "You know why we had to move here. It wasn't safe—"

"Yeah, I get it," Ty cut in, irritated. "I know exactly why we moved to this shithole and why we can't leave. I also know why I'm not supposed to talk about it, too."

Stunned, Kenna stared at her son, feeling like she was looking at a stranger. Where was the boy who used to cuddle with her in the dark, wiping away her tears and promising that it would be all right? Where was the kid who called 911 when she'd smashed her skull into the marble, leaving her unconscious and bleeding out? "Ty, I promise you, it's going to get better. Everything is going to get better—"

"Sure it is," he said, shaking his head with a dark look that cut into her soul. "Are we done?"

"Yeah, I guess so," she murmured, hating this disconnect between them. Ty had always been her partner in crime, her little buddy. Had she lost him forever?

No, she refused to give in to that kind of thinking.

Onward and upward, as Nancy used to say. No sense
in looking backward if they weren't headed that direction. They'd find a way to get through this, and then
all this ugliness would be a chapter they happily forgot.
Maybe she'd light some candles and burn some sage like
her ancestors used to. She wasn't as connected to her
indigenous roots as she'd like to be, but that was going
to change. She might not have grown up on the reservation, but she was still Macawi—and she'd do whatever
was necessary to chase away the negative energy swirling around her family. Surely her ancestors were on her
side, right? God, she needed all the help she could get.

"Well, let me know if you change your mind," she
said, letting him off the hook. He would come to her
when he was ready. Pushing someone only made them
run in the opposite direction. Ty shook his head as if to
say, *keep dreamin', lady*, and disappeared into his bedroom, slamming the door behind him.

She winced but let it go. *This is a phase*, she told her-
self. Everyone reacts differently to a traumatic event.
Ty would get through this, and they'd turn the page.
Someday this would be a nasty memory.

*Yeah, but most kids don't live through the hell you've
dragged that poor boy through*, a nagging voice reminded her.

Stop it. She curled her hands into tight fists and fought
the urge to scream. *We're safe—that's all that matters
now.*

Someday, when Ty was older, she'd be able to explain
how everything had gone down and how she'd had no
choice but to run.

That day was not today.

Currently, her son was an angry, hurt little boy who
didn't know how to deal with his pain in any other way

but to lash out, and she'd weather whatever cuts and bruises she had to for him to heal.

It's what mothers do.

She blinked back tears, grinding the moisture out and quickly wiping her cheeks. It was her day off. Maybe she'd make Ty's favorite dinner tonight. The kid was a sucker for her lemon chicken pasta and fresh, crusty bread slathered with butter.

Yep, nothing a hearty comfort meal couldn't help.

The idea soothed her ragged heart and set her in motion.

Whenever things were bumpy in their lives, Kenna had always been able to smooth the rough edges with a good meal, just like the baking she'd done earlier.

Humming, she made a grocery list and called out to Ty, "I'm heading to the store. I'll be back in a bit," adding as a reminder, "If you need anything, you can call my cell from the landline, okay?" She waited for his response, frowning when nothing but silence bounced back. "Ty?"

Sudden loud music drowned out any possibility of Ty hearing another word.

Lemon chicken, please don't fail me. I need this to work.

She absolutely couldn't bear losing her son on top of everything else that'd been taken from her.

Please.

Chapter 5

"Are you sure you're okay to close up?" Isabel asked, unsure, but Kenna waved her on with a smile. It was Friday night, and Isabel had a hot date to get ready for. Far be it from Kenna to keep anyone from possibly finding Mr. Right.

"I'm fine, I promise. I like spending time with the animals anyway," she assured her coworker. "This will give me a chance to spend a little extra time with Bianca. She came in so scared today. I want to make sure she goes to sleep okay before I lock up."

"Yeah, she's definitely skittish," Isabel agreed, swinging her purse over her shoulder. "Little sucker tried to bite me before I gave her the sedative to calm her down."

Bianca, a Jack Russell terrier with a broken leg, had been logged into the infirmary for overnight care. Although another vet was scheduled to come in later tonight to watch over the patients, Kenna hated the idea of the Jack Russell being away from home and scared all alone.

"You're a good egg," Isabel said, blowing her a kiss before rushing out.

Kenna followed and locked the front, turning the sign to Closed. It seemed a lifetime ago that she'd been excited about going on a date. Now the idea of dating gave her instant anxiety. A shudder rippled through her before she pushed away the thought with distaste.

She doubted there would ever come a time when the idea of dating didn't create a cold sweat.

And if she suffered the tiniest moment of sadness that life hadn't turned out the way she envisioned, she tried not to spend more than a heartbeat in that feeling.

Her cell chirped right as she was shutting down the office computer. Thinking it was probably Ty, she scooped up her phone and glanced at the messages.

You were always on my mind.

Kenna stared at the message, her heart stopping painfully in her chest. Her mouth dried up as her hands began to shake. The message had come from an unknown sender, but tears sprang to her eyes when his voice whispered in her memory as he crooned the classic Elvis song while stroking her hair and wiping her tears even as she lay dazed.

A second text came through.

Show that special person you care by booking a Caribbean cruise with Ocean Adventures. Booking agents are standing by!

Kenna barked a near-hysterical laugh. Stupid spam!

She wiped her damp forehead with the back of her hand, still shaking from head to toe. *Get a grip, Kenna.* It was nothing. She was turning into a Nervous Nelly, afraid of her own shadow. She took a deliberate minute to straighten everything on her desk with military precision while calming her breathing. *See? No boogeyman. Just your overactive imagination.*

But the damage had been done. She couldn't help but feel eyes on her when, seconds prior, she'd felt perfectly safe and secure alone at the office.

Damn you, Leon.

But she knew the only way to push past the fear was to face it, so she forced herself to go about her routine, ignoring her vulnerability and the deep terror that Leon might try to find them instead of losing interest when the chase became tedious.

It wouldn't be the first time she'd been accused of being naive, but for her sanity's sake, she had to believe that Leon's interest in her only lasted as long as it was convenient to have her around. No doubt he'd replaced her the moment he realized she was gone.

Wasn't that what malignant narcissists did when they became bored with their old toys? Kenna suffered no illusion that she'd been anything more than a convenient plaything, or punching bag, depending on the day. For all she knew, Leon was glad to be rid of her. *Please let that be so.*

A part of her felt guilty for not being stronger and pressing charges when she had the chance, but Leon had scared the courage out of her before she'd even left the hospital. He'd been quick to remind her of his connections, his sterling reputation and how no one would believe anything she said. Not to mention the threat of more violence that'd radiated from his hard gaze even as he stroked her hand like a concerned lover and not the monster who had put her in that bed. She'd chickened out, too afraid to move a muscle against him, but she'd started her escape plan all the while playing the contrite little woman who'd seen the error of her ways.

It made Kenna sick to her stomach to remember any detail of her recovery time. She'd had to hide the way her skin had crawled lying next to him, listening to him as he slept like a baby without a single ounce of guilt at the mottled bruises covering her body or the hairline fracture nearly splitting her skull.

Leon hadn't lost a minute of sleep over any of it.

Kenna smothered a shudder as she drew a deep breath to calm her racing heart. *We're starting over. Leon is someone else's problem now. Leave the past in the past.*

And while she silently said a prayer for the next unfortunate person in his life, she had to think of herself and Ty.

She walked briskly to the back room, which served as their infirmary, and smiled when she saw Bianca sacked out, oblivious to her surroundings. *Such a sweet pup.* "Dream of chasing gophers and catching birds," she whispered as she gently snapped off the overhead light, leaving the room in soothing partial darkness, dimly lit only by the few strategically placed nightlights.

After checking on the handful of other animals staying overnight, she left notes for the incoming night doctor and had just returned to the front to set the alarm code when something caught the corner of her eye from the darkened window.

Her heart leaped in her chest, immediately thundering. A sharp *whack* against the window made her jump. She nearly tripped over her office chair as the brief flash of a face pressed against the glass made her stumble back with a cry.

Even though improbable, she saw Leon in that split second and nearly wet herself in panic.

No, no, nooooo! Tears tickled her sinuses as fear drenched her synapses. It couldn't be! Impossible! But the fight-or-flight button in her brain took full control and reason had left the building.

Stumbling over the rolling chair, she scrambled to grab her cell phone with shaking fingers, dialing 911 in a blind terror. When the dispatcher picked up, she could barely form words. "I need help, please!" she managed to whisper. "I—I think there's someone trying to get into the vet clinic. I—I'm all alone. Please hurry."

"We'll send an officer right away," the dispatcher said in a voice meant to keep the caller calm, but Kenna could barely hear above the pounding of her heartbeat in her eardrum. "Are you in a safe place?"

"I don't know. Maybe. The clinic is locked, but I don't know if it's secure enough," she answered in a choked voice, immediately thinking of the back door, which didn't have a dead bolt but a flimsy lock that a hard kick would bust open. At this moment, not even a steel door would make her feel secure. "Just hurry."

"An officer is en route to your location. Please stay on the line until he arrives."

"Okay," she promised, gripping her phone hard and trying to breathe. *It's going to be all right. Stay calm.* But her pits were soaked with sweat as adrenaline poured into her veins and her heart threatened to pop from her chest. Her gaze roamed her desk, looking for anything that might serve as a weapon, but nothing more dangerous than a stapler caught her eye. Still, she scooped the stapler up with her free hand, determined to go down swinging if need be.

It could've been five minutes or fifteen—Kenna wasn't sure because time froze as she sat trembling on the floor behind her desk. A sharp rap at the front door and accompanying announcement of "Cottonwood PD" set her into immediate motion, rushing for the door.

It was Lucas Merritt, the new K-9 cop, looking like a knight in shining armor. She nearly wept with relief and threw herself into his arms, clinging to him as a sob escaped her.

"Whoa there, are you okay?" he murmured, his touch gentle but firm as he held her. "Are you hurt?"

For a long moment, she lost sight of everything but the comfort of how safe she felt in his arms, but a heartbeat later, she realized with instant mortification how over-the-top her reaction must appear and pulled away abruptly with a stammered apology.

"I—I'm so sorry," she started, her cheeks burning. "I don't know what came over me. I was so relieved to see an officer that I reacted out of pure instinct." She wiped at her eyes and tried to compose herself. "Um, did you find anyone out there?"

"I did a perimeter search, and it seems whoever gave you a scare didn't stick around. Are you okay?" Lucas's concerned gaze was nearly her undoing even as she fought to find her composure now that all was fine. "Are you sure you saw something? Sometimes when we're all alone, our brain can play tricks on us."

Kenna's brain replayed that awful moment, and she knew without a doubt, someone's face had pressed against the glass, almost leering at her. But if Lucas had done a search and found no one, whatever she'd seen was long gone. Fresh embarrassment choked her throat as she returned sheepishly, "It was probably a bum or kids playing a prank. I shouldn't have panicked. I'm sorry for wasting your time."

"Never apologize for calling if you feel threatened. It's always better to be safe than sorry," Lucas said, gently relieving her of the stapler still in her clenched hand. "You look pale. Why don't you sit down for a minute and let me take a look at you?"

"Oh, thank you," she murmured, wincing as fresh blood supply returned to her palm, explaining forlornly, "It was the only thing I could find."

"I wouldn't want to take a stapler to the head," he said with warm approval, even if it was to make her feel less foolish. "Come sit down," he repeated, gesturing to the chair.

But Kenna was reeling from embarrassment and wanted to go home, "No, it's okay, I'm fine," she assured him, but a wave of dizziness made a liar out of her, and she had no choice but to sink into her office chair as he suggested.

She blushed as Lucas peered into her eyes, checking her pupils. "I'm going to call EMS to come check you out," he decided.

"No, please don't. I'm fine. I'm probably hungry. I forgot to eat lunch, and then the adrenaline rush likely pushed me over the edge. A little low blood sugar isn't cause for an ambulance. The last thing I want is a big bill for emergency services that I don't need. I promise I'm okay."

Lucas didn't seem convinced, but he didn't push, and she was grateful. He helped her rise from her chair, and she realized Noble wasn't with him. "Where's your K-9 partner?" she asked.

"I put him back in the rig after the perimeter search."

"Well, I suppose if Noble didn't pick up any scent of someone lurking, I'm probably safe," she said, relaxing more, finally able to breathe without fearing someone had their hands around her throat. She risked meeting his gaze with a tremulous smile. "Thank you for coming. I know it was probably nothing, but I was really scared."

The corners of his lips tilted as he tipped an imaginary cowboy hat. "That's what I'm here for—rescuing damsels in distress."

"A damsel in distress," she repeated in a murmur as a ripple of awareness cascaded through her. *If he only knew.* For a split second, she wondered if things would've been different if someone like Lucas had stood between her and Leon that first time he'd hit her. Before she'd been in an abusive relationship, she'd assumed walking away would've been the easiest decision to make. It wasn't until she was in the thick of it that she'd realized with horror, getting out felt like stepping off a cliff. "Well, I appreciate your kindness, even if I overreacted to the situation."

Whatever had spooked Kenna had done a fine job of shaking her up. Despite her promises to the contrary, she still looked like she'd seen a ghost. In his experience, women who reacted like Kenna had had been taught reasons to know fear at a visceral level.

"Kenna, can you think of why someone might be interested in messing with you?" he asked.

Kenna swallowed as she blinked, her eyes wide. "No."

That's a lie.

Lucas was good at spotting lies after years of dealing with Becca, but he couldn't make Kenna talk if she didn't want to share. He bit back a sigh and grabbed his pocket notebook. "Tell me exactly what happened. Don't leave out any detail," he instructed.

Kenna fluttered a shaky hand through her thick, dark hair, seeming embarrassed. "Honestly, the more I think about it, the more I think I made a mountain out of a molehill and wasted everyone's time."

"Indulge me," he said. "I gotta have something to put in the report."

She chuckled ruefully. "Okay, but it's not much to go on." Kenna drew a deep breath before continuing, her brow furrowing slightly as she recalled, "Normally Isabel helps me close, but I let her go early so she could meet her date. I spent a few minutes in the infirmary, making sure the patients were tucked in for the night, and then I left some notes for the incoming night doctor. Just as I was about to set the alarm code, I heard a loud whack, and then seconds later, I thought I saw a face pressed against the glass. But now that I'm going over it in my head, I can't tell if it was my imagination running wild."

"It could've been a kid playing a prank," he acknowledged, but he was more interested in her reaction. He shouldn't press, but there was something about how she was trying to hide the subtle tremors that activated his need to make sure she was okay. "How about I give you a ride home?"

"Oh gosh, no, that's not necessary," she said quickly. "I've already taken up too much of your time."

"Not at all. I'm on the clock. I'm getting paid to make sure you're safe," he said with a disarming smile, hoping to settle her nerves.

"No wonder all the single women are angling to be the future Mrs. Merritt," she murmured, ducking her gaze briefly. "You know how to turn on the charm when you need to."

"Is that so? I don't think anyone's ever accused me of being the center of attention when it comes to the ladies," he admitted. That'd always been his brother's department. Before drugs had taken over Brock's life, ruining his skin, sucking every ounce of fat from his body and leaving him a wasted shell of a man, he'd been a handsome devil. "As far as looking for any future Mrs. Merritt, I'm more focused on getting familiar with my new town, enjoying the different scenery and keeping drama far away from my day-to-day."

"That's a nice change," she admitted with a surprised smile. "Most guys are the opposite when they come to a new place."

"You mean, most guys act like dogs?" he finished for her, and she blushed. He chuckled. "Yeah, I'm not like most guys. Right now I'm more interested in finding the best hiking spots than filling my nights with random hookups."

The small talk seemed to be doing the trick, as color returned to Kenna's cheeks and she looked less like a frightened rabbit. At the mention of hiking, she perked up with wary interest. "You like to hike?"

"Love it. Nothing like fresh air and a quiet trail to put things right in your head. You hike?"

"Not as much lately. I used to enjoy it, though." She added, "But to be honest, I'm woefully out of shape at this point. I'd probably twist an ankle and end up flat on my behind."

She looked strong and capable of handling a moderate hike, but he suggested, "Start small until you get your feet back under you." She was a strikingly beautiful woman, with delicate, high cheekbones and full, sensual lips—which was the least appropriate thing he should notice while on a call. He shifted on his feet and headed toward the door, gesturing. "Well, I'll walk you to your car if you're ready."

"Thank you," she said, casting him a quick smile as she grabbed her purse. After setting the alarm, she locked the front door, and even though he was standing beside her, her gaze darted from right to left as if still not entirely sure someone wasn't out there ready to pounce and drag her into the bushes. For good measure, he scanned the area one last time, if only to reassure Kenna she was safe, and waited as she unlocked her car, opened the door and climbed inside.

"Let me know if anything else weird happens. Don't hesitate to call, okay?"

"I won't," she promised, murmuring a quick "I really appreciate your professionalism."

He nodded and watched her drive away. Her kid was supposed to be in court next week on the vandalism charges. She had a lot on her plate with that one.

But he'd seen real fear in those dark brown eyes.

And he couldn't help but wonder if Kenna Griffin had more than skeletons in her closet.

Walk away, a voice whispered.

Sound advice, but he knew he wouldn't.

Hell, some red flags were just too mesmerizing to ignore.

Chapter 6

"Lucas, can you come into my office for a minute?"

Lucas looked up from his paperwork and nodded, ready to take a break from staring at the dizzying statement given by a drunk who swore someone had stolen his beer and, consequently, his job, and that the government was planning to inject everyone with nanotech to control their brains.

As if that guy's alcohol-soaked brain was worth the government's attention.

He walked into Detective Luna Griffin's office and closed the door behind him when she gestured for privacy.

"Is everything okay?" he asked, concerned.

She went straight to the point. "I know I should keep my nose out of things, but I couldn't help but notice your report of the suspicious circumstances at the vet office the other night. I saw that Kenna made the 911 call, but she never mentioned anything about it when she came home."

He frowned. "That's surprising. She was pretty shook up. Something really spooked her. She looked like she'd seen a ghost or something. I asked her if there was anyone who might have cause to mess with her, but she clammed up real quick."

Luna nodded with a pensive frown. "And you didn't find any evidence of a possible intruder?"

"No, ma'am. Did a full perimeter search with Noble, and not even his nose picked up a scent."

"That's good," she said, but that troubled look remained. The fact that Kenna had told her sister nothing about the incident set off alarm bells in his head again. Luna tried shrugging it off, saying with wry amusement, "It was probably that guy you picked up, sauced out of his gourd. Have you heard some of his conspiracy theories?"

"Unfortunately, I got an earful when I brought him in. He needs a psych eval."

"Probably, but resources are strained, and unless he's threatening to harm himself or others, we don't have much of a choice but to turn him loose as soon as he sobers up."

"He's still in the drunk tank?" Lucas asked, amused. "Probably the best night of sleep he's gotten in ages."

Luna checked her watch. "Yep. Although his stay at Club Cottonwood is about to be over. As soon as you finish his report, we can turn him loose with a slap on the wrist."

"Catch and release, the new age of police work," Lucas said with derision. "Seems that's about the same no matter where you go. My old precinct had similar issues with misdemeanor criminal offenses. The overcrowding in the jails only left room for the most hardened criminals."

Luna sighed. "Yeah, no argument there. Not that Cottonwood has too many of those, thank God." She paused a minute before switching gears unexpectedly. "I've been thinking—something bad happened to my sister before coming back to Cottonwood this time around. She won't talk about it and I haven't pressed, but it must've been pretty bad if a simple scare sent her into a panic. I'm a little worried, but she's real quiet when it comes to her private life, and we've never been that close, so I don't think she feels comfortable confiding in me. Makes me feel like I've been a terrible excuse for a big sister."

He knew a thing or two about guilt when it came to siblings, but he doubted Luna's troubles with Kenna were on par with what he went through with Brock. Lucas chose his words carefully. "I agree your sister seems like a private person. I don't want to say anything that might upset her about the incident, especially if she didn't choose to share what happened. All I can say is, she was embarrassed for calling, but I told her not to worry about that stuff. We're here to help."

Luna seemed to appreciate his concern and restraint. A new spark of respect gleamed in her eye. "The department won the lottery with you, Lucas. You're a good man and a good cop."

He wasn't accustomed to such easy praise. "Just doing my job, Detective," he said, ducking his head as his cheeks heated a little, but he felt compelled to add, "Your sister seems like a good person."

"With a big heart," Luna agreed without hesitation, "but sometimes she's trusted the wrong people. I'm a little worried there's more to the story than she's letting on. The question is, how do I find out without alienating her?"

He didn't have the answer. "That's a tough one. I wish I knew."

"You and me both. Anyway, thanks for handling the situation with kindness. My sister could use some of that in her life right now."

He smiled. "My pleasure," he said before returning to his desk, his thoughts stubbornly centered on Kenna.

Up until a few months ago, when a shocking homicide case rocked the small town, one might argue Cottonwood was the kind of place people only saw in the movies. A friendly vibe to the town extended to its residents—but no place was perfect. Even pretty places had dark shadows somewhere.

However, it was likely Kenna had gotten spooked by someone playing a prank.

But that's the thing about change—it happens, and when it comes, it's usually jarring to the people in their comfort zone.

Did Kenna have something to be worried about, or was she jumping at shadows from her past?

Not my problem, he reminded himself. Kenna had a great support system with her sister, so he didn't need to spend more time wondering about her situation.

He needed to make heads or tails of Mr. Dobney's statement before he clocked out.

And that was going to take all his brainpower.

But before he could return to his report, Wes popped his head into the room, saying, "Hey man, you've got someone in the lobby interested in talking about the K-9 program. You want me to take his number? I know you're pushing hard to finish that report."

Even though he was pressed for time, he wouldn't do

anything to jeopardize the program's popularity, which meant plenty of good PR, no matter how it presented itself. "No, I got this," he said with a short smile. "I could use a break from this word salad anyway."

"Mr. Dobney?" Wes guessed with a knowing grin. "He's nuttier than a squirrel turd."

"Oh, you know him?" Lucas returned the grin. "And yeah, completely cuckoo. It's too bad that alcohol curdled his brain."

"What if, in a rare twist of events, Mr. Dobney is the only sane one around here? What if…he's riiiiiggghh-hhttt," Wes said, exaggerating the last word with theatrics worthy of a community actor. "Space lasers are going to kill us all!"

"God save us," Lucas quipped, leaving the report room to go to the lobby. An older man, sturdy, well-built, and equally well-dressed, stood admiring the academy pictures on the wall. Lucas cleared his throat to politely get his attention. "I'm K-9 officer Lucas Merritt. How can I help you, sir?"

The man turned, flashing an impeccable set of teeth and a respectable smattering of gray woven into his dirty blond hair, extending a hand in welcome. "Ambrose Elliott. Pleasure to meet you. Thank you for taking time out of your busy schedule to talk with me."

"No problem," Lucas assured the man. "I was told you wanted to know more about the K-9 program?"

"Actually, a slight misrepresentation. I'm actually interested in Noble—or rather, how I can get my own Noble, if you will."

"Well, Noble comes from a breeder in Germany that only sells to law enforcement, but there are plenty of breeders who specialize in precision training for civilians. May I ask, what do you do that you need a military-grade dog?"

The man chuckled as if caught, admitting, "Quite possibly to remind me of my glory days. I'm former military, but also, I own several businesses, and theft has become a problem these days. I feel if I had something with sharp teeth patrolling the grounds, it might be a better deterrent than a few signs warning that trespassers will be prosecuted."

Lucas nodded with a smile, agreeing. "A well-trained dog is an asset, but it's also a huge responsibility. I can give you a few names of breeders that might be worth looking into, but I can't give you Noble's breeder information."

"Understandable and fair," Ambrose said. "I'll take what you can give me."

Lucas took a minute to jot down some names of reputable breeders on the back of a business card and handed it over. "So, are you a resident of Cottonwood?" he asked.

"No, not so lucky as to call this haven home," Ambrose admitted with a sigh. "Just here for a short time and saw the article in the newspaper about the K-9 program. Thought I'd pop in and ask. I figure, nothing ventured, nothing gained, right?"

"Good policy to live by, sir," Lucas said, liking the guy's demeanor. "Well, I'd love to chat some more, but paperwork never sleeps, you know?"

"That I do," Ambrose answered with a friendly smile, extending his hand for another shake. "It was a real pleasure to meet you. Maybe I'll see you around town while I'm still here."

"Maybe so. If you do, don't hesitate to say hello."

"Will do."

Lucas waited until the gentleman exited the lobby

and returned to his nonsensical report, ready to go home, prop his feet up and enjoy a cold beer.

And not think about the mystery of Kenna Griffin.

Kenna had just finished putting away the leftovers when her sister Luna walked in with an expression Kenna knew well.

"Can we talk?" Luna asked.

"Are you hungry? I just put the tuna casserole leftovers in the fridge, and they're probably still warm," she answered, sidestepping the question. She had a feeling she knew what Luna wanted to talk about, and Kenna had zero interest in touching that hot stove.

"Thanks, but I grabbed something from the vending machine at work—"

"That sounds awful."

"It was," Luna admitted, "but I'm used to it. Now, back to the question at hand. I think you know where I'm going with this."

"I do, and honestly, I don't really want to talk about it. I never should've called 911. I'm embarrassed that I got spooked by something so small. It was probably someone being a jerk and nothing more."

"Probably," Luna agreed. "But that doesn't change the fact that you were scared out of your mind. Talk to me, Kenna. Does this have anything to do with why you left Kentucky?"

The mere mention of the state she'd run from was enough to send a shudder down her spine—and Luna didn't miss her reaction, either.

Luna pointed emphatically at Kenna. "See? Right there! What are you hiding? What the hell happened in Kentucky that you're practically shaking in your skin at the memory?"

"I—I said I don't want to talk about it," Kenna reminded Luna, her voice hitting a higher octave. "Seriously, why do you have to poke and prod at everything? It doesn't matter what happened. All that matters is what happens now. We're rebuilding, and I don't need to spend my time looking backward for no reason."

"But there is a reason if you're terrified of something—or someone—coming after you," Luna pointed out gently. "Sis, I'm here for you. Please, let me help you."

Kenna wanted to tell her sisters what happened, but once that thread was pulled, the whole sweater would unravel, and she couldn't stand for her family to know the whole of what had happened once she hooked up with Leon.

The man was the devil in disguise. If she could go back in time, she'd call in sick from work so that she never caught his eye and never fell into his sticky web.

She remembered every detail of their first meeting. She used to think it was a romantic story, but now she saw it differently.

Her head throbbed where the hairline fracture was still tender, but she tried to hide the sudden wince from her sister's eagle eye. "I need you to trust that whatever I left behind, it is in the past and that's where I intend to keep it, okay?" Kenna assured Luna. "I appreciate everything you've done for us. We wouldn't have been able to start over without you and Dad." At the mention of her father, tears sprang to her eyes, but she ground them away quickly. "And everything from this point forward will be better. I can feel it."

That last part was false bravado delivered with a bright smile, a skill Kenna had perfected, but Luna wasn't so easily fooled.

However, she also knew how to read a room and could tell Kenna wouldn't budge. She sighed with resignation. "Okay, just promise me that if trouble does follow you here to Cottonwood, you'll tell me before it's too late."

"It won't follow me," she insisted.

"Kenna, just promise me."

Kenna drew a deep breath, seeing the worry in her sister's eyes, which made her feel like a toad for putting those creases between her brow. "I promise," she said, if only to ease her sister's concern. Then she rose and pulled a cheesecake from the fridge, grateful she'd decided to make Luna's favorite on a whim. "Look what I have here… I think it's exactly what you need to erase the memory of that vending machine burrito."

"Who said it was a burrito?" Luna asked, yet she was riveted by the cheesecake in Kenna's hands.

"Wasn't it?"

"It was," Luna relented with a heavy sigh. "Okay, I'll take a small slice. A real small one."

Kenna chuckled, relieved to have navigated that pitfall. "One small piece, coming up."

One bite, and Luna was groaning with delight, conversation forgotten—for now. "You know, if you keep plying me with sweets like this, I'm not going to be able to fit on the back of Benjamin's bike, and I've just started appreciating our rides when I visit him in Arizona."

"I'm not worried. Benjamin would love you at any size. I've seen how in love with you that man is. You caught a good one."

Luna's smile shone with unabashed love, and Kenna's heart contracted. Would anyone ever look at her in that same way?

Not likely.

All she seemed good at attracting was abusive psychopaths.

Best to stay single.

Hey, at least she could bake a mean cheesecake.

That was something.

And then Luna suggested between bites, "You should bring your lemon muffins to the station."

"Yeah? You think it might help with Ty's case?"

"No, but I think I heard that lemon was Lucas's favorite. Might be a nice gesture."

Kenna shook her head, ready to murmur, *hell no*, but she bit her tongue instead. Lucas had been real sweet to her the other night when she needed it. He could've been condescending or made her feel bad for getting so easily spooked, but he'd been nothing but professional and kind.

That was worth a muffin or two, right?

Maybe.

"I'll think about it," she finally said, leaving Luna to finish her dessert in peace but already collecting ingredients in her mind.

Except within a heartbeat of her decision, she second-guessed herself. She didn't want to send the wrong message by showing up with baked goods for a man she barely knew—but why not show a little appreciation for his basic human kindness? That's what was messed up with the world—no one was nice anymore.

Kenna reached for the flour, her thoughts stuck in a dizzying loop of indecision. Was it appropriate to bring muffins for a man simply doing his job?

This is how people go insane, she grumbled. It starts with having arguments in their head over an issue that shouldn't be an issue.

She was going to make the man muffins. It wasn't a big deal if she didn't act like it was a big deal.

The ancient kitchen wall phone rang and nearly sent her soul straight to heaven. Good grief! She'd forgotten how loud landlines could be. She wiped her hands and answered on the second ring, bemused that anyone was using the old number when everyone she knew had her cell.

"Hello?" When nothing but silence answered, she tried again. "Hello? Is anyone there?"

Puzzled, she wondered if landlines could get bad connections like a cell phone but then heard the distinct sound of human breath on the other end and hung up the phone with a gasp.

Her heart hammered in her chest as instant fear curdled her stomach, but she forced a few calming breaths even as tears sprang to her eyes. *It's not him. It's not him. He's not in Cottonwood.* He didn't have her number, much less her parents' landline. It was probably some kid trying to be funny. Teenagers prank calling people was a rite of passage, right? A bubble of forced laughter popped from her mouth as she shook her head, determined to find her footing.

If she continued to let Leon live rent-free in her head, she'd never really escape him. People recovered from bad experiences all the time—she would, too.

Swallowing the lump in her throat, she continued with her baking prep and tried to delete the icky sound of disembodied breathing lodged in her memory.

Chapter 7

"Oh, I can drop these off in the break room—no need to bother anyone."

Lucas perked up at Kenna's voice and immediately dropped everything he was doing to investigate. He rounded the corner and saw Kenna, dressed in a bright yellow sundress, her hair in a messy bun with tendrils coming down to frame her face, holding a plate full of yellow muffins covered in white icing. He started drooling instantly, but he wasn't sure if it was because of the lemon goodies or the fact that Kenna looked like the dream girl he'd never realized he wanted.

At his appearance, Kenna blushed, embarrassed as she shot her sister a dark look, saying, "I'm so sorry. My plan was to leave these and go, but my sister seemed to have different plans."

Luna smiled as if she were an angel with nothing but good intentions, but the same as Kenna, he smelled a setup, except he didn't mind nearly as much as he should've. His resolve seemed suspiciously weak around Kenna, which was probably something he ought to curb—but she intrigued him.

"My sister makes the absolute best desserts," Luna said. "I challenge anyone to beat her lemon muffins. I mean, maybe it's *technically* a cupcake because there's icing on top, but I call them muffins so no one looks sidewise at you for eating one for breakfast."

Lucas could get on board with that thinking and eagerly selected one from the plate. "I can be an impartial judge. I happen to have a discerning palate when it comes to all things sugary and lemony."

In spite of herself, Kenna giggled. "Well, then, please let me hear the verdict."

Perfecting his best Gordon Ramsey stance, he prepared to render judgment with some semblance of reserve, but the minute that muffin/cupcake hit his mouth, he groaned like someone else had taken over his body. "Damn, that's good. That's fancy-restaurant good," he admitted, stuffing the rest of the muffin in his mouth and finishing it, though now he needed milk immediately. "I may not have thought this through," he admitted, swallowing the pastry. "You didn't by any chance bring some milk or coffee to help wash it down?"

Kenna laughed. "Sorry, you're on your own for beverages."

"Fair enough." He opened the break room fridge and pulled out someone's iced coffee, cracking it open and taking a deep guzzle. "Ahh, perfect."

"Was that yours?" Kenna asked with amusement.

"Nope," he answered with a grin. "But I'll replace it, I promise."

But Luna knew who it belonged to, because she

started laughing and warned him, "You better hustle. That belonged to Betty, the head dispatcher, and if you haven't figured out by now the reason why she has the nickname Betty the Ballbuster, you're about to."

He slid his gaze to Kenna. "Seeing as it's sort of your fault that I'm in this predicament, I think you should walk with me to the café to pick up a replacement," he said, half joking but hoping she'd find the humor and agree.

The easy camaraderie between them took a turn, and the bright light in Kenna's eyes dimmed as she withdrew like an African violet that'd been touched too much. "Sorry, I can't stay," she said, shooting Luna another look. "I'm glad you like the muffins. Please feel free to share. I made plenty for the station. Have a great day."

And then she practically ran out of the room like the devil was on her heels.

"Was it something I said?" he asked, bewildered. Immediately, he felt the urge to run after her, but that seemed like the wrong call. He looked to Luna in apology. "I guess that's what happens when I try to be witty. That was always my brother's department. Seems I should've left it that way."

"No, no, it's not you," Luna assured him with a frown. "My sister is just… Um, well, I think she's unsure of herself right now and terrified of making a mistake. If anyone was being pushy, it was me. I'm the one who suggested she make the lemon muffins."

"You? Why?"

Luna looked caught but came out with it. "Because I like you," she admitted. "You're a good man, and I think you and my sister would hit it off under the right circumstances. I guess I was trying my hand at being an amateur matchmaker." She looked a little sheepish. "Sorry. I should stick to police work."

Lucas didn't fault Luna for trying to do something nice for her sister, but it had probably worked out for the best. He wasn't exactly ready to date anyway, which was why he'd made himself a promise to get his head screwed on straight before he started admiring anyone of the opposite sex.

But he hadn't expected to run into a woman like Kenna. In that yellow dress. Bearing cupcakes that tasted like sunshine. Seemed kinda unfair, to be honest. He was only human, for crying out loud.

"Don't worry about it. As long as Kenna is okay and knows that I didn't mean anything pushy by my joking. In the future, I'll leave the comedy to the comedians." Lucas grabbed another muffin, saying, "Well, I think with that, I'll take this on the road and go get that replacement iced coffee before I get caught and skewered."

"Good idea," Luna said, smiling.

With Noble walking beside him, Lucas realized he was still replaying the scenario with Kenna in his head, possibly looking for an alternate way he could've handled the situation. He really needed to put the brakes on whatever he felt for Kenna. He didn't want a relationship with anyone, much less someone emotionally fragile. In the past, Becca always managed to get in the way of his romantic life, even if she hadn't been trying, but it was hard to explain to a romantic partner the entanglement between him, Brock and Becca.

He supposed even though Becca had always chosen Brock when it mattered, Lucas had still carried a torch for the woman in his secret heart of hearts. As time wore on and their addiction had spiraled into a dangerous situation for everyone involved, Lucas had realized harboring any kind of hope that Becca might someday change was a toxic pill to force down his throat. Not to mention, what kind of brother was he since he'd been secretly in love with his brother's girl for years?

Becca had manipulated that private shame for far too long.

Leaving Kansas behind was a reminder that he wasn't going to perpetuate unhealthy cycles, that he would choose himself first going forward.

But even as he reiterated that reminder in his head, he scanned the sidewalks in the hopes of catching where Kenna ended up. Had she dropped off the muffins on her way to work? Maybe she's at the vet clinic today? No, that dress was definitely not work attire. He distinctly remembered Kenna wearing scrubs when he first met her at the clinic with Noble.

So today was her day off, and she'd decided to bring muffins to the station—specifically lemon, his favorite.

He wasn't Einstein by any means, but was it a sign that Kenna was interested?

Or was he reaching?

Now he'd gone and confused himself.

This was why he wasn't planning on dating anyone for a year after moving to Cottonwood—he didn't need this kind of disruption in his life.

He really needed to stretch his legs and go hiking. The trails were gorgeous this time of year, and the weather was beautiful. What the hell was he waiting for?

Maybe a hiking partner.

Or a hiking partner with long dark hair and eyes that absolutely stunned in a yellow sundress?

He looked down at Noble with a deep exhale, admitting, "I'm in trouble, buddy."

Noble whined as if to agree.

Yep. Big trouble.

What was she thinking, bringing muffins to the station, knowing full well she'd hoped Lucas would notice? And then she was instantly petrified when he did.

What a fine mess you've made.

Tears burned her eyes as that mean voice in her head berated her without mercy. She was trying to make demonstrable changes in her life, and the first cute guy to look her way had her all aflutter like a teenager, which she definitely was not.

She sat heavily on the park bench, drawing deep, calming breaths to steady her heart rate and get a handle on her thoughts. *Okay, reset.* It wasn't that bad. So, she'd embarrassed herself—big deal. It only mattered if she planned to date Lucas, which she didn't. Laugh it off, forget about it. She had bigger problems than what Lucas Merritt thought of her.

Such as Ty's court appearance. Never in a million years had she ever thought those words would cross her mind. *But here we are.*

All her life, she wished she was more like her sisters. Somehow Luna and Sayeh had inherited a steel backbone—neither took any crap from anyone—while she'd been gifted a backbone of putty.

Unlike Sayeh, she rarely thought of her birth parents. She'd been very close to her adopted mother, Nancy. She missed her so much. Right about now, she'd give anything for one of her big, squeezy hugs that promised everything would work out. Tears sprang to her eyes. Nancy would've had great advice to share, something full of kindness and quiet wisdom that Kenna sorely needed.

Instead, she felt adrift with no one to anchor her to the ground, and the current was pulling her farther from shore.

Her adoptive dad, bless his heart, had always been closer to Luna, but losing him in such an awful way had been a cruelty to their family.

And to Ty.

Her son was drowning right before her eyes, and she didn't know how to save him because she could barely save herself.

"Kenna Griffin? Is that you?"

She looked up sharply at the inquisitive query only to see the person she'd least like to see since moving home. "Mya," she said with a fake smile. "How are you?"

Mya Houckette, the frenemy of her childhood, stood with a bright smile and a speculative gaze that immediately made Kenna anxious. "I heard that you were back, but I didn't believe it, because if I knew anything about Li'l Miss Proudfoot, she absolutely couldn't wait to get out of this town. What are you doing here?"

It was an innocent question, but coming from Mya it felt malicious. "My family needed me, and it was time to come home," she said, giving Mya nothing to gossip with as she forced an airy laugh, adding, "And, with maturity comes the realization that home wasn't so bad after all. I wanted my son to experience what I had."

"Only one?" Mya asked, surprised. "I thought for sure you'd have at least *four* kids by this point in your life. You were always so motherly—and let's face it, you fell in love at the drop of a hat with every single boyfriend. I swear it's a mystery how you got through high school without a single pregnancy scare!"

Kenna pretended to laugh as if sharing a great memory, but she felt the sting of Mya's veiled insult. "Do you have any kids?" she asked, hoping and praying that Mya wasn't in charge of any child's care.

"God no, can you imagine me a mother?" Mya answered, laughing. She gestured to her trim figure. "This body can still rock a bikini in Ibiza, and I'm not trading that for anything. Maybe at some point I'll adopt. I don't know, I haven't decided."

The way Mya talked about adopting a child was as cavalier as the effort she'd put into choosing her breakfast and just as fickle. "Well, you look great," Kenna said, hoping that would signal the end of this little reunion.

But Mya settled beside her as if invited. "Actually, it's so good to see you. We have to catch up. You might've noticed my signs all around town—I'm a Realtor now, and very successful, I might add. What do you do?"

"I—well, I just started working at the vet clinic. I love working with the animals."

Mya wrinkled her nose. "I could never. Sick animals—ugh, the smells alone would send me running for the hills. Anyway, you were always better with gross things than me. Remember when we were partners for the biology dissection lab? I couldn't bear to touch that slimy frog, but you had no problem gutting the poor thing."

That wasn't how Kenna remembered that situation. Kenna had agonized over cutting into the frog and begged Mya to do it, but Mya threw a fit over her fresh manicure and spent most of the time flirting with Craig Butler while Kenna struggled to get the assignment done.

But there was no sense in arguing with Mya when she got something in her head, and Kenna didn't want to waste the energy. *Seems some things haven't changed.* Kenna checked her watch, pretending to keep track of the time. "I hate to cut our chat short, but I have an appointment that I need to get to in a few minutes."

Mya pouted with disappointment. "I really wanted to catch up. I've missed you, girl."

Kenna could say without hesitation that she had not missed Mya. "It was great to see you," Kenna lied, rising. "I'm sure we'll run into each other again soon."

"That's a promise," Mya said. "Let's do lunch sometime. My treat."

Kenna would rather chew on a nail sandwich. "Yeah, we'll put something together," she said without committing. "Have a great day!"

Before Mya could say anything else, Kenna left her behind.

It wasn't until she was driving back home that she released the breath trapped in her chest. She hadn't had time to analyze things when she'd decided to return to Cottonwood.

For her, Cottonwood had never been a bad place, but being here only reminded her how malleable she'd been to everything around her. She'd never stood up to Mya in all the years that the woman had abused her kindness, treated her badly or tried to destroy her reputation with malicious gossip.

Instead of calling her out, Kenna had always rolled over and let it slide, trying to believe that Mya truly was her friend and defending her when people saw what Kenna refused to acknowledge.

But she wanted—no, needed—to be different. To open her eyes to the reality of a situation instead of trying to reframe the facts to fit a more comfortable narrative.

Maybe if she'd done that when she first met Leon, she would've noticed the red flags flapping in front of her—and she would've run far and fast in the opposite direction.

She couldn't do anything about the past, but she damn well could start changing for the future.

Chapter 8

"The minor Tyler Anthony Griffin stands charged with malicious mischief on public property," the judge intoned, looking over the paperwork beneath her black-rimmed glasses. From what Lucas could glean from shop talk around the station, Judge Vermeulen was the least lenient of the three judges circulating through the juvenile court system. He could feel Kenna's distressed vibration as she sat perched on the old wooden pew, awaiting her son's sentencing.

In the face of his consequence before the judge, Ty was no longer spitting fire and brimstone but was more subdued—looking more like a ten-year-old kid than a streetwise hooligan—and Lucas felt bad for the boy.

Maybe he should've let the kid off with a warning, but his gut told him that this was the only way Ty would learn, and better to learn now than later when the consequences were steeper. However, he would do what he could to help. "Your Honor, if it pleases the court, I feel Tyler would benefit from community service and probation," he began, glancing back at Kenna, trying to reassure her. "The Cottonwood PD has a great Explorer program that routinely performs various acts of community service under the supervision of the Explorer program supervisor, who is a uniformed officer. I think Tyler would make a good cadet with the right direction."

The judge's expression didn't change, but she gave an imperceptible nod to indicate she'd heard. She looked square at Tyler, openly judging him as if she could see into his soul with the power of her hard gaze. Man, he wouldn't want to be on the wrong side of this judge's court. Finally, she said straight to Ty, "I'm not known for taking a soft approach to crime in my court—no matter the age. But I've read your file, and I see your family has recently been through a terrible tragedy. While I'm not soft, I'm also not cruel. To that end, I will grant Officer Merritt's request and allow your community service to be served through the Explorer program, but I will expect you to keep your nose clean, do your work with a good attitude, and I never want to see you in my court again. Got it?"

"Yes, ma'am," Ty answered in a subdued tone, but he held eye contact, which showed strength of character. Lucas was impressed.

"All right. I mean it, Tyler. If I see you on the wrong side of this court, I will bring the hammer down so hard on your head it'll leave an imprint on your soul."

Ty swallowed but jerked a nod. "Yes, ma'am. You won't see me again."

"Good." She adjusted her glasses before adding pointedly, "I'm also ordering juvenile anger management with a licensed therapist. Court is adjourned." She rapped the gavel, and it was over.

Lucas motioned for Kenna and Ty to follow him outside the courthouse.

In spite of the win, Kenna looked pale. Maybe she wasn't aware of how lucky Ty was to get such a light judgment. "That went better than expected," he said, hoping that would make her feel better.

"Oh, um, yes! Absolutely," she said, bobbing a short nod, but she looked uneasy. Then, with a short laugh that sounded a little brittle, she shared, "I was taken aback by the therapy requirement. It's not like Ty is an angry kid or anything. Can the judge change her mind?"

"Judges don't change their mind." Lucas chuckled ruefully, honestly perplexed by her question.

"Why not?" she asked.

"Because once judgment is rendered, it's final," he answered, surprised at how Kenna looked willing to march into the judge's chambers to persuade Her Honor to rethink her decision. "And judges don't take kindly to that level of disrespect."

"Maybe because no one has ever asked."

"Kenna, is there a reason you don't want Ty going to therapy?"

Her bright smile seemed at odds with her subtle stiffening. "Of course not. Just thrown off guard, I guess."

Lucas relaxed, waving off her worry. "The court-ordered therapy will be a piece of cake. Ty will be just fine."

Ty started pulling at the little tie around his neck, uncomfortable. "This thing's choking me," he groused as he handed it to Kenna with a short look. "And this shirt is itchy."

"But you made a good impression on the judge, so

stop your fussing," Kenna admonished, stuffing the tie in her purse. It might've been his imagination, but he thought her hands were shaking. Before he had a chance to take a second look, she thanked him profusely for his part. "Thank you so much for your input. I think it really made the difference. You didn't have to do that, but we appreciate it."

"If he hadn't arrested me in the first place, none of this would've happened," Ty grumbled, but Kenna gasped and flicked his ear with a glare. "Ow!" he yelped, rubbing at his ear.

"Tyler Anthony! If you hadn't been vandalizing public property, this wouldn't have happened," she returned with heat in her eyes.

Bravo, Mom, Lucas wanted to say but wisely held his tongue. Maybe there was hope for Ty if Kenna made sure the kid knew it was time to act right.

Satisfied Ty was going to watch his mouth, she returned to Lucas. "Like I said, we are very appreciative, and when you see Ty again, I can promise he'll have an attitude adjustment."

He chuckled—he figured the kid probably wouldn't, but that's okay. He didn't get his feelings hurt by boys too big for their britches. The kid would learn, one way or another. "I'll get you the paperwork you need to sign him up for the program, and you're in luck—I'm actually taking the cadets for a hiking excursion this weekend on the Bear Claw Trail. I could use a chaperone if you're interested."

Damn his own mouth. He was doing a bang-up job of staying in his lane when it came to Kenna. He tacked on, "I just mentioned it because I thought it might be a way for you and Ty to do something together—a way to connect, you know?" *So smooth.*

The quick save worked, but before Kenna could answer, Ty piped in with a sour "My mom doesn't hike."

Kenna corrected Ty sharply. "That's not true. I love hiking." Seeming to decide at that moment, she answered, "I'd love to chaperone. I think it'll be fun."

If he got the impression Kenna was agreeing to make a point with her son, he didn't complain. He couldn't shake the little butterflies that erupted in his stomach nor the smile that followed.

"Great! I'll get you everything you need. I can send it home with Luna. Does that work for you?"

"Perfect." She paused a minute and then told Ty to wait for her in the car. Once her son was out of earshot, she said to Lucas, with eyes brimming, "I can't tell you how grateful I am that you stuck your neck out for Ty. He's a good kid, and I hate that you haven't seen that side of him yet, but you will. I promise."

"He's going through something, and I'm guessing he's not ready to talk about it. I get that. I was a young kid once, and I remember feeling out of sorts about the stuff going on in my life. The outdoors always helped me. Maybe it'll be what Ty needs, too."

She wiped at her eyes, smiling. "You know, I feel the same way. I've always loved being out in nature, and I hate that I got away from it for so long. I'm looking forward to going hiking. Thank you for asking."

"No problem," he said. Maybe now wasn't the right time, but he needed to clear the air. "Hey, about the other day with the muffins—"

"Oh gosh, water under the bridge. We don't even need to mention it. I'm glad you enjoyed the muffins," she said, pulling away with a smile. She waved with a cheery "See you this Saturday!" before leaving him behind.

Well, at least he knew where Ty got his penchant for avoiding stuff.

He chuckled and headed back to the station to start the paperwork.

"That went better than we could've hoped, but we'll need to prepare before you go to that therapy appointment," Kenna said to Ty as she drove them home. She was already trying to think of every possible question that could pose a problem. Ty needed to avoid talking about what'd happened to them in Kentucky. All it would take would be something to pique the therapist's interest to start looking into Kenna's business, and they'd find out she'd been a frequent visitor to several state hospitals, and everything would go downhill. "It's best to avoid talking about certain things, okay, Ty?"

"Like what?" he asked sullenly.

"You know what," she answered with a hard look. Now was not the time to play dumb. "It's just better if we, maybe, pretend like it didn't happen."

"Why?"

"Because I—*we* can't afford people asking questions. We don't want to take the risk that Leon might find us. We can't let that happen, okay?" That wasn't the biggest reason that had her shaking, although the threat of Leon was an ever-present shadow in her mind. But if a therapist discovered details of her time in Kentucky, Kenna might lose Ty, and she couldn't take that risk. Leon had made her do illegal things—things she suspected Ty knew—and if CPS got involved, they might decide Kenna wasn't a good enough mother and put Ty in foster care. Kenna would swallow knives before she let that happen.

At Leon's name, Ty stopped pressing, but his attitude remained.

She released a shaky breath. *We can do this. A little coaching and everything will be fine.*

She and Ty were a team, and they'd figure this out.

Switching tracks, she said, "From what I remember, Bear Claw Trail is an easy hike. You'll like it." Kenna was looking forward to lacing up her hiking boots and stretching her legs. It'd been too long since she'd enjoyed the simple pleasure of God's country.

"Who said I like to hike?" Ty said, his face screwing into an annoyed expression. "Dirt, and bugs biting me. Sounds like a great time."

"Tyler," she said, exasperated, "work with me here. Officer Merritt did you a kindness, and you're being a real toad about it. I swear, I thought I raised you better than that."

Ty shrugged as if he didn't care about her opinion on the matter, and that hurt something fierce. "I'm hungry. Can we get something to eat?"

"We have food at home. I'll scramble you some eggs and bacon."

"Never mind."

In the past, she might've caved, but she didn't this time. Ty had to learn that he couldn't act like a jerk and get rewarded with treats. She swallowed the hurt and said, "Okay, your choice. Guess you'll have to wait for lunch then. In the meantime, you have a fresh schoolwork packet waiting for you. I expect you to have your work finished so I can go over it."

"Don't you have to work?" he returned petulantly.

"I took the day off for court," she answered. "So I'm home all day."

"Yay."

She sighed, hating this disconnect between them. Twisting the wheel abruptly, she veered the car off to the side of the shoulder, kicking up dirt and gravel and shocking Ty. "Mom! What are you doing? Trying to kill us?"

"No, I'm trying to figure out when this mean, foul-mouthed changeling is going to return my sweet, loving son. I don't know what's going on with you, because you won't talk to me, and that's fine. I understand your need for space, but that doesn't give you the right to treat me like dirt. I'm your mother, and you need to remember that fact. I have loved you since the day you were born and I'll love you to the day I die, but right now, I don't like you very much, and it kills me to admit that. Now, as I see it, you've got two choices—dig your heels in and be an even bigger jerk to every single person trying to help you and end up in a worse situation, or you can swallow your damn baby pride and realize that you've been given a second chance and not many people get that in life, so suck it up and start acting right."

"I don't want to be here anymore!" Ty shouted back, shocking her with his outburst. "You never asked me if I wanted to give up everything in my life to end up in this boring, stupid town, and then I had to watch my grandpa die right in front of me. I want to leave and never come back!"

Her eyes stung at his raw truth. He was correct that she hadn't asked him, but what choice had there been? She swallowed and chose her words carefully. "Tyler… we had to leave because Leon… Well, you know what he did. It wasn't going to stop. I had to get us out of there before it was too late, and there was no way he would let us leave unless we made it so inconvenient for him to follow. If we'd stayed in Kentucky, he would've dragged us back. I was scared. Not only for me, but for you, too."

Ty sniffed back angry tears, wiping at his nose. "We lived in a nice house, with nice things. I had my own room. Leon was going to sponsor my baseball team. Why'd you have to make him so mad?"

"Breathing made Leon mad some days," she answered quietly, remembering all the times she'd tiptoed around his moods to avoid getting hit or verbally abused. "And it wasn't going to stop with me. He was already starting to push you around in ways that scared me." She reached for his hand and held it tightly. "I would die if anything happened to you. Do you hear me? I would die. You're my life. So we had to run. And that's why I'm asking you to try and make a good life here for now. If you want to move when you're eighteen and on your own, I'll help you pack, but for now, this is home, okay?"

"Okay." Ty gave Kenna an imperceptible nod, but those tiny sniffs poked at her heart. He remembered every hit, every broken bone, but she hoped to God Ty didn't know the true extent of Leon's cruelty, the part she'd take to the grave. However, Ty had another concern pressing on his mind. "I don't like the way that cop looks at you," Ty warned with a glower. "I think he likes you."

She paused, a ready denial on her lips, but she couldn't quite get the words out, because she knew it would be a lie. She wasn't quite sure if Lucas was interested in her romantically or if he was just being kind, but a tiny spark of something existed between them that scared and excited her.

Heaven help her, she was trying to keep her head on straight, but there was something about Lucas that softened her resolve like butter left near the hot stove.

"He seems like a nice guy," Kenna offered, hoping Ty would take some reassurance in that observation, but Ty cut her with a look.

"They *all* start off nice."

Ouch. She couldn't argue with Ty's flat statement. She swallowed, admitting, "I've been real bad in the relationship department, haven't I?" At Ty's subtle nod, she sighed with resignation. "I know. I'm trying to get better at that. I promise."

"Then why are we going on this hiking trip with the cop who arrested me?"

"Because that same cop seems to care about whether or not you turn into a true juvenile delinquent, and I do, too. Plus, I really do love hiking."

"Since when?"

Kenna chuckled and ruffled her son's hair, which he low-key hated but tolerated. "Since I had a life before becoming a mom. When I was younger, I used to hike all the time. There's something relaxing about being in the woods, walking a trail and enjoying the sunshine on your face. You'll see," she promised. "Besides, it's just a hiking trip, not a marriage proposal."

"And what if that changes?"

She laughed with derision, sure of one thing. "It won't."

"You promise?"

"Of course," she answered with confidence, relieved to feel the tension dissipating. "You know what? On second thought, I think you're right. Let's splurge and get something to eat at the café. They have the best blueberry pancakes, possibly better than mine."

"Not possible. Everyone knows you make the best," Ty returned with the smallest hint of her sweet boy, but she'd take it. He met her gaze. "Mom, do you think we're safe here?"

She ignored the slither of dread at the memory of that weird phone call at the house and pasted a bright smile on her face for her son's benefit. "Absolutely. Leon is a lot of things, but he hates being inconvenienced. I think once we left, he didn't think of us again."

Ty wasn't sure. "I heard Leon once say that if he couldn't have you, no one could. What did he mean by that?"

Kenna stilled, wondering when Ty had overheard Leon threaten her like that. It was hard to say—Leon had often whispered terrible things in the privacy of their bedroom, or when he thought they were alone, things for her ears only so no one would ever believe what a monster he was if she tried to get help. "Leon was a bully, and bullies are all talk," she answered, fighting to keep her voice strong. "Like I said, Leon has probably forgotten all about me, or at the very least, he's grateful to be rid of me."

Ty's pensive frown struck at her heart. No kid should have to shoulder that kind of worry for their parent. She swallowed and reached for his hand, clutching it tightly in her own. "I'm so sorry we were in that bad situation for way too long. I'm doing everything I can to make it right. I promise, Ty. All I ask is that you work with— not against—me. Okay?"

Ty nodded but slowly pulled his hand free. "Can we go to the café? I'm starving."

"Right," she said, wiping at the tiny tear that threatened to slide down her cheek. "Blueberry pancakes await."

Maybe things weren't perfect—hell, maybe they were broken in all sorts of places—but she'd damn well take whatever victory she could get, because anything had to be better than where they'd been.

Sometimes you had to be happy with the bruised fruit, because at least it wasn't rotten.

Chapter 9

"Are there going to be snakes on the trail?" a voice called out from the line of cadets preparing to head out.

"Yep, so watch where you step," Lucas answered with a grin, adjusting his backpack with all their lunch supplies and extra water. He caught the smothered smile on Kenna's face as she helped secure her son's water bladder, and it made something inside him warm.

Some might call Lucas crazy for agreeing to tromp through nature's playground with a group of preteens and teenagers ranging in age from ten to seventeen, but he was looking forward to the adventure and the chance to finally see the local trailhead.

The thing was, he liked volunteering with the kids—a fact that caused him to receive no small amount of teasing at the office when it appeared he'd drawn the short straw to be the Explorer cadet coordinator. Kids were easier to teach than adults. Adults were set in their ways and content to let their wheels keep falling into a rut. Kids, on the other hand, were malleable and enjoyed learning new things. Well, most kids. Ty looked as happy as a wet cat.

He turned to the group. "All right, eyes on me," he instructed firmly. "This is a relatively easy hike, but you still want to watch where you plant your feet. You can still break an ankle or find yourself on the wrong end of a danger noodle if you ignore what you're doing."

"Officer Merritt." Fifteen-year-old Spring Johnson, one of the Johnson twins, raised her hand with an uncertain expression, "What do we do if we come across a, um, danger noodle?"

"First and foremost, don't panic. They are more afraid of you than you are of them. No sudden movements. Give the snake a chance to get away, which it will more than likely do the minute it can."

"And what if it doesn't go away?" Spring countered with a frown.

"Let's cross that bridge when we come to it." He clapped his hands together with an excited smile. "Who's ready to see some nature?"

"Everything but the danger noodle," grumbled Spring.

"Why are we doing this?" Ty asked, shooting a look at his mother. "There's bugs everywhere."

"Which is why I brought bug repellent," Kenna said as if Ty was helping her remember something important. She rummaged in her pack and pulled the can, shaking it to start spraying the kids. "Ticks are nasty buggers."

Lucas withheld the chuckle at how deftly Kenna maneuvered around her son's not-so-enthusiastic response to an outing. The kid's expression wasn't hiding anything. The disdain for everything around him was hard to miss, but Kenna was charging forward as if all was good in her world. He envied that level of dogged determination in spite of perceived opposition.

"Look, I know it's probably more fun to spend all day on your phone or in front of the TV or something, but there's a lot out there that's far more interesting than whatever you watch electronically. There's something about nature that calms the soul—I know, that's a little deep this early in the morning, but humor me and give it a chance. You never know what you might find. Okay, cadets, *heyyyy-O!* Head out!"

Lucas took the lead with the cadets in the middle and Kenna bringing up the rear. The trail wasn't long, but the Yellowstone River ran along the cottonwood-fringed path, thick with green underbrush and alive with the various chirps, scuttles and rustling of wildlife and insects. He drew a deep breath as they walked, feeling the tension fall from his shoulders. This was exactly what he needed.

While entertaining the cadets with little nature facts about the area, which he'd studied a little before that morning, he forgot about every stressor currently sapping the joy from his life.

Like Becca.

Three missed calls in a row but no message left. He didn't know if she was letting him know she'd gotten into the program she'd mentioned or if she'd bailed on the idea and still needed money.

Either way, he hadn't called her back. He was trying to create distance between them, but she kept finding reasons to insert herself into his life.

He was inordinately grateful there was spotty cell service where they were going.

Besides, he didn't want anything getting in the way of enjoying the day with Kenna and the cadets. The weather was damn near perfect, and the water glistening with sparks of sunshine was postcard-pretty. What more could a guy ask for?

"Officer Merritt, how come you didn't bring Noble today?" asked Hayden Mockley, the oldest cadet in the group, and the one most serious about a future career in law enforcement, possibly even becoming a K-9 officer.

"He's getting pampered and groomed today," he answered. "Noble would've loved all of this nature, but that's more of a solo outing for the two of us. Besides, now I can focus all of my attention on you cadets."

The plan was to follow the trail and then break off, following an unmarked trail along the riverside, which would then rejoin the main trail farther up the way.

"The Macawi tribe would hunt for elk, deer and antelope for their skins, but they also seasonally hunted buffalo and beaver," he shared. "And did you know the Macawi people were expert horsemen? Horses and the Macawi have a long, rich history together. Legend has it the Macawi people were born with the ability to speak to horses. How cool is that?"

"I didn't realize you were interested in the Macawi culture," Kenna called out to Lucas with a warm smile that bordered on bashful as they walked. "I was born on the Macawi Reservation."

"Really? I didn't know that," Lucas said, surprised. "You'll have to tell me more when we break for lunch."

"Well, I didn't actually grow up on the reservation," she admitted. "Me and my sisters were adopted when we were young."

"Still, pretty impressive to have that cultural background," he said with a grin. "One of the first things I did when I realized Cottonwood bordered the Macawi Reservation was read up on the people. I have great respect for those who came before us. It's my opinion that we could stand to learn a thing or two from the people who understood the language of the land."

"What does that mean?" Ty asked, reluctantly intrigued. "You think, like, the dirt talks to you or something?"

He chuckled. "Not so literally, but there's a possibility that the land does speak in a language we've forgotten how to hear. Did you know that a scientist hooked up special equipment to various mushrooms growing in the wild and discovered their energy signature, when transformed into sound, created sophisticated melodies? We all know that some mushrooms are edible and some are poisonous, but did you know each one could sing?"

"That's weird," Ty said, but he looked at the ground, searching for mushrooms.

Ariana Coates, a thirteen-year-old girl who'd joined the cadets to "build up her résumé," as she called it, was intensely serious, but even she appeared curious about his mushroom story. "I'd like to hear these singing mushrooms," she said.

"Well, I don't have the right equipment, but I bet I could find the link to the article and I could email it to you all," Lucas said, catching another look from Kenna that bordered on sweet before she ducked her gaze. Did she have any idea how beautiful she was? Women often played coy to get his attention, but Kenna had this genuine sense of shyness that tugged at him, even when he tried to shut down his response to it. He'd already made a big production about staying single for a while after relocating to Montana, but damn if being around Kenna didn't have him second-guessing that decision.

Maybe he'd been too hasty in making that call. Becca wasn't around to mess with his head anymore. He had a clean slate and plenty to offer a partner, right?

Lucas caught Kenna's laughter, and the sound was like someone had poured pure joy into his tank. Hell, since when was life about playing it safe? Sometimes the best adventure was right around the bend.

It was silly, yet listening to Lucas talk about her people with such respect and reverence made her tingle in places she thought had been shut down permanently.

He answered every question the cadets lobbed his way with ease, and if he didn't have the answer, he promised to find one for them. She found his calm confidence very sexy, which was a huge difference from the men she'd always been attracted to.

She'd since learned there was an ocean between arrogance and confidence but somehow had always mixed up the two.

But not anymore.

And that's what Lucas oozed without even trying.

When they reached the campsite and claimed a picnic bench, it was nearly noon. Everyone was sweating and eyeing the water with envy. "Can't we just jump in once?" asked Arrow Johnson, the other twin, his dark mop of hair damp with sweat. Kenna didn't blame the kid—a dip in the water seemed like a great idea to her, too.

But Lucas shook his head. "Sorry, buddy, not this trip. Safety first. I don't have enough chaperones to ensure everyone's safety in the water. Maybe a different trip. You can pour some water on your head and you'll cool off."

"That's not the same," Arrow grumbled, but he doused

himself anyway. Within minutes, everyone but Ariana was doing the same. Ariana was busy studying an anthill at a safe distance, watching the tiny ants go about their tasks. Kenna remembered being the quiet girl when she was young, lost in her own world, but Ariana had more ambition than Kenna had ever aspired to at that tender age. Both Luna and Sayeh had been graced with drive, whereas Kenna had been content to drift and enjoy the scenery. She'd discovered too late that drifting had a tendency to dump you on rocky shores.

"I wonder if ants have a song like the mushrooms," Ariana said.

"I don't know," Lucas admitted as he unpacked their lunches, handing them off to Kenna so she could pass them to the cadets. "If anyone needs a refill for their water bladder, here's a fresh water jug."

"Seeing as they all just dumped their water over their heads, I'd say they probably do," Kenna said, chuckling, but she was glad to see Ty actually smiling. He and Arrow Johnson had seemed to hit it off, and they were laughing about something, even as droplets of water slid down their faces in the summer sun. She gestured to the boys. "Come and eat your sandwich." She smiled as they raced each other to the table.

Kenna sat opposite Lucas, which wasn't planned, but she couldn't say she minded. He was ruggedly handsome, but there was something wholesome about him, too, she thought as she took a bite of the plain turkey and cheese.

"How's the sandwich?" Lucas asked, winking because he knew it wasn't much to write home about, but she was ridiculously tickled that he'd spent the time to pack seven lunches—five for the cadets and one for each adult—for this excursion, even though it shouldn't be that big of a deal.

But it was.

In all her dating life, she'd never been with anyone who put the safety and care of others before their own needs. Her brief stint in college ended with Bad Boyfriend Number One, Zane. When he'd made it so difficult to attend class, she eventually dropped out and never managed to make it back. Bad Boyfriend Number Three always used her car (to cheat on her, no less) and then left her without gas, which she only discovered as she was leaving for work the following day. After that, there was a slew of boyfriends—most short-lived—who followed the same selfish, self-absorbed patterns, but none had been like Leon.

He took the cake.

She used to think that people used the term *narcissist* a little too freely, but having been trapped by one for almost two years, she no longer passed that cavalier judgment.

"That good, huh?" Lucas cut into her thoughts with a teasing smile, and she realized she'd dropped into her own head and gotten lost there for a good minute.

"Sorry," she said, insisting with a blush, "No, they're really good. Filling and hearty, which is perfect for a hiking lunch."

"You're being kind," he said, the corners of his mouth tilting adorably. "But my tender ego appreciates it. Thank you."

Was that a dimple? *Oh please, not a dimple.* Dimples were her kryptonite. She leaned toward Lucas, sharing in a conspiratorial whisper, "I think Ty is actually having a good time. It's the first time I've seen him smile since his grandpa died."

Lucas sobered at the mention of her dad. "That's a tough thing to go through for anyone. How's your family holding up?"

"I think we're all dealing with it in our own way. Luna has her boyfriend, Benjamin, and the job to keep her mind busy, and Sayeh is off chasing a mystery involving our birth parents as well as fighting against a sexual harassment situation at work that nearly got her fired," she clarified quickly when she noticed Lucas's flash of confusion. "Oh, my sister Sayeh defended herself against a coworker for sexually harassing her, but she may have gone a little overboard. I guess the guy had a broken nose and jaw. Something about excessive force. Anyway, she's definitely got her hands full. No time for grief."

"And how about you?" he asked.

She forced a short laugh. "Um, well, I'm a mom to a troubled kid, so I don't really have time to focus on my grief at the moment. When I get some free time, I'll have a mental breakdown, but until then, gotta stay the course."

He chuckled. "You're a strong woman. I admire that in you."

"Me? Strong? Oh gosh, you've got the wrong impression of me," she said, shaking her head with a rueful laugh. "Unlike my sisters, I'm made of pudding."

"I don't believe that for a second. For one, like you said, you're a mom, and I've never met a mother who wasn't stronger than any man I've ever known. I once saw a mother lift a car off her child from sheer adrenaline. Moms are badass, so don't even try to tell me that you're not."

She warmed to his praise, shyly accepting the compliment. "I guess so. I never looked at it like that."

"Back in Kansas, I got called out to a domestic disturbance—cops hate those calls, not because we don't want to help but because they're unpredictably dangerous to everyone involved. Anyway, we got there and the guy was long gone, but his wife was slumped over in the corner of the living room at an odd angle. As we approached, we heard the muffled cries of a baby and discovered the mother had shielded her child using her own body."

Kenna blinked, her throat closing. She would do the same for Ty in a heartbeat. "What happened?"

"Dad came home drunk, got it in his head that the kid wasn't his. When he tried to get his hands on the baby, the mom protected her child, which only enraged the man further. He beat his wife to death, but the baby lived. The man is now serving life in prison, and the kid was adopted. Last I heard, the kid was living a good life, but it'll never erase the loss of his mother."

"I don't know how you can handle those kinds of calls," she admitted, swallowing the bite that'd suddenly congealed in her mouth. If luck hadn't been on her side that night when Leon threw her across the room, Ty would be an orphan being raised by one of her sisters. She was intimately aware that her story could've ended as badly as so many before her. Kenna cleared her throat with a sip of water, adding, "Well, like I said, I know I couldn't do it."

"That's why I'm working with the K-9 unit now," he shared. "That case hit too hard. Every cop has a case that changes them—that one was mine." He broke the heavy moment with a quick, rhythmic tapping of his knuckles on the wooden picnic table, saying with chagrin, "I usually save that story for when I'm meeting the family."

That made an unexpected laugh pop from her mouth. "Oh, is that so? Good choice. Nice icebreaker."

"Go big or go home, right?"

They laughed, and the moment's heaviness disintegrated like a soap bubble under pressure. Was she surprised to discover Lucas was more than just a handsome face? Maybe. She knew he was kind and generous, but she hadn't expected to see such depth in his character. Was she wistfully wondering what having a partner like Lucas would be like, maybe a little? Yes, but she'd forgive herself this time. The day was too nice to spoil with dark thoughts and the heavy press of guilt.

Way too soon, the time to go arrived. Even Ty seemed reluctant to leave the idyllic camp spot, and that gave Kenna confidence that her boy was in there somewhere. Maybe hiking could become their thing. The thought gave her comfort and hope, two things she sorely needed in her life right now.

They packed up, made sure they left the campground clean and headed back to the trailhead.

Kenna was light as air, and a smile hovered on her lips even though a part of her tried to stamp it down. *But it feels so good*, she wanted to argue with that annoying voice nagging at her. Maybe Lucas was different. Even Luna liked him, and she had a far better compass when it came to guys than Kenna did. So, perhaps it wasn't so bad that she felt drawn to him in dizzying ways.

By the time they reached the trailhead, the parents of the cadets were waiting. It was quick work of sending the kids off on their way, and then just Ty and Kenna and Lucas remained.

"Go ahead and wait for me in the car," she told Ty.

Ty's smile faded to a look of suspicion, but he did as she asked.

Once he was out of earshot, Kenna said, "Thank you again for what you've done for Ty. I can't tell you how much it meant to me to see him smiling again. He really needed this."

"Like I said, fresh air, dirt and sunshine, the best cure-alls in the world," Lucas said. "But you're welcome. Happy to help. He's a good kid underneath all that attitude. Reminds me of someone."

"You?" she guessed.

"Nope, my little brother."

"You have a little brother?"

"Had. He passed away."

She frowned. "Oh, I'm sorry. May I ask how he died?"

Lucas hesitated briefly but shared, "Uh, a drug overdose."

"Oh, I'm so sorry. That must've been so painful for your family."

"No family to speak of, but losing Brock was the worst pain of my life."

Kenna wanted to reach out and hug Lucas but settled for a quick squeeze of his hand to show she understood.

"Me and Brock were always close, but drugs will sever even the strongest of ties."

"I can only imagine," she said, so grateful she'd never fallen into that particular trap, but she'd known plenty who had. "I'm sorry for your loss."

Lucas accepted her kindness with a smile, admitting, "Yeah, it was rough, but seeing Ty reminded me of him in some ways. I'll be honest, it's hard for me to stand back and let another kid fall through the cracks when he needs help."

Kenna tried not to read too much into his statement, but no mother liked to hear that their kid was poten-

tially at a turning point that could go either way—and
one of those ways ended with dying.

Lucas must've seen the apprehension in her expression and rushed to clarify. "I don't mean that Ty is anywhere near where Brock ended up. I just mean that
catching a kid before they stumble too hard is the best
way to help them from falling to their knees. Does that
make sense?"

The fact that he was anxious to alleviate her fears
instantly made her gooey. He genuinely seemed to care
about her feelings, which was something she wasn't
used to getting when it came to men. How low had she
been placing the bar in the past? *Pretty much on the
damn floor.*

Lucas had such a good heart. He deserved someone
far better than her, but maybe she would be a little selfish this time and see what happened.

"Um, so, if you ever want another batch of lemon
muffins—"

"Yes."

He said it so quickly that she couldn't help but laugh.

"Yes," he repeated, only this time those dimples
popped out again, and she almost melted into a puddle
right there.

"Okay," she murmured, risking a look from beneath
her lashes. "Monday?"

"I'll bring the iced coffee so I don't have to steal from
Betty the Ballbuster."

"That's a terrible nickname," she admonished playfully.

"She's a terrible grump but an excellent dispatcher,
so you take the good with the bad," he said with a shrug,
his gaze zeroing in on her lips.

Would he kiss her? No, she couldn't do that with Ty

watching. She slowly and reluctantly broke the spell weaving around them, forcing a bright, cheery smile as she backed away. "Okay, then, thanks again, and I'll bring those muffins on Monday."

She gave an awkward wave and then climbed into the car as if her heart weren't thundering in her chest, and the most ridiculous urge to start singing at the top of her lungs didn't have her feeling like a kid again.

Until she met her son's stony gaze.

Damn it. She might've made a promise that would be too hard to keep.

Chapter 10

"You promised!"

Ty's hurt glower cut into her heart, prompting her to set him straight immediately. "I haven't broken any promises to you, Tyler," she admonished as they drove home after the hike. "Bringing a plate of muffins to Officer Merritt is a gesture of goodwill. He went out of his way for you and he didn't have to. Didn't you have fun today?"

"Yeah, but that's not the point. I saw the way you two were looking at each other and I know what it means. I'm not a baby, Mom."

But he *was* a baby, she wanted to cry out, frustrated that circumstances had stolen parts of his childhood from him. He was way too observant for a kid his age, and that was her fault. She'd leaned on him too hard, needing her own child as a buffer from some of Leon's abuse. It wasn't always a foolproof method, but Leon knew he couldn't protect his reputation if Ty started talking about how Leon liked to beat the crap out of Kenna behind closed doors. To the outside world, Leon was a great guy—personable, likable and witty. It was only with Kenna that he showed his true colors.

"I know you're not a baby," she said solemnly, searching for a way to be honest without misleading her son about Lucas. She couldn't say that she wasn't affected by Lucas, because the butterflies in her stomach made that statement a lie.

She swallowed the urge to soothe his feelings with another promise that felt dangerously close to lying. The fact was, she was attracted to Lucas. She didn't know what to do with that acknowledgment—likely nothing—but she didn't want to lie to her son.

"I promised you I wasn't looking to date anyone right now. That hasn't changed, but I never said I wouldn't be friends with people," she said, dancing around the truth.

"Friends don't look at each other like you two do," he returned, daring her to correct him. "I've seen it plenty of times."

She was going to stick to the facts as she knew them. "Even if I liked Lucas as more than a friend, right now just isn't a good time to be thinking about that kind of stuff. I'm trying to get my life together and get us both on solid ground again. Okay?"

"So you *do* like him for a boyfriend? I knew it."

"You're a smart kid, but you're not listening. You're picking and choosing because you're mad. I am not looking for anything more than friendship, no matter how I might feel. Do you understand?"

"What if he tries to get you to like him as more than a friend?"

She sighed, admitting something that hurt to say. "Ty,

once he learns a bit more about me, whatever feelings he might have will go away. I can promise you that."

"Why?"

"Because—" She stopped herself—Ty didn't need to hear that stuff—and switched gears. "Doesn't matter, because I'm not looking. I'm open to friendship, and that's it."

Her response was sensible and the best thing to say, but it felt wrong, which only created confusion in her head. Shouldn't it be a relief that she was finally doing the right thing instead of falling headlong into the first situation that her heart said was a green light?

"I saw you hit it off with one of the cadets, Arrow?" Kenna said, steering the conversation away from Lucas.

"Yeah, he's cool, I guess," Ty answered with a non-committal nod, but his energy had shifted from angry and scared to grudgingly less so. "He wanted to be a skydive instructor, but his mom said that jumping out of a perfectly good airplane wasn't a real job, so he decided he'd become a cop instead."

Kenna laughed. "They both seem a little on the dangerous side. How about you? What do you want to be when you grow up?"

Ty shrugged. "I don't know, haven't thought about it."

Her smile faded. Had she robbed her son of a normal childhood because of her lifestyle? Shouldn't he be thinking of that kind of stuff by now? Or was she paranoid and Ty was too young to think that far off in the future? She didn't know anymore. Everything she did made her question the action before it. As usual, it was enough to drive her insane.

"Let's order pizza tonight," she decided, too pooped to think about dinner. "What do you say? Pepperoni, sausage and extra cheese?"

A real smile broke out on Ty's face. "I won't turn down pizza."

"I know you won't," she said with a grin, grateful to have navigated that sticky situation. At least pizza was still her son's currency. Not even pizza would save the day if things didn't get better between them.

She kept the conversation fun and light, encouraging Ty to continue talking about his newfound friendship with the older cadet. By the time they picked up the Take-n-Bake and arrived home, Ty's mood had lightened considerably, almost back to being the son she remembered.

Ty ran to his bedroom to play on his Xbox (a gift from his auntie Sayeh when they first arrived—Lord have mercy on the karma that woman was going to get when she decided to have kids), and Kenna relaxed with a beer on the patio.

Luna came outside to join her. "I thought I heard you guys come back. How was the hiking trip?"

"It was really good," Kenna answered with enthusiasm. "It's been a long time since I've been out to Bear Claw Trail, but it was just as I remembered. Beautiful, easy hike along the river."

"Did you see any snakes?"

"Gratefully, no. We did see a beaver dam, though, which was very exciting for the cadets."

"I was never one for hiking like you, but I do remember Bear Claw being relatively tame, with a beautiful view of the Yellowstone."

"Yep. Still the same," Kenna said.

"And how did things go with Lucas?"

"Great!" Kenna forced a bright smile. "And if things don't work out for Lucas as a K-9 officer, he definitely has a career as a trail guide. He was quite thorough on the bugs, flora and even the history of the Macawi and their relationship with the Yellowstone River. Oh, and horses."

Luna laughed. "I didn't realize Lucas was so enamored with local history."

"And the Macawi culture," Kenna exclaimed with a short laugh. "He put me to shame. I didn't know some of the facts he was sharing, and that's our tribe!"

Luna shared Kenna's amusement and chagrin. "Man, I'll admit it's been weird learning about our heritage as an adult rather than growing up with the culture. With Sayeh getting more involved with the Macawi Reservation, it's been an eye-opening experience to realize how disconnected we were from our past."

Kenna sobered, agreeing. "I want to start learning again. Especially with Ty. He doesn't know anything about our culture, and that feels wrong. We might not have grown up on the reservation, but our blood is still Macawi."

Luna nodded, sipping her beer. "So why do you think Lucas was so interested in the Macawi facts?"

Kenna shrugged. "I think he wanted to make the excursion interesting and so went out of his way to pepper them with fun facts. The cadets seemed to eat it up, so I think it worked."

"Excellent. We've needed a good replacement for the cadet coordinator since Vernon retired. I'm glad to hear that Lucas is a solid fit."

"He's really good with kids," Kenna murmured, trying not to overthink how sweet and handsome he was. "I'm surprised he's not married."

"Me, too," Luna admitted, although she frowned as she shared, "I don't know for sure, but I think he had a bad situation back in Kansas that's made him a little gun-shy."

"You mean with his brother? Lucas told me his younger brother died from a drug overdose."

Luna frowned in surprise. "Maybe. I didn't want to pry, and he hasn't really given up much detail. I'm a private person, so I understand not wanting to share personal stuff. Did he say if he and his brother were close?"

"Very. It was real hard for him," Kenna shared, feeling a pinch for Lucas's loss. As much as they squabbled, Kenna couldn't imagine losing either of her sisters.

"That's terrible. Although I'm not sure how losing his brother has kept him away from a relationship. A guy that looks like Lucas doesn't usually find himself alone for long."

"Maybe he's taking the time to heal?" Kenna supposed, wondering herself.

"Possibly. He's already turned down a few eager ladies in town who were aggressively chasing him down, which leads me to believe he's serious about staying respectfully single."

Kenna chuckled. "Respectfully? What do you mean?"

"Well, he's so damn nice about it even when he's turning them down. Seemed the best way to describe how he handles the sticky situation when rejecting them."

Why did she find that even more adorable? Even when he was under no obligation to care about a stranger's feelings, he was kind? Lord, was this guy for real?

Luna noticed her sudden mood shift, asking, "Are you okay?"

"Yeah, just reflecting, I guess."

"I'm here if you want to divulge," Luna offered.

Even though Kenna and her sisters had grown closer

since the tragedy with their dad, it still wasn't easy to open up. It was a work in progress that still needed lots of time.

"Actually, I think I'm going to shower," she said, finishing her beer. "I'm still sticky from the hike, and I need to start the pizza soon."

Luna nodded and let it go; she understood.

And for that, Kenna was grateful.

It wasn't that she didn't want to talk to her sister about things—she just didn't know how to form the words.

Especially the ones that would cut like glass coming out of her mouth.

Lucas was still riding a high from the hike, replaying that last conversation with Kenna in his mind. Something in her smile, the way her eyes lit up, created a forest fire in his brain that he couldn't quite stop.

And she was bringing him muffins Monday.

He picked up Noble from his pamper day at the doggie spa and headed home. If he didn't talk to someone about the situation with Kenna, he'd burst. "Sorry, bud, it's you," he said to Noble as he drove home. "So, there's this woman I think I'm crazy about, and I barely know her. I know, I know, I said I wanted to stay single for a year in my new place, but she's unlike any woman I've ever met. She's the wrinkle I never expected, you know?"

Noble whined and licked his chops as if to say, "You're on your own, pal," but at least he was a good listener.

"She's a single mom with the biggest heart I've ever seen. She's the kind of woman who would do anything for the person she loves, and I'd be lucky to have that kind of attention from a woman like her. I don't know, maybe I'm rambling, but I feel giddy, like a teenager, and it's a little embarrassing, I'll give you that, but it feels amazing, too. She's incredible. I know, it's just muffins, you say, but muffins can lead to lunches, which can lead to dinners and then, who knows? Maybe a kiss?"

Could a dog roll his eyes? Lucas was almost sure Noble had done just that. Not a matchmaker, that one.

"Try to imagine the hottest standard poodle sashaying in your path, then you might understand," he joked.

Noble chuffed and groaned.

"Oh? Not a poodle guy? You like the short queens? Okay, how about a sassy corgi with those heart-shaped fluffy butts?"

He was in too good of a mood, but it felt fantastic. If he could sing, he would've belted out a few notes, but he wouldn't subject Noble to that level of torture.

As soon as his feet crossed the threshold of his house, his cell phone sprang to life, and he eagerly checked the caller ID—only to see Becca's name flash.

His good mood evaporated. He didn't want to take the call, but he'd already missed several of her calls. What if it was an emergency? He wanted closure, but old habits died hard.

"What's up, Becca?"

"Lucas, I've been trying to get ahold of you for days. Haven't you seen any of my missed calls?"

The sad desperation in her voice softened his tone. "I saw your calls, but you never left a message. I figured if it was important, you would've said something. You didn't, so I went about my business."

"There was a time when you always took my call," Becca recalled with a sniff. "Have things gotten so bad between us that you can't even stomach hearing my voice?"

"Of course not," he said with a heavy exhale. This was exactly why he didn't want to answer her calls. When Becca was high or drunk, she leaned heavily on the sad-girl card, and for a long time, it had always worked on him, but he'd gotten wise to her every play. "What do you need? Did you get into the program?"

"I'm trying," she said in earnest, "but I'm on a waiting list. They could call me at any time, though."

"Good," he said, repeating his original question, "so why do you keep calling?"

"It's real hard to stay sober when you don't have any support," she said, her voice getting small. "I mean, when you were here, you were able to help me, and now I'm all alone, and all I do is think of Brock and that makes it worse. At least when you were here, I was able to keep things in check a little better."

"Your memory is selective," he told her. When Becca had wanted to get high, nothing had stopped her. He couldn't count the number of times he'd gone to find her when she'd dropped off the face of the planet only to find her curled up in a stupor in some rat-infested trap house. "Becca, you can't get sober for anyone but yourself. Me being there wasn't helping you—it gave you a convenient excuse to keep screwing up because you had a safety net. Me leaving was the best thing I could've done for us both."

"That's not true," she protested, and he knew the crocodile tears weren't far behind. "Please, I can't do this without you. I'm begging you to help me."

"I am helping you."

"No, you're abandoning me."

"I'm not having this argument," he said. *Again.* "Are you high or drunk right now?"

"No! How could you ask me that?" she asked, indignant and offended, but his gut instinct told him she was lying. "Fine, obviously you're not interested in helping me, even though you promised me that you'd always be there at Brock's funeral. I guess your promises aren't worth much, are they?"

His temper threatened to flare, but he let it go. Becca was hungry for any kind of reaction, even anger. He wasn't going to play her games. That promise had been a mistake. Becca wasn't the girl she'd once been, and for that matter, he wasn't the same boy, either. It was possible the last remnants of the boy he'd been had died with Brock.

"Good night, Becca."

"No, wait—"

But he'd already clicked off, and then he did something he'd never dared to do.

He blocked her number.

I'm sorry, brother. I can't do it anymore. I just can't.

Hopefully, if Brock was watching, he understood, because, goddamn, Lucas had tried to do right by Becca, even if he'd failed his brother.

He really had.

Chapter 11

Kenna was a wellspring of nervous energy as she zipped around the kitchen putting the finishing touches on her basket of muffins that Monday morning. She'd been up way too early—couldn't sleep because of her racing mind—so she'd crept into the kitchen at an unholy hour and not only baked the lemon muffins but also prepared Ty's favorite chocolate chip pancakes so they would be ready for him when he woke up.

Not only was she bringing in the muffins today, but Ty was also starting the court-ordered anger management with the therapist, and she wanted to vomit.

She'd spent Sunday making sure Ty knew what to say—or more specifically, what to avoid—and she felt reasonably confident he could handle the assignment, but she feared she was the worst mother in the world for asking him to do this in the first place.

But she consoled herself with the promise that they

were going to be okay once they got through this. This was a bump in the road, not a sinkhole.

However, starting the day off sweet with some chocolate pancakes wouldn't hurt, either.

Luna came in first, dressed in her uniform and ready for the day. She sniffed the air in the kitchen and saw the stack of pancakes and the picnic basket with the lemon muffins. "Tough choice," she admitted, eyeing that basket. "But I think I'll stick with coffee and a banana today. Benjamin wants to book a Caribbean cruise soon, and if I keep eating your pastries, I'll need a whole new wardrobe."

"Haven't you heard? Curves are sexy," Kenna returned with a smile.

"Maybe so, but I can't afford to keep buying new clothes. Not with this economy." Luna poured a mug of coffee and took a sip before offering, "I know today is Ty's first therapy appointment—"

"Technically, it's not even *real* therapy, just an anger-management class, which he doesn't even need," Kenna corrected with a short smile. "Lucas said that it's standard practice for these kinds of cases."

"Yeah, probably," Luna agreed, "though it wouldn't hurt for Ty to talk to someone about his feelings. Grief is tricky under normal circumstances, much less what Ty went through with Dad's murder. It's not a terrible idea to have a professional helping him deal with that trauma."

"He's fine," Kenna said, irritated with Luna constantly pushing the therapy angle. "I know my son, and he's fine. We will get through this and put it all behind us."

Luna wisely shut her trap about things she didn't need to be talking about, and Kenna blew out a short breath, her nerves strung taut. "I'm sorry, that was—yikes, where'd that come from?—I didn't mean to snap like that."

"No worries. You're under a lot of strain. I understand." But Luna looked a little hurt in spite of her assurances to the contrary. They had a long way to go to building the type of relationship that you saw on TV shows, but Kenna didn't need to make the gap wider just because she was dealing with her own guilt.

"Yeah, this case with Ty has me on edge," Kenna murmured, thankful for her sister's cool head. If Kenna had snapped at Sayeh like that, they'd probably be brawling on the kitchen floor.

Speaking of. "Have you talked to Sayeh lately?"

"Not for a few weeks. She's got her hands full with that IA investigation. Turns out that guy she clocked has gotten handsy with a few other female coworkers, and they're all coming forward."

"That's good news," Kenna said, proud of her little sister for being the catalyst. "Any other news on the soil samples taken from the reservation?"

"If there's news, she hasn't shared," Luna answered, taking another sip. "How do you feel about that whole situation?"

Kenna sighed, considering the question. It was complicated. Unlike Sayeh, she'd never felt a pressing need to know more about their birth parents, but their deaths had created a void deep inside that she couldn't seem to fill no matter what she threw in there. Since discovering it was likely they were murdered, Kenna didn't know how to feel. Sayeh was hoping that the soil samples revealed a lack of caustic chemicals often left behind during meth lab explosions, which would prove the police report had been wrong and that the fire was used to cover up their biological parents' murder. Kenna wasn't sure it was a great use of time or resources, but it seemed important to Sayeh, so she tried to be supportive. She shrugged, unsure. "I want to know what happened to them, but the outcome doesn't really change my life either way. I'm more interested for Sayeh's sake. She's really invested in finding the answers, and I want her to finally be happy."

"And you think finding out if our parents were murdered will make her happy?" Luna returned with a quizzical expression. "Seems like the opposite would happen."

"Maybe that's the closure she needs."

Luna nodded, considering that possibility. "Well, maybe so. I guess we'll just have to wait and see." She finished her coffee, rinsed her mug and grabbed a banana. "Hey, if you want, I can take the muffins in so you don't have to make a special trip."

A wise woman trying to avoid complicating things would eagerly take her sister's offer, but Kenna wanted to see Lucas's face when she delivered the muffins. "That's okay, I got it. It's no big deal. I plan to stop after I drop Ty off."

"Okay, sounds good. Hey, I just remembered to ask, do you have any objections to having the landline turned off? No one uses it, and now that Dad is gone, I thought we might as well cut the expense. I tried to talk Dad into letting it go years ago, but he insisted we keep it."

Kenna forced a chuckle, recalling the mouth breather from the other day. "I wouldn't mind. Everyone who would need to get a hold of us has our cell phone numbers. I certainly wouldn't miss another one of those prank calls."

"What do you mean?"

"Oh, it was nothing. I was in the kitchen and the phone rang—scared the soul out of me, though—but when I picked up, there was nothing but some weirdo breathing heavy on the other line. I hung up, and they didn't call back. Do you remember prank calling people as kids? Maybe it's still a rite of passage. Maybe I should be grateful that technology hasn't completely overridden everything from our childhood."

Luna offered a troubled smile but let it go. "Okay, I'll call the phone company and get it taken care of."

Kenna smiled and moved on, already thinking about her muffin delivery. It was such a small thing, but the thought of seeing Lucas's face light up when she arrived, basket in hand, gave her a giddy sense of happiness that felt too good to stop.

Safe to assume wisdom wasn't one of her strong suits, but nothing was wrong with being friends with Lucas, she justified as she tidied up the kitchen, even though it was practically spotless already.

Everyone needed a friend who looked distractingly good in hiking boots, a ball cap and a pair of dimples that stopped her heart.

Was it terrible that all she'd thought of last night was what it'd be like to kiss Lucas?

Friends don't kiss, a voice reminded her.

Stop being a party pooper. Some do.

But you don't.

She closed her eyes and exhaled loudly. No kissing friends.

Crap.

He knew he was grinning like a fool but couldn't stop himself as soon as Kenna entered the building and walked into his section of the station. She seemed to float into view, her dark hair in a cute ponytail, wearing dangling silver earrings and a long, funky, hippie-chick dress that fit her perfectly. Her smile brightened as they made eye contact, and he jumped out of his seat to greet her.

He had all the adoring energy of a puppy dog but couldn't help himself.

"Special delivery," she joked, handing over the basket. "There's plenty to share, so don't be stingy."

Lucas made a show of peeking beneath the gingham covering and shook his head. "Sorry, I'm going to have to disagree. This is clearly a delivery for one. The rest of the station can get their own magical muffins."

She giggled and blushed. "Magical? You're laying it on a little thick. They're just lemon muffins."

"Agree to disagree."

"Okay," she said, nodding with a bashful smile. "Did you remember to bring the iced coffee?"

"I did," he said, setting the basket on the desk and disappearing for a quick minute to grab the coffee from the break room refrigerator and two cups. "And a big enough container to share."

"That's so sweet, but I shouldn't stay," she said, gesturing. "I just wanted to drop these off in person to tell you that I can't say enough good things about Saturday's hiking trip. Not only did you manage to break through that hard shell around Ty—if only briefly—but you reminded me of something I'd forgotten about myself, and that's damn near priceless to me."

"Then let's do it again," he suggested.

She laughed at his eagerness, but she didn't shut him down. Not immediately, anyway. "What will people think about Cottonwood's most eligible bachelor tromping around the wildness with someone like me?"

"I don't know, that I'm a lucky guy?" he answered with a quizzical frown. Why did she have such a dim view of herself? As far as he could tell, Kenna was a rare gem that dazzled, but everyone in this town seemed to be blind to that. But not him. "On second thought, how about dinner?"

He held his breath. Kenna stilled as her eyes widened. She wanted to say yes, he could feel it, but something held her back. Was it him? The answer came to him in a thunderclap of awareness, and he adjusted his offer. "Bring Ty. It'll be fun."

Kenna swallowed, and her eyes watered, which was the opposite reaction he'd been going for. Why was he floundering so badly? Had he completely lost his touch? He started to apologize, but she stopped him. "No, it's not you. It's me. Can I be honest with you?"

"Of course."

"I like you. I really do, but I made a promise to Ty that I wouldn't date anyone right now. We came from a difficult situation, and moving home was my vow to my son that I'd finally get my life together. It's embarrassing to admit, but it seems I have some unhealthy patterns that I'm trying to change, and I can't do that if I keep falling into the same rut."

He understood that feeling all too well. Becca was his rut, and he'd run away from an entire state to get out of his pattern. What or who was Kenna running from? "May I ask what those ruts were?"

"Falling in love with the wrong people." She swallowed, looking incredibly vulnerable.

"Hell, we've all done that," he murmured. "I wouldn't beat yourself up too badly on that score."

"I wish it were that simple. In the past, I've picked some questionable men to be in our lives, and the last one, well, he was really bad."

"How bad?" he asked.

She shook her head, apparently not wanting to go into details. "Bad enough. Anyway, that's in the past, but I'm still rebuilding our lives, and I'm not sure I can do that when I'm in a new relationship."

"I get it. It's kinda funny—I made a promise to myself that I wouldn't date for the first year in Cottonwood so I could get my head on straight and figure out how to watch for red flags instead of trying to collect them like party favors, but I never planned on meeting someone like you," he admitted. "You kinda wrecked my plan."

She chuckled wryly. "Well, I hate to break it to you, but I'm the reddest of flags out there. I'm doing you a favor by reminding you to steer clear of bad patterns."

He wasn't going to lie and say he wasn't disappointed, but she was trying to save him from himself, and he appreciated that she cared enough to warn him off. Except he kinda found the challenge even more enticing. *Talk about some reverse psychology at work.* However, he wasn't going to push something she wasn't ready for, no matter his feelings.

"So, we stay friends until it's a better time to try something different," he suggested.

"But that's not fair to you," she protested. "You're a catch. You shouldn't sit around waiting for me when I don't know if I'll ever be ready."

"Look, I like you a lot, and I want to get to know you and Ty better. I can put that other stuff on hold. Let's go hiking again and maybe catch some dinner and a movie. If all goes well, maybe we go camping or something. What I'm trying to say—in case it wasn't clear—is that I like spending time with you, and I'll take what I can get until—if—we're both ready to offer more."

Unexpected tears welled in her eyes. "You would do that for me?"

"In a heartbeat," he said without hesitation. "Besides, they say a lasting relationship is built on the foundation of a solid friendship, and I've never tried that before, so I'm down for giving it a shot."

"And what if we find out that we're better as friends?"

"Then I've gained a kick-ass friend who can vet future potentials and vice versa. I don't see a downside."

She laughed and wiped at her eyes. "You're unlike anyone I've ever met, you know that?"

"I'll take that as a compliment, given the guys you said you're used to dating," he said with a wink.

"Fair enough," she said, her laugh deepening. Kenna glanced at the muffin basket. "We should eat so you can get back to work and I can time it perfectly to pick up Ty from his anger-management session."

"Sounds like a plan," he said, pouring the iced coffee into two red plastic cups while Kenna served up the muffins using small paper plates. Lucas lifted his cup with a smile, feeling light as air. "Here's to a beautiful friendship and whatever else it may or may not become."

She smiled and lifted her cup in agreement.

It was a start, and he'd take it.

Women like Kenna didn't come along often, and he knew having her in his life, in any capacity, was worth trying.

But as he watched her leave, he couldn't shake the

feeling that he needed to know more about the bad boy-friend before they went any further. In his experience, bad boyfriends had a tendency to linger—no matter if they were invited or not.

Chapter 12

Kenna left the station with a smile from ear to ear. How was it possible that Lucas was this good? Was it an act? Was he really this kind and generous? A trickle of doubt threatened to rain on her positive mood, but she pushed it away. No, she couldn't hope for a fresh start if she was determined to see ghosts from her past around every corner.

Her saving grace was that Luna was a huge fan of Lucas's, and her sister was a harsh judge. If Lucas had even the slightest bit of weirdness, her sister would've sniffed it out.

But why would he be interested in her if there wasn't something terribly wrong with him?

Stop spiraling.

No need to spend energy worrying about something that wouldn't happen. They'd agreed a relationship wasn't in the cards right now, but there was nothing

Loyal Readers
FREE BOOKS Voucher

We're giving away **THOUSANDS**
of **FREE BOOKS**

See Details Inside

Get up to 4
FREE FABULOUS BOOKS
You Love!

To thank you for being a loyal reader we'd like to send you up to 4 FREE BOOKS, absolutely free when you try the Harlequin Reader Service.

Just write "YES" on the Loyal Reader Voucher and we'll send you 2 free books from each series you choose and Free Mystery Gifts, altogether worth over $20.

Try **Harlequin® Romantic Suspense** books featuring heart-racing page-turners with unexpected plot twists and irresistible chemistry that will keep you guessing to the very end.

Try **Harlequin Intrigue® Larger-Print** books featuring action-packed stories that will keep you on the edge of your seat. Solve the crime and deliver justice at all costs.

Or **TRY BOTH and get 2 books from each series!**

Your free books are completely free, even the shipping! If you continue with your subscription, you can look forward to curated monthly shipments of brand-new books from your selected series, always at a discount off the cover price! Plus you can cancel any time.

So don't miss out, return your Loyal Readers Voucher today to get your Free books.

Pam Powers

LOYAL READER
FREE BOOKS VOUCHER

YES! I Love Reading, please send me up to 4 FREE BOOKS and Free Mystery Gifts from the series I select.

Just write in "YES" on the dotted line below then return this card today and we'll send your free books & gifts asap!

➡ ___ YES ___ ⬅

Which do you prefer?

☐ **Harlequin® Romantic Suspense**
240/340 HDL GRS9

☐ **Harlequin Intrigue® Larger-Print**
199/399 HDL GRS9

☐ **BOTH**
240/340 & 199/399
HDL GRTL

FIRST NAME	LAST NAME

ADDRESS

APT.#	CITY

STATE/PROV.	ZIP/POSTAL CODE

EMAIL ☐ Please check this box if you would like to receive newsletters and promotional emails from Harlequin Enterprises ULC and its affiliates. You can unsubscribe anytime.

HI/HRS-622-LR_LRV22

HARLEQUIN Reader Service —**Here's how it works:**

Accepting your 2 free books and 2 free gifts (gifts valued at approximately $10.00 retail) places you under no obligation to buy anything. You may keep the books and gifts and return the shipping statement marked "cancel." If you do not cancel, approximately one month later we'll send you more books from the series you have chosen, and bill you at our low, subscribers-only discount price. Harlequin® Romantic Suspense books consist of 4 books each month and cost just $5.49 each in the U.S. or $6.24 each in Canada, a savings of at least 12% off the cover price. Harlequin Intrigue® Larger-Print books consist of 6 books each month and cost just $6.49 each in the U.S. or $6.99 each in Canada, a savings of at least 13% off the cover price. It's quite a bargain! Shipping and handling is just 50¢ per book in the U.S. and $1.25 per book in Canada*. You may return any shipment at our expense and cancel at any time by calling the number below — or you may continue to receive monthly shipments at our low, subscribers-only discount price plus shipping and handling.

▲ If offer card is missing write to: Harlequin Reader Service, P.O. Box 1341, Buffalo, NY 14240-8531 or visit www.ReaderService.com ▲

BUSINESS REPLY MAIL
FIRST-CLASS MAIL   PERMIT NO. 717   BUFFALO, NY

POSTAGE WILL BE PAID BY ADDRESSEE

HARLEQUIN READER SERVICE
PO BOX 1341
BUFFALO NY 14240-8571

NO POSTAGE
NECESSARY
IF MAILED
IN THE
UNITED STATES

wrong with having a friend. She didn't need to second-guess every person who came into her life for fear that they would turn into a monster behind closed doors.

Deep in the swirling chaos of her thoughts, she opened her car door, preparing to pick up Ty, when she jumped back in shock, holding in a horrified screech.

A tabby cat, dribbling fresh blood, eyes glazed over in death, lay sprawled across her driver's seat as if someone had tossed it there and walked away. Her heart thundered in her chest. The saliva in her mouth dried to dust. She swept the parking lot, looking for anyone who might've done such a horrible thing, but no one seemed particularly suspicious. Shaking all over, she backed away, unsure what to do.

Luna would know. She hurried back to the station and went straight to Luna's office, nearly babbling and barely making sense. Lucas saw her make a beeline for her sister and immediately followed.

"What's wrong?" he and Luna asked almost simultaneously.

"I—I have a dead cat in my car," she blurted, her hands shaking so hard she had to clutch her purse to hide the obvious tremors. "It's—I don't know how it got in there, but I need help getting it out. I thought, um, animal control could come and get it?"

An icy draft had slithered down her spine and anchored in her tailbone, because her teeth began to chatter and she couldn't control it.

"Of course, I'll have them go right now," Luna assured Kenna, shooting Lucas a look to take over while she handled the cat. "Wait here, okay?"

Kenna nodded numbly, still seeing that poor cat on her seat. Who would do such a thing? And why?

Lucas gently rubbed her shoulders, forcing some circulation through her veins. If she didn't know better, she'd think the blood in her body had simply frozen, and she was seconds away from becoming a pillar of ice, even though it was hot as Hades outside.

"Tell me what happened," he instructed in a calm voice.

"I left the station to go pick up Ty and—" Her eyes widened in alarm. She'd completely forgotten about her son. "Oh no! I'm going to be late to pick up Ty! He's going to freak out. I have to get there. Can you take me, please?"

She knew she sounded desperate and a little unhinged, but that was an accurate assessment of her mental state. Lucas didn't blink an eye and went into crisis mode. "No problem. I'll drive you. Can you tell me more about this cat situation while we drive to the therapist's office?"

That seemed a reasonable compromise. She jerked a nod, and Lucas put Noble safely in his kennel before they went out to his vehicle. Kenna felt an odd sense of dissociation creeping over her. "Like I said, I was walking to the car, getting ready to pick up Ty, and I saw that poor thing bleeding all over my front seat." *So much blood for such a small thing*, she noted, almost as if making an observation from outside herself.

"Did you have your windows down?" he asked.

She paused a minute to recall, her mind going oddly blank. All she could see in her mind's eye was that damn cat. Lucas's calm voice guiding her, settling her nerves, helped to clear her memory. She slowly nodded, realizing she had left the window down because she hadn't figured she would stay and eat the muffins with Lucas, but then she had. "I did leave my window down," she admitted, nibbling on her cuticle as her nerves started to crawl. "Do you think the cat was injured and jumped into my car to die?"

"That sounds plausible," he said, pulling into the therapist's parking lot. He put the car in Park and turned to her, his gaze soft and concerned. "But is there any other reason that might make sense of why a dead cat would be in your car?"

Leon.

His name hovered on her lips, but she swallowed the impulse to tell Lucas. It was doubtful Leon was here in Cottonwood. How would he have found her? She'd never told him where she'd grown up, and she didn't have anything in her name here. Everything was in her sister's name or her dad's. She paid cash for everything, and she kept to herself. The chill slowly thawed from her body as reason calmed her nervous system. She rubbed her forehead, wincing at the sudden booming headache behind her eyeballs. Now she had to do damage control. *Again.* "I think I was freaked out at seeing the blood. You're right—it was probably injured and looking for a safe place to rest and then died."

But Lucas's keen gaze saw something she didn't want to share. "Kenna, if you're in some kind of trouble—"

"I'm not," she assured him with a fake smile that barely reached the edges of her mouth. "I'm a big ol' baby who can't stand the sight of blood, and I overreacted. I'm sorry."

"We agreed to be friends, right?" he reminded her. At her slow nod, he said, "Well, friends don't lie to each other. You're pale as a ghost, and it looks a lot like that night when you thought an intruder was outside the vet clinic. I've seen enough cases of PTSD from abuse victims to know it when I see it. Who hurt you, Kenna? Was it one of your exes?"

She desperately wanted to jump out of his vehicle and shut him out, but something in his eyes made her want to fall into his arms and sob, to release the burden of her secret to someone who cared.

But this wasn't a fairy tale, and happy endings weren't part of her future. She swallowed the sticky lump in her throat, knowing that if she didn't give him something, he'd keep digging, and she couldn't afford for him to do that. "Remember that bad boyfriend I mentioned?" she said. Lucas nodded gravely. "Well, he was mean, and that's why I left. So, yeah, I might be a little jumpy, but it's just because it's hard to feel safe even when you are."

"You're sure he's not here?" he asked.

"Positive," she answered with more confidence than she felt. Logically, it made no sense for Leon to not only expend the effort to chase her but to end up in Cottonwood just to torture her. "He has no reason to follow me. He's probably already moved on to his next woman. I literally meant nothing to him." *A fact Leon had often thrown in her face to drive home the reality that she had zero value.*

"I could run his name through the system just to be sure," he offered.

"No, that's not necessary," she said quickly, checking her watch and using that as an excuse to get away from his questions. "I better get Ty before he has a meltdown or something."

She left the car before Lucas could ask anything else, but the sensation of wanting to throw up came again, like earlier in the morning.

Her cell phone chirped with a text message notification from Luna.

Animal control picked up the cat and sprayed the seat with disinfectant, but you'll need to have it deep cleaned. That was really gross. Are you okay?

Kenna responded quickly, All good, sorry for freaking out. Blood does that to me. I'll be back as soon as I get Ty, and she hustled to get her kid.

Leon's not here. Leon's not here. Leon's not here.

But no matter how many times she repeated the mantra in her head, she couldn't shake the feeling that he was watching and waiting to snatch her when she least expected it.

And that caused bile to rise in her throat.

Lucas knew fear when he saw it. There was no faking what he'd picked up from Kenna. Pure, unadulterated fear had ricocheted through her body and put every sense on alert—over a dead cat.

It was gruesome and tragic, but was it cause to freak out like that?

No, not in his experience. How evil was this ex-boyfriend? Had he knocked her around? *Likely.* But why was she deliberately evasive whenever he asked about her past? What kind of skeletons were banging around in her closet? People with stuff to hide usually did anything possible to keep their secrets hidden.

He wanted to help, but if she was determined to keep him out, there wasn't much he could do.

Frustration welled in him, but he held it in check as Kenna and Ty exited the building. She was talking to him, leaning toward him, Ty's face slightly angled away from her. If body language revealed the truth, he didn't want to hear whatever Kenna was whispering to Ty— and he didn't think it was about the cat. His hunch was confirmed as Kenna climbed into the car and launched into the cat details, almost for Lucas's benefit. "I found a dead cat in my car when I came to pick you up, so Lucas agreed to give me a ride."

"How'd a dead cat get in your car?" Ty asked, seeming macabrely intrigued and grossed out at the same time. "Can I see it? How dead was it?"

"Tyler," Kenna said with a frown, "dead is dead, and no, you can't see it. Auntie Luna has already taken care of it." She shuddered. "There was a lot of blood. I'll have to get the car cleaned."

"But how'd a bloody cat get into the car?" Ty asked, confused.

"I left the window open, and I think maybe it was injured from fighting or something and it jumped into the car to hide."

"That's a bummer," Ty said, but he seemed unmoved, as if something else was bothering him. "Can we get something to eat?"

"I made you pancakes this morning," Kenna reminded him with a perplexed expression. "You can't still be hungry?"

"I'm a growing boy," Ty replied with a shrug. "Can we?"

"Um, I don't know. I have to find a way to get the car cleaned," Kenna answered, biting her lip with an anxious frown. "I don't even know where to start. Seems like blood cleanup isn't your everyday cleaning request."

"I know a guy who's great at interior car detailing," Lucas offered. "I could give you his card. He does all the police department vehicles, and he's certified for hazmat cleanup as well."

Her relief was evident as she exhaled a long breath.

"Thank you, that would be great," she said with the flash of a smile. "That would be so helpful. I hope he's not too expensive. I'm on a budget that doesn't include a line item for dead-animal detailing."

"Given the circumstances, I'm sure he'd be willing to cut you a good deal," Lucas said, silently making a note to talk to George himself. If he had to, he'd chip in. He glanced at Ty, who was staring out the window, watching the scenery go by with an inscrutable expression. He'd give anything for a peek into those thoughts. "I've still got a whole basket of muffins at the station if you want to grab one, Ty," he offered.

But Ty wasn't interested. "I hate lemon," he said.

Kenna looked at her son sharply but didn't call him out. There was a test of wills happening between mother and son, and by the looks of things, he wasn't sure Kenna was going to win.

One thing was for sure—he didn't envy the fight on her hands.

Chapter 13

Later that evening, Kenna joined Ty in his bedroom and quietly closed the door behind her. Ty glanced up from his Xbox but quickly returned to his game. She sat gingerly on the edge of his bed, trying not to feel like an unwelcome guest in her son's room, but the chill he was throwing her way was hard to miss.

"Ty? Can we talk for a minute?" she asked.

"I'm busy, Mom," he returned without losing his focus on the game.

"C'mon, it's important."

Maybe it was the subtle pleading in her voice or the fact that she wasn't coming at him like an authoritarian, but Ty sighed and paused his game. "What?" he asked.

"I was wondering if we could talk about your therapy session. How'd it go?"

He shrugged. "Fine. I lied just like you told me to."

She winced, hating how that sounded. "I mean, did

you need to lie? What kind of questions did the therapist ask?"

But Ty had his own questions. "Why was there a dead cat in the car?" Kenna was taken aback by his about-face and the mature look in his young gaze. Before she could reiterate the running theory, he asked, "Was it Leon?"

Immediate panic seized her by the throat. "N-no, of course not," she answered with a slight stammer. "He has no idea where we are. I'll admit, at first I was scared, but I can't keep jumping at shadows. Leon is in the past and we're safe here."

"Like Grandpa was safe here?" Ty shot back as he rubbed his thumb against the game controller in his hand with a hard motion. If he kept it up, he'd break it. She reached for his hand gently to stop him. Ty met her gaze. "Don't tell me we're safe. Nowhere feels safe from anything."

She blinked, horrified at the pain and fear in her son's eyes. What was she doing to her sweet boy? This was her fault. She had to make it right. They couldn't leave Cottonwood; her support system was here, and she sorely needed help. In the past, that'd always been her biggest problem—being afraid to ask for help—and look where it'd landed her. Nevertheless, she was determined to make changes.

And yet, here she was, asking her son to lie for her and trying to make everything better with chocolate pancakes and lemon muffins—lemon, which Ty didn't hate, but he'd known that would hurt her feelings.

"I'm sorry," she said in a small voice, feeling defeated. "I shouldn't have asked you to lie. I was afraid of losing you after everything we've done to get here. I'm trying to keep you safe, but I probably just mucked things up even more."

Ty blinked back tears, but he wiped them away quickly, a tiny glimmer of her boy shining through as he said gruffly, "It's okay, Mom. I know you're trying."

Maybe she'd try brutal honesty for once. "Ty, the truth is, I don't know what I'm doing most times, and even then it seems every decision I make is the wrong one. There's a saying that seems to be tattooed on my damn forehead and it's 'the road to hell is paved with good intentions,' and that's my life in a nutshell. I want to believe that Leon isn't here because it scares the piss out of me to believe otherwise, but I can't be sure of anything anymore."

"You need to tell Auntie Luna. She'll be able to help," Ty insisted. "Even Auntie Sayeh. I bet if you put Auntie Sayeh in a room alone with Leon, only Auntie Sayeh would come out alive."

It wasn't funny, but her kid always managed to make her laugh when she least expected it. "You're right," she agreed, missing Sayeh, admitting, "On both points. Geesh, kid, how are you so damn wise when I'm supposed to be the adult?"

Ty shrugged. "Grandpa used to say I was an old soul. Sounded weird coming from someone who was so old, but maybe that's what he meant."

At the mention of her dad, fresh tears sprang to her eyes as a memory came to her that she'd forgotten. But it wasn't her dad who'd made the observation about her infant son—it'd been her mom.

As Nancy had *oohed* and *ahhhed* over newborn Tyler, the second his little eyes had opened in her arms, she'd proclaimed with gentle authority, "This one is an old soul. You can tell from the eyes. He's going to be a wise one."

The fact that her dad had shared that with Ty had

been his way of keeping Nancy alive, if only in spirit, and that punctured Kenna's heart with fresh grief. In hindsight, Kenna wasn't sure if she'd ever properly allowed herself to grieve Nancy's death from cancer all those years ago, and now with her dad gone, too, it seemed like the bill was coming due for both of them.

All she'd been doing was running from one catastrophe to the next instead of dealing with what needed to be dealt with—and she wanted off that psycho merry-go-round.

Crap, she groaned, realizing what needed to be done. She rose and pressed a kiss to the top of her son's crown, wrinkling her nose a little, saying, "When you finish your game, you need a shower, old soul," and left him to go find Luna for a long-overdue conversation.

Kenna prayed for the strength to be honest and the courage to listen to what she didn't want to hear.

Even from her sister.

Lucas ended his shift, the basket of leftover lemon muffins in his hand, Noble trotting at his side and his thoughts centered squarely on Kenna's troublesome situation, even though he knew it was none of his business.

He'd resisted the urge to dig into her background, feeling in his gut that it would be a terrible misstep, but that didn't stop him from running through her every reaction to situations that created an odd discord in his intuition.

He wanted to believe that Kenna was everything she seemed—intelligent, beautiful and kindhearted—but she was definitely hiding something.

Ignoring his intuition had only screwed him in the past. He was determined to be better going forward. Still, a part of him didn't want to find out if Kenna was hiding something monstrous, because he liked her too much to be devastated.

Well, if something turned up with Kenna that made him uncomfortable, he had no one to blame but himself. Hadn't she already admitted she was a walking red flag? But red on Kenna looked so pretty, he wanted to argue. Except that'd been his weakness with Becca, too. He'd had plenty of reasons to give Becca a wide berth and yet, he'd pined after the one girl he should've known was off-limits.

He needed something to take his mind off Kenna and her situation; otherwise, he'd sit and stew. One of the things he'd planned to do once he got settled was to organize a weekend backpacking trip, and to this point, he hadn't done much preparation, which he was going to rectify tonight.

He'd already invested in a brand-new Osprey Atmos backpack, and he was itching to put it to good use. His old one was still in good condition, but he'd splurged on a new backpack to perhaps have an extra for a plus-one, should he meet a person who would be interested.

And he was already eyeing Kenna as his plus-one, even though he probably should have his head examined.

Back in Kansas, when he'd been mapping out his new home state, he'd immediately been taken with the idea of backpacking through the Absaroka-Beartooth Wilderness. The alpine beauty took his breath away, and now was the perfect time of the year to traverse the trails of the ten-thousand-foot mountainside.

After his nightly routine of feeding Noble and giving him some quality playtime, Lucas pulled his gear from the spare bedroom and inspected his original pack, making sure it was still sturdy and safe, then he repacked it tightly and grabbed a beer to enjoy the night sky before bed.

He loved Montana, and he didn't miss Kansas—particularly the seasonal threat of a tornado ripping through your house—but he wished he could've gotten Brock out of there before things had gone sour.

He'd turned a blind eye to Brock's addiction, telling himself it wasn't all that bad and that he'd grow out of his hard-partying ways, but it only got worse. Becca didn't help, either. They'd all grown up together, and he'd mistakenly thought he could count on Becca to help him get Brock sober, but she'd been just as hooked as his brother, and there was nothing an addict liked less than an intervention.

But a beautiful and damaged woman was kryptonite for a man who wanted to be her hero. God, he'd wanted to save them both, but he'd been so in love with Becca he would've done whatever he could to keep her from drowning. As a consequence, he'd missed how Brock's head was completely underwater, and by the time he'd figured it out, Brock was gone.

It took Lucas too long to figure out that Becca had been a cancer in their lives.

He rubbed his forehead, deep in thought. He wasn't what he'd consider deeply introspective, but it was hard not to slip into philosophical territory after everything that'd gone down.

Leaving Becca behind had been the best decision of his life. So, why did he feel some sort of residual guilt? They weren't kids anymore and Becca wasn't his responsibility, yet he was pushing against the feeling that he'd abandoned her when she needed someone the most.

Hell, this circular thinking could drive a man crazy.

He finished his beer, crushed the can and started to

head back into the house, but the sharp crack of a branch in the dark made him stop. Unlike his place in Kansas, his house in Montana was surrounded by trees. It was one of the things that had drawn him to this particular property. He peered into the inky darkness, the tree line a pitch-black silhouette against the moon's glow. A warning prickle danced along his nape as he stared harder into the unforgiving night. Maybe Kenna's jitters were contagious, because he wished he had his gun within grabbing distance. But as nothing but regular night sounds followed the tense moments, he relaxed.

Nothing but nocturnal critters, he told himself, shaking his head at his sudden nerves as he went inside, but he made sure to turn the dead bolt on the heavy door and close the curtains.

Good sense reminded him he needed to make a decision about Kenna. Either he was all in or he was backing out and letting her figure things out independently.

They'd agreed to friendship. Would he bail on a friend because they had a complicated life? He knew the answer to that—he wasn't the kind of person to bail on anyone, and that'd been the problem.

Becca had cost him his brother. Maybe if he'd been less concerned about trying to save them both, he could've spent that energy solely on Brock.

Kenna wasn't asking him to save her, though. If anything, she was pleading with him to save himself, which was a huge difference and he didn't know how to feel about it.

The hard truth was, he didn't want to back out.

He wanted to take her to dinner—which made him question if Kenna was right and friendship wasn't enough. Maybe he was lying to himself, because right now, he wanted her in ways that had nothing to do with being friendly.

One problem at a time, he supposed.

He closed up the house and turned off the lights, but before he turned in for the night, he took a final look out the window, not sure what he thought he'd find, but he couldn't shake the unsettled feeling that something out there was watching him.

Damn jitters. If this was how Kenna felt all the time, he pitied her, because this sucked.

Hopefully, whatever lurked outside didn't know how to jimmy a lock, because he was heading to bed.

The high-end, military-grade night-vision goggles gave the man a crystal-clear, albeit emerald green, view of the house nestled in the forest canopy.

Bad things happen to people all alone in the woods. He could easily slip in through the back door, slit the guy's throat and be out in minutes, leaving no trace. No one would ever find him because he was The Ghost.

Rage simmered in his veins. This was the guy sniffing around his woman. He could see the hunger in the man's eyes, the lust to taste her sweet skin and the silk of her long dark hair sliding through his fingertips.

Leon's grip curled more tightly around the goggles, wishing it were the man's neck. This was Kenna's fault. She should've known better. She would have to be punished for being a bad, bad girl.

Except her punishment wouldn't be so easy as the cost of her flesh—no, he wanted her to know how badly she'd screwed up, and the cost would be her new boy toy.

And her son.

It could've been so different. He would've raised the

boy like his own and taught him the right way to be a man—none of this soft bullshit of today. A boy needed a strong man with a hard hand to teach him the ways of the world.

But Kenna, the faithless whore, had to go and break the rules.

This was on her.

He melted into the darkness. *Patience*, he reminded himself as he pulled away. The plan wasn't complete yet.

Soon.

Chapter 14

As it turned out, Kenna didn't see Luna until the following evening, which gave her plenty of time to back out, rethink her strategy and then ultimately return to her original decision to play it straight with her sister, but her nerves were shot.

"You look like a long-tailed cat in a room full of rockers," Luna remarked, noting how Kenna was making a second pass through the already spotless kitchen. "If you keep cleaning that countertop, you're going to wipe away the smooth layer protecting the quartz underneath. What's going on? You are like Martha Stewart on crack when something is bothering you."

Yep. Her tells were pretty obvious. She peeked out of the kitchen to check and see if Ty was around. Satisfied he was in his room, she motioned for Luna to follow her outside onto the porch.

Luna, seeming to sense something was truly wrong, became serious. "Are you okay?"

"I need to be honest with you," she said, drawing a deep breath. "I was afraid to tell you the whole truth about why we left Kentucky, because I just wanted to put it behind us, but I've been selfishly expecting Ty to shoulder all of my secrets, and it's not fair to him."

"That sounds serious," Luna admitted. "Is this why you've been so adamant about Ty not needing therapy?"

Kenna nodded in misery. "I know, I'm a terrible mother. Go ahead and say it, because I already feel it."

"You're not a terrible mother. Why would you think that?"

Kenna shook her head. "You don't know everything."

"Okay, so tell me," Luna said, reaching for her hand to hold it tightly. "Whatever it is, I'm sure it's not as bad as you think."

That's cute. If only that were true.

Kenna floundered, unsure of where to start. Drawing a deep breath, she decided to only share what was truly necessary. "We had to leave Kentucky because the last time my ex attacked me, I almost died." At Luna's shocked expression, Kenna winced but kept going. "I was threatening to leave, and we got into a huge fight. He hit me so hard I fell to the floor, but when I went down, my head clipped the corner of a marble statue and it cracked my skull." She gingerly pointed to the place where her head remained tender. "Right here is where there's a hairline fracture."

"Oh my God, Kenna," Luna cried, horrified. "Why didn't you call me or Sayeh? We would've come get you."

"I couldn't. He had all of my cash, my credit cards and my cell. When they released me from the hospital, he took control and wouldn't let me leave the house— it was under the guise of taking care of me, but I was a prisoner. I pretended to still love him and acted appreciative of his care so he would let his guard down. A few days later, I scooped Ty out of bed in the middle of the night and we ran. That's how we ended up here that night."

"And that's where you got the shiner," Luna remembered.

She nodded, embarrassed, but continued, "Yes, but we're finally free and that's all that matters as far as I'm concerned."

"So, where is this asshole now?" Luna asked.

Here came the tricky part. "I'm hoping still in Kentucky, but I can't stop looking over my shoulder. That's why I've been so jumpy. I mean, it's highly unlikely he followed me here to Cottonwood, but the dead cat really freaked me out."

Luna nodded, thinking. "We should file a protection order against him so if he comes within ten feet of you, I can legally shoot him."

"You can do that?" Kenna asked, tentatively impressed.

Luna sighed, relenting, "No, not really, but it's a nice thought."

Kenna chuckled. "Yeah, that's true."

"But we should still file the order so it'll start a paper trail."

"That's exactly what I don't want," Kenna explained, knowing her sister would struggle to understand her reluctance. "I've done everything I can to keep Leon from knowing where we are. I've used cash for everything, nothing is in my name, and I'm hoping that Leon feels I'm not worth the effort to chase me."

"Why would he think that?" Luna asked, confused. "Weren't you living together?"

"Yes, but Leon has no reason to chase after me. He never failed to tell me that I was easily replaceable, and I believe him. Leon is rich, handsome and charismatic. Women were always flocking to him. I have no doubt that once I was gone, he simply moved on to his next supply."

"It's possible, but there's a volatile and unpredictable element to men like this Leon. I don't like it."

"I'm telling you because I don't want Tyler to have to keep my secrets anymore. I didn't want anyone to know about the abuse, but hiding it only made it worse for Ty, and I don't want to put him through anymore of my bullshit."

Luna nodded, squeezing her hand. "You're a good person, sis. Please believe me when I say you have the best heart and your son is lucky to have a mom like you."

Tears sprang to her eyes. "I don't know about that, but thank you," she whispered. "Can you help me get through this with as little paper trail as possible?"

Luna nodded, promising, "I'll do what I can."

Relief flooded through Kenna. More had happened during her time spent under Leon's thumb, but some secrets she would take to the grave. Not even Ty knew about everything, and that was how it would stay.

"Thank you, sissy," Kenna said, accepting a big hug from Luna. "I appreciate everything you've done for me and Ty. Someday I hope I can repay you."

"There's no running tab with family," Luna said, pulling away and wiping her eyes. "Taking care of each other is just what we do."

Kenna smiled, so grateful for Luna's understanding. "Please don't tell Sayeh just yet. She has enough on her plate. I don't want her to worry—or worse, chase after Leon."

"Probably wise for now, but we'll need to tell her sooner or later."

Kenna knew that, but for now, having the coolheaded sister in the know was enough. The hothead would have to wait.

She also wanted to tell Lucas, but that impulse was more challenging to unravel. She didn't like the idea of secrets between them, even though they'd only agreed to friendship for now. Still, not telling him seemed like a recipe for disaster, but she also didn't want to scare him away.

Luna, perceptive as always, seemed to read her mind. "You should tell Lucas."

Kenna met her sister's gaze, uncertain. "I don't know. Seems like something I should keep private."

"He likes you," Luna said, adding bluntly, "and *you* like *him*. It's better to start things with honesty."

"We aren't starting things," she assured her sister hastily, but her heart ached to say the words. "We agreed to be friends."

"Even friendship should have a foundation of honesty, don't you think?"

"Not necessarily," she disagreed, shuddering to think of Lucas looking at her differently if he knew her secret. "Friendships should be safe havens. Besides, I don't want to burden him with my drama. He left Kansas to start fresh, and I don't want to ruin that for him."

"Why would that ruin it for him?" Luna asked, seeming confused. "Real friends should be there for each other, not only when it's convenient."

"Yeah, of course, but why ask someone I barely know to carry a boulder for me?"

Luna chuckled quizzically. "Kenna, everyone has something in their past that they're not proud of. I hardly think what you're carrying around is a boulder."

If only that were true. Kenna wanted to change the subject. "Did you schedule the landline for termination?"

"I tried to, but then I was talked out of it."

"What?"

"Yeah, I should've thought of this, but it's a safety thing. With Ty here, I think it's best to have an operational landline."

"I don't understand. Why?"

"Because if there's ever a reason someone has to call 911, dispatch will get the address right away, rather than being routed to the cell towers and then sent to the local dispatch. It could mean valuable seconds saving a life."

Kenna swallowed, immediately thinking of their dad. If only they'd had a few extra seconds to warn their dad that an intruder was coming to threaten their family. *Don't go there.* She shook off the sadness that threatened and renewed her focus. "Tomorrow I'm dropping Ty off at summer camp on my way to work."

Luna rose an eyebrow. "Ty wants to go to summer camp?"

"Um, not really, but I don't feel safe leaving him home alone."

In light of Ty's recent stint with crime, Luna didn't argue. "Okay, I'll see you in the morning. I'll lock up."

Kenna nodded, watching as her sister went through her routine, the same as her dad used to throughout her childhood, coaxing a smile from her lips at the memory.

It felt better to share at least some of her story with her sister, but now she had to decide how much she was willing to share with Lucas.

Because she might talk a good game, but when she thought of Lucas, more than friendship warmed her heart—and she was terrified of chasing away the first good man she'd ever attracted in her adult life.

Maybe she'd have a clearer idea after a good night's sleep.

Now, if only she could sleep.

Damn you, anxiety. Will you ever not be a part of my life?

Lucas had made up his mind. He was asking Kenna to dinner—he had the place picked out, nothing too fancy, but a business with an excellent reputation for finger-lickin'-good barbecue—and all he had to do was swing by the vet clinic at closing time and ask her out.

Having a plan put a smile on his face and a spring in his step that was undoubtedly noticed by his coworkers, including young Wes, who had started to gravitate toward him as a mentor.

"Whatever you're having, let me have some," he joked as he paused at Lucas's desk. "This must have something to do with Kenna," he guessed.

"What makes you say that?" Lucas asked.

"Because you get that same goofy look on your face every time you see her and she's got muffins in her hand."

"Maybe I really like muffins," Lucas countered.

"No one likes muffins *that* much. It's her, but I get it. She's gorgeous. I mean, she's hard to ignore. You think I didn't have a raging crush on Detective Luna when I first came on? Try being fresh out of the academy on your first job and the person you're assigned to shadow is distractingly beautiful. It was rough. But I got through it. I mean, it helped that she only had eyes for that guy of hers. Damn lucky bastard. Anyway, I'd be careful of Kenna, though."

Lucas stilled as an alarm bell clanged in his head. "Yeah? And why is that?"

Wes cracked a grin. "Because she's a mad baker. You end up with a woman like her, you'll end up round as a circle. We've all seen your weakness for her lemon muffins. Can you imagine that on a full-time basis? No, man, I wouldn't be able to control myself around a pastry chef–level wife. Just sayin', think about it."

Lucas laughed at the young pup, sharing, "Someday you'll realize that there's more to life than six-pack abs. I think growing old, *round* and happy with the right person sounds like goals."

Wes's expression twisted into an incredulous frown. "You got weird goals, man."

Maybe so, but when he thought of cuddling up to Kenna, with all her soft curves, he couldn't imagine anything sweeter, including her lemon muffins.

Curious, he asked, "Have you met the other sister, Sayeh?"

Wes nodded, his eyes widening as he said, "Now *that* one, not gonna lie, she scares me."

"And why is that?" he asked, amused.

"Sayeh has this witchy energy to her that's super aggressive. I mean, those Griffin women were blessed in the looks department—that Native American blood is blessed by God or something—but Sayeh looks like the kind of woman who would suck out your soul and spit it out at your feet for looking at her the wrong way." Wes affected a fake shudder. "No, sir, I don't have what it takes to look sidewise at Sayeh, and I'm not sure the devil himself would take her on. Not that any of us have to worry here. She's a big ol' New York FBI agent, so she's rarely in Cottonwood."

"Impressive," he murmured, but he preferred the sweetness of Kenna's disposition to a badass soul eater, anyway. Still, good information should things progress the way he hoped with Kenna. "Well, Kenna and I—"

But he didn't get to finish his sentence, because the older gentleman he'd met a few weeks ago was heading his way.

"Just the man I was hoping to find," the man said, extending a hand. "Not sure if you remember me—"

Lucas did. "Ambrose Elliott," he recalled, accepting the offered gesture. "You're an easy man to remember. You were asking about Noble. Did you end up finding a breeder that suits your needs?"

"Not yet, but hope springs eternal," he said with an easy smile. "Actually, my business has me in the area for a little longer. I happened to chat with one of the parents of your Explorer cadets, and she said you're an avid hiker."

"I am," Lucas confirmed. "You looking to do some hiking?"

Ambrose nodded eagerly. "I was hoping you could tell me where the best trails are around here. I need to blow off some steam and get some fresh air. I feel like I'm slowly suffocating in my office."

He knew that feeling. "I'm fairly new to the area myself, but I'm planning a backpacking trip through the Absaroka-Beartooth Wilderness pretty soon. You should check it out. There's a number of great trails, and it's only about a four-hour drive from here."

"Not bad. I like a little road time to think before I punish my body with a grueling hike," the other man joked.

"I say there's nothing like nature to heal the mind," Lucas shared with a grin.

"The Absaroka-Beartooth Wilderness, you say? I'll definitely check it out. Which trail, in particular, were you looking at?"

"Not sure yet. I'm still working out the details. It might depend on if I hike it alone or with a hiking partner."

"Smart. Well, if you end up needing a partner, I'm open to hitting the trail. I'm a fan of the buddy system for safety purposes, particularly if you're new to the area."

"All righty, sir. I'll definitely keep that in mind."

Ambrose left Lucas with his business card and waved goodbye. Wes ambled back over to him. "He seems like a nice guy."

"Yeah," Lucas agreed, but there was something about the man that he couldn't put his finger on that rubbed him the wrong way.

And the thought of hiking into the wilderness with him? Just didn't feel right at all.

Chapter 15

Kenna checked in on a sweet rottweiler with terrible allergies and returned to the front desk, where Isabel was eager to share gossip. While Kenna wasn't much for gossip, Isabel's callow enthusiasm reminded her of her youth, when life was still full of infinite possibilities. That seemed like a lifetime ago.

"Seeing as you've got Cottonwood's most eligible bachelor mooning over you—"

"I do not," Kenna corrected her with a blush, although secretly, she enjoyed the idea of Lucas crushing on her. "Lucas and I are just friends."

"Yeah, whatever. Everyone can see how he looks at you. So gross—and also, admittedly, swoonworthy. I wish someone was looking at me that way," Isabel said with a slight pout. "But I might have found the next best thing."

"Oh? And who might that be?" Kenna asked, intrigued.

"First, let me preface this with, I don't usually date guys who are older than me, but there's something so sophisticated about this guy that I can't seem to help myself."

"How much older is he?"

"I don't know, maybe twenty years? Hard to tell. He's in crazy good shape, and he's just delicious."

Kenna chuckled. "Well, be careful. Sometimes older men gravitate toward younger women because they are easier to control."

"Girl, no one is controlling me, I can promise you that," Isabel said with an airy laugh. "If anything, I've got him wrapped around my little pinkie." Isabel shook her behind with a sassy expression, saying, "He's all over this booty, if you know what I mean."

Kenna laughed. "Okay, I believe you. Just speaking from experience, sometimes older men can hide terrible personality traits that younger women don't catch until it's too late."

"You sound like a therapist," Isabel quipped, rolling her eyes. "Sometimes it's just about the fun, nothing serious, you know?"

"You're right," Kenna said, realizing she was being a wet blanket to the younger woman. Her experience with Leon had colored her lens. Maybe this guy was different. She had to learn to accept that not all men were monsters in disguise, something Lucas was helping her see. Kenna throttled down her alarm to ask, "So where'd you meet him?"

Isabel was delighted to share. "It was crazy, almost like it was fate or something. My horoscope told me that I was going to meet the love of my life soon, but I never thought it was going to be *this* soon! Remember that night you let me leave early to go out with friends—

and then you had your little freak-out and I felt super bad? Sorry about that. Well, I was going to meet him in person for the first time, and we hit it off almost immediately. It was crazy!"

An odd, discordant chord twanged in her head. "Wait, what do you mean? You met in person for the first time? Is he from around here?"

"We met online, you know, through a dating app. And for once, the man actually looked like his profile picture. You'd be shocked at how many times men use pictures that are ten years old and now they're fat and bald. And no, he's not from here. Somewhere south, I think. Honestly, I forgot where he said he was from. He's in town on business, which is so crazy, because who travels to freaking Cottonwood on business? But also, kinda sexy, not gonna lie. I like the idea of a successful renaissance man. He's so smart, he knows a lot about everything and Lord, is he in good shape!"

Kenna loathed the idea of dating apps and had never used one. She was much too reserved to put herself out there like that, and it seemed dangerous given the state of the world nowadays. "You're not worried you might inadvertently attract the attention of a psychopath?" she asked, curious. "How do you know he's who he says he is? What if he's married? Or worse, wants to wear your skin like a hat?"

Isabel laughed as if Kenna was adorably skittish about nothing. "You can't be scared of everything out there. You have to live life, you know? Besides, what are the odds that I'd run across a weirdo here in Cottonwood? This place is so damn wholesome, I almost wish someone weird would come along to spice things up."

Kenna hated to be the buzzkill but reminded Isabel, "Be careful what you wish for. It was only a few months ago that an entire family was killed in their own home. No place has a bubble around it to keep bad people out. You need to be careful. Especially since he's not from around here. It's not like you can check his references. He could be lying through his teeth."

Isabel sobered with embarrassment. "God, I'm such an insensitive ass sometimes. Of course, that was awful and shocking, what happened to that family, but the odds of anything like that happening again… I mean, I think we're talking somewhere in the unlikely range of winning the lottery."

"Let's hope so," Kenna murmured, still thinking about Leon. When she'd first met him, he'd seemed like Prince Charming. He'd swept her off her feet with compliments, lavish gifts and big, sweet promises that slowly changed into vicious cruelty, but by the time she realized she was in trouble, it was too late. She drew a deep breath, shoving thoughts of Leon away. "Well, just do me a favor and always tell someone where you're going and who you're with. Maybe I'm too cautious, but it's the mom in me. I can't help it."

Also, the hairline fracture in her skull was a great reminder that fangs could hide behind charming smiles.

Isabel switched gears with the mercurial speed of her short attention span. "So, what's the deal with you and Mr. Hunky Cop? Have you kissed yet? If not, *wh-hhhhhyyyy* the hell not? I'd climb that man like a spider monkey on a tree. He's yummy."

Kenna blushed. Lucas *was* yummy, but she didn't have the luxury of giving in to her desires, and it made her feel like a bruised piece of fruit trying to explain why. "I'm trying to focus on rebuilding my life. Right now, my son is my focus."

"Yeah, you're a good mom," Isabel admitted with a

sigh. "That's how I know I'm not ready for kids. My needs come first and I need quality sexy time, if you know what I mean."

Kenna barked a short laugh, trying to remember the last time she'd felt excited about sex. She'd thought Leon had ruined that part of her, but lately, she'd been definitely thinking about Lucas in ways that weren't PG. "You're young. Have fun," she said, leaving it at that, but she added one last time, hoping it would stick, "Just be careful, please."

"Okay, *Mom*," Isabel said with a teasing smile, promising with an exaggerated eye roll, "I'll be careful."

Kenna figured that was the best she could hope for. No one could've told her to slow down or watch for snakes when she'd been Isabel's age, but she sure wished she would've listened.

In her case, wisdom had been hard-earned—and she had the literal scars to prove it.

Lucas's day hadn't exactly gone as planned, and by the end, he hadn't been able to get over to the vet clinic to talk to Kenna, and that was all he could think about. Being the only K-9 officer in the small town kept him busy, which he loved, but it made it hard to carve out any personal time between professional responsibilities.

Now that his shift was over, he was anxious to clock out and head over to the clinic, but as luck would have it, that beautiful Native American goddess appeared like magic at his desk. His heart rate kicked up a notch, and an immediate smile found his mouth. "Well, this is a nice surprise. How did you know you were on my mind all day?"

She blushed. "Oh, is that so? And what exactly were you thinking about?"

Loaded question. He wanted to tell her that he thought of her every second of every day, that her smile did weird things to his insides and her laugh reminded him of sunshine, but instead, he shrugged, playing it casual. "I don't know, I thought dinner might be nice."

"Yeah? I might be open to that," she answered shyly. "As long as Ty can come, too."

"Sure, bring him along." He knew she and her son were a package deal, and he was okay with that. Besides, even though Kenna hadn't shared a lot of details about her past relationships, he recognized the signs of an abused woman, which meant Ty had seen some things. He wanted Ty to know he wasn't like those other men, and the only way to do that was with his actions. "The place I was thinking of serves great barbecue."

"Here in town?" Kenna asked.

"Nope. Billings."

Kenna smiled as if delighted he wanted to take them outside town, that he'd put some effort into picking the place, and he was heartened by her reaction. "Sounds fun," she said. "Should I meet you there or…?"

"Hell no, I made the offer, I drive. All I want you to do is get yourself ready, bring your appetite, and I'll pick you and Ty up. Sound good?"

"Yes."

Well, this is going over well, he thought with an almost giddy smile. There was a sweetness to Kenna that he could happily drown in for the rest of his life if given half the chance.

Noble whined at his feet and yawned as if to say, *Slow your roll—it's just dinner, Romeo.*

Right, good reminder. Lucas cleared his throat and adjusted his utility belt, but his smile never left. He was so enraptured by Kenna and how well things were going that he didn't see the tornado coming his way.

"Lucas?"

Both Lucas and Kenna swiveled their heads toward the female voice, and all good feelings crashed to the ground.

"Becca, what are you doing here?" he asked, stunned and dismayed to see his secret childhood crush and his brother's girlfriend standing forlornly, casting a suspicious and openly hostile look Kenna's way, as if she'd caught him cheating and she was the victim.

And everything happened in a heartbeat.

One minute Kenna was open and shyly interested, and the next, she closed up tighter than a drum and put distance between them. "This seems personal. I'll let you go. 'Bye." And then she left before he could run after her and explain.

He swore under his breath, swiveling his gaze squarely toward Becca with a stiff jaw.

"You don't seem very happy to see me," Becca observed with hurt feelings.

"I'm not," he returned flatly. "What are you doing here? How'd you find me?"

She ignored his question. "You're being so mean when I've come so far." Her bottom lip trembled. "Lucas, I wouldn't have come if you would've helped me. I had nowhere to go."

Confused, he asked, "What do you mean?"

People were starting to stare. Becca asked quietly, "Can we talk someplace private, please?"

He didn't have a choice. As much as he wanted to put Becca on a bus back to Kansas, he wasn't about to give everyone a show with their drama. Lucas swallowed his anger and gestured curtly for her to follow him to the interrogation room. Once the door was shut, he faced Becca with arms folded. "Okay, what the hell are you doing here, Becca?"

Her eyes watered. "This isn't exactly the response I was hoping for. You truly hoped to abandon me? Am I such a bad person that you couldn't wait to run away? What the hell did I do that was so wrong?"

The laundry list was too long, but damn that woman for knowing how to push his buttons. He didn't believe Becca was a bad person, but she was so deeply flawed that she couldn't help the chaos she brought with her no matter where she went. Not to mention she was an unrepentant drug addict who refused treatment. He pinched the bridge of his nose, trying to find patience. "Becca, what happened to the treatment facility you talked about?"

"I tried to tell you, I was on a waiting list," she answered glumly. "But my landlord didn't care and threatened to throw me out unless I did things for him. I didn't want to ask you for money, but I refused his offer and I couldn't make rent. So, here I am. Homeless with nowhere to go. I spent the last bit of money I had to get here."

That explained why she was here but not how she'd found him. Knowing Becca, she'd sweet-talked someone to give out his forwarding address at his old station. When she wanted to be, the woman could be extraordinarily manipulative. Well, she was here now, and once again, she was his problem.

"I've missed you," Becca said tentatively, glancing at him from beneath her lashes as if she weren't a hellion wrapped in the disguise of a sweet and demure woman. "Ever since you left, I've been thinking that I should've treated you better, but I'm ready to change—"

"Don't bother with the act, Becca," he said, cutting her short. "I'm not in the mood for your bullshit. You shouldn't have come."

"Where was I supposed to go?"

"Not my problem."

"Harsh, Lucas. Real harsh."

He shrugged, still seeing Kenna's expression in his mind. He could only imagine what she thought she saw, and the only thing he wanted to do was run after her to explain, but Becca knew he wouldn't leave her on the street if she was on his doorstep. *Damn her.* "Are you sober?" he asked.

"Yes."

Lucas eyed her with open suspicion, but she seemed to be telling the truth. For now. He gestured. "Let me see your purse."

"Lucas!"

Her outrage landed on fallow ground. "Either let me check your bag or I walk."

Tears sparkled in her eyes, but she thrust her purse at him. "Fine, *Officer.* Feel free to rummage in my personal bag if it makes you feel better."

He ignored her. Grabbing safety gloves from his utility belt, he treated her no differently than he would anyone suspected of illegal substances. He searched her bag thoroughly, even going so far as to double-check the lining to see if anything was secretly sewn into the bag. Satisfied, he returned the bag to Becca.

"Have we really fallen so far that you don't believe anything I say?"

"Yep."

Becca glanced away, but not before Lucas caught the sheen of tears. No, he refused to feel bad. Becca had brought this on herself, as usual, and was expecting him to bail her out. This wasn't the first time she'd been evicted, but he'd mistakenly thought that if he left Kansas, Becca would have to finally stand on her own two feet.

"Was that your girlfriend?" Becca asked, dragging her gaze back to him. "She doesn't seem your type."

"You don't know my type."

She chuckled as if he were lying to himself. "Okay, sure."

Lucas hated that they were handfasted together. "Listen, I told you when I left Kansas I was done with you and all your manipulative bullshit, and I meant it. Just because you thought you'd dump yourself in my lap doesn't mean you're getting a soft touch. You brought all of this on yourself, and you're not staying with me."

"Where am I supposed to go? I don't have any money and I don't know anyone here. I'm all alone."

"That's on you. You've pushed away every single person in your life who ever cared about you, and now you're expecting me to fix the mess, but I'm not going to. Get your life together, Becca. You're a goddamn adult. Start acting like one."

Becca blinked at his harsh statement, her eyes watering. He expected her to launch into her usual guilt trip, but she didn't. Instead, she nodded, clutching her purse more tightly to her body. "You're right," she admitted in a small voice. "I've made a lot of mistakes and most I can't even say I felt bad about, but things are different now."

"Sure they are," he said, shaking his head at her claim. "What makes things different now?"

Becca swallowed, shifting with discomfort, unsure of how to continue. He'd never seen this particular play in all the years he'd known Becca. She actually seemed genuinely lost and scared.

"Becca?"

She finally met his gaze, admitting with a slight tremble to her lip, "I'm pregnant."

And just like that, Becca had wedged herself into his life once more.

Chapter 16

Lucas felt the ground slide out from beneath his feet. He knew the baby wasn't his, because he and Becca had never been together, but they'd had a complicated relationship that only became more entangled after the death of his brother.

An immediate tension headache clamped down on his skull. "Are you sure?" he asked. "Did you see a doctor?"

Becca nodded stiffly, rummaging in her purse to produce a grainy ultrasound photo. "This is from the clinic I went to. I'm ten weeks pregnant," she said. "I knew you wouldn't believe me if I told you over the phone, so I brought this to show."

Lucas stared at the thin ultrasound paper, searching for any evidence that it might be fake, but he saw Becca's name and birth date and the approximate age of the fetus printed on the paper, and he knew she wasn't lying.

"Who's the father?" he asked.

"I don't know," she admitted in an embarrassed whisper. "I was partying pretty hard for a while after you left, and I don't remember a lot."

A baby. An innocent life—with Becca as its mother. *Good grief.* Now he had to ask an even more difficult question. "And you're choosing to keep the baby?" he guessed.

She shrugged. "I mean, yeah."

"Have you considered adoption?" he asked. "Do you really think you're up to being a mother?"

He tried to ignore the hurt in her eyes. Becca was notorious for ignoring the consequences of her actions and expecting everyone to forgive her when she smiled their way. It'd sure worked on the Merritt brothers for a long time. "You think I can't be a good mother?"

"No." He wasn't going to sugarcoat anything for her. "You're a drug addict who won't get help. How can you possibly parent a child?"

"I've been clean since I found out," she protested.

"And when was that?"

"Two weeks ago," she admitted. "But I haven't even wanted to use. I've been pretty sick to my stomach."

"Yeah, what happens when you get to the second trimester and you're no longer so sick? What then? You need help to stay sober, and you're not exactly open to changing your life."

"Lucas! C'mon, I'm really trying here, and all you're interested in doing is grinding me into the floor. News flash, I already do enough of that on my own. I don't need you to do it for me."

"I don't know what you expect of me, Becca," he said, exasperated. "You got pregnant with God knows whose baby and you show up barely clean and begging for my help when you've never followed through on any promise to get clean in the past. What am I supposed to think?"

"It's all different now. I want to be a good mom, but I need your help to get back on my feet. After that, I'll leave and you'll never have to see me again."

He didn't believe that for a second. Becca was a master at picking the currency that worked best to achieve her objective, but he couldn't deny she was pregnant, because that grainy slip of paper would be difficult for someone like Becca—who wasn't the least bit tech-savvy—to fake.

"Do you really hate me so much that you can't extend me a little kindness?" she said, wiping at her eyes. "You're all I have and you know it. Maybe you're not happy with that, but it doesn't change the facts. If you turn me away, you'll be putting me on the streets, and how's that going to look for the newest cop in a small town?"

There it was, the slightest twist of cruel manipulation.

"What would your new girlfriend think of a man who could do that?"

"She's not my girlfriend," he growled, "and leave her out of this."

Becca's expression softened as if Kenna not being his girl meant anything. The days were long gone that he felt anything more than guilt and responsibility for Becca.

"I don't hate you," he returned sharply. "I just know you, and I know you're not ready to be a mom."

"Maybe not, but I want to try," she said in earnest. "You're the only one who can help me get there. Can't you please, just one last time, try and help me? For old times' sake? Before, you know, everything got screwed up?"

For a brief second he saw Becca as the girl he first met the summer he was twelve and Brock was ten—the girl from their childhood—lost, wounded and curled up in a ball with tears streaking down her young face, hiding in an abandoned car out in Turner's Field that the neighbor kids had turned into their personal hideout. Lucas and Brock had often ended up there when their dad was on a rampage. Sleeping outside seemed a safer bet than anywhere in the house when their dad was in a mood to break things—his boys included.

Becca, the same age as Brock, had had a busted lip, and her thin body had looked malnourished. He and Brock had known at a glance that her home life was bad, and a bond immediately formed.

After that moment, they'd become thick as thieves. Until both Brock and Becca fell into drugs and Lucas went into law enforcement.

But those old bonds always tugged at him—more so after Brock's death, when guilt and shame overrode his good sense when it came to Becca. When he left Kansas, he'd come to the realization he couldn't save Becca if she didn't want to be saved.

But here she was now, pregnant and alone, claiming she was ready to do the work to really get sober this time. Was he being cruel to turn her away?

He honestly didn't believe Becca could care for a child once it arrived, but maybe she'd be more willing to consider adoption once she'd had time to think about it.

"Please?"

She had him by the short hairs and knew it. Becca didn't know how to be anything but manipulative, even if she wasn't openly trying—it was part of her messed-up programming. He didn't want her in his house, but until he found a better solution, he couldn't have her sleeping on the streets. "Fine," he bit out, "you can stay with me temporarily until I find a better solution, but Becca, hear me when I say if I find out you've so much as taken a single drag from a damn cigarette, you're gone. On the other hand, if you can show me that you truly want to change, I'll do what I can to help, but I'm done wasting my time on someone who is determined to self-destruct. Got it?"

She nodded, wiping at her eyes. "Thank you."

The earnest gratitude was a surprise, but Becca had a long way to prove that she wasn't still running a game to get her way.

But as shocking as Becca's bombshell was, he was more preoccupied with the need to explain things to Kenna before she heard a twisted version of the story that was half fiction and possibly distorted by Becca herself.

Perfect timing, he groused to himself as he clocked out and took Becca to his place. Just when he and Kenna were turning a corner, this had to go and happen.

"So you're still not going to tell me who the girl was?" Becca said, breaking the tense silence in the car.

"I told you she's none of your business, and I meant it," he said.

"Okay, fine, you don't need to bite my head off," Becca returned sullenly, glancing at Noble in the back seat. "Does this dog go with you everywhere?"

"Yes."

"Is he dangerous?"

"Only if you're a criminal," he answered.

"He's looking at me funny."

"He's an excellent judge of character."

"Ha-ha, very funny," Becca returned with a sour expression. "Well, he looks mean. Hopefully, you have a kennel or something to keep him in."

"Let's get one thing straight—you're the unwelcome guest in my home, not Noble. So try to remember your place."

Becca swallowed whatever she was going to say next. His expression was made of stone, and there was no arguing the point. At least she knew how to read his tone well enough to zip her lip and change her tune. "Don't get me wrong, I love regular dogs, you know, the ones who are sweet and cute and sit on your lap, but your dog gives off a vibe that's intimidating."

"Like I said, only to those who are doing things they shouldn't. If you keep your nose clean, you won't have a problem with Noble."

"Is he drug trained?" she asked with a note of worry.

Even though Noble was only apprehension trained, Lucas lied to keep Becca honest. "Yep."

"It's a good thing I'm clean, then," she said.

"For your sake, I hope so," Lucas said, leaving it at that.

They walked into the house, and while Lucas was tending to Noble with their nightly routine, Becca wandered the place, taking it all in as if she were sizing it up to make it her own. "This is really cute," she said. "It could use a woman's touch, of course, but it has potential."

The only woman's touch he wanted was Kenna's. "You won't be staying long enough to put your touch on anything," he reminded her. "I'm going to look for alternative lodging for you first thing tomorrow."

"I could help you out," she said, trying to negotiate. "If you remember, I'm a decent cook, and I could keep the house clean for you. All this dog hair can get out of control real quick. I'd be happy to pitch in as my way of saying thank you for helping me."

"Becca, don't push it," he warned. "You've made a royal mess of my fresh start and I'm trying to keep my cool, but you're stomping on my nerves each time you open your mouth."

Becca pressed her lips together as if wounded by his statement, but she jerked a short nod, saying, "If you don't mind, I'm exhausted. Can you show me where I'm sleeping for the night?"

Lucas nodded, relieved Becca didn't keep poking, which was her usual mode of operation. "The guest bedroom is all yours," he said, opening the bedroom door to show her. "Bathroom is down the hall. The kitchen has some food if you're hungry. I need to handle something before it gets too late."

"Thanks."

He accepted her thanks with a grunt and quickly left. All that mattered was getting to Kenna and explaining before the glimmer of interest that'd sparked between them died beneath the unwelcome stomp of Becca's foot.

Kenna's thoughts were a tangled mess. Who was that woman? Clearly, they'd had history. Kenna knew the vibe of possession from another woman when she saw it, and that woman had been staring daggers Kenna's way.

The last thing Kenna needed was a jealous woman making life difficult. What if Lucas had lied about being single? Maybe she was his wife or, at the very least, girlfriend? Had the warning Kenna had given Isabel about dating strange men from the internet just unfolded right before her eyes? Embarrassment flushed her cheeks, and she shifted against the discomfort building in her chest. She desperately wanted to believe that

Lucas wasn't like that, but what did she know about the man?

Maybe she'd dodged a bullet, and this was a blessing.

What was she thinking, anyway, entertaining romantic thoughts about Lucas? She should've stuck to her guns and shut him down hard.

Luna was working the night shift, so Kenna and Ty were home alone. She hated to admit it, but recent events had left her more spooked than usual, and she kept glancing out the window to make sure there was no one out there and double-checking the front door lock.

Ty was in his room, which left Kenna to stare morosely off into space with nothing but the ongoing drama in her head to occupy her thoughts.

Headlights pulled into the driveway, and Kenna's heart nearly stopped beating. She knew it couldn't be Luna, and Kenna didn't know anyone well enough to expect a visitor. Panic threatened to steal her ability to breathe, and she immediately started to think of an exit strategy when a knock at the door broke the silence.

Calm down. It could be a neighbor or something equally innocent, she chided herself even as her body began to shake.

Or it could be Leon, another voice whispered fearfully.

She stopped that thought. Like Isabel said, she couldn't live in fear for the rest of her life. The odds of Leon being in Cottonwood were astronomically small. If she allowed Leon's memory to steal every ounce of joy from her fresh start, it wouldn't be a fresh start.

Swallowing, she went to the door and asked with only a slight tremor in her voice, "Who is it?"

When Lucas's voice answered, "It's me, Lucas," she breathed an audible sigh of relief, and her knees threatened to buckle. She took a minute to collect herself and opened the door to a visibly concerned Lucas. "Can we talk?" he asked, getting straight to the point.

It wasn't in her to be rude, and she reluctantly nodded, allowing him to enter.

Lucas explained himself immediately, as if knowing he needed to put her mind at ease. "I'm sorry for showing up unannounced, but I couldn't let you go the whole night without giving you anything you might need to feel secure."

"That's not necessary," she said, forcing a short laugh that she didn't feel. "You don't owe me an explanation."

"I want to," he said. "Kenna, I don't want you to question my character for a second. I want to be completely transparent with you."

She shook her head, not wanting to be swayed by his display. Anyone could say the right words if they knew what buttons to push. "Your business is your own," Kenna said. "You really don't have to explain yourself."

"Becca is…a childhood friend and my brother's girlfriend," he blurted almost desperately. "I left Kansas because every time I tried to distance myself from her and the chaos she brings, she followed me. I thought leaving the state would finally give me the closure I needed, but damn if she didn't just follow me here, too. I had no clue she was going to show up uninvited like she did, and honestly, I'm doing my best not to be a jerk about it, but we've got a complicated history that I'm really trying to leave in the past."

Kenna wasn't expecting his earnest explanation. She could almost feel his need for her to understand, and, in spite of herself, she was moved by his determination to be completely transparent. "What do you mean by complicated?" she asked, curious.

"We've never dated or anything like that," he explained but there was something else behind his eyes that worried her, and for Kenna, nondisclosure was a huge trigger. "But we used to be close. For a long time after my brother died, I was her entire support system. I tried my best to help her, but Becca has issues that she refuses to get help for, and I realized that if I didn't put distance between us, she was going to take me down with her."

"What kind of issues?" Kenna asked.

"Remember how I told you my brother died of a drug overdose?" At Kenna's slow nod, he continued gravely, "Well, Becca was with him, because they were both drug addicts. Pills, mostly, but when she's in her party mode, anything goes. There's no telling what's been flowing through her system. Like I said, she's always refused help and insisted on doing it herself, but the end result was always the same, and I was tired of the merry-go-round. I came to the realization that she was never going to change, and I left."

"So, why is she here now?" Kenna asked.

Lucas looked miserable and frustrated, but he admitted, "Because now she's pregnant and has nowhere to go. She spent the last of her cash to get here and knew I wouldn't throw her out."

Kenna blinked in surprise, reeling from Lucas's admission. On the one hand, she found his refusal to toss a pregnant woman out on the street admirable, but on the other, did she really want to invite this kind of drama into her life? Drama that wasn't her own? No, she did not.

"I appreciate the clarification," she said, framing her words carefully. "But I don't—"

"Wait," he cut in, stepping closer, his expression

haunting her in ways she didn't expect. "I know we talked about being friends, but I have to be honest… I have feelings for you that are deeper than friendship and I don't think I'm off base when I say I think you do, too."

Caught, she could only stare up at him, floundering in the face of his brutal honesty. She wasn't going to deny that somehow, in spite of her best efforts, she'd developed feelings for him, but they'd agreed to strictly friendship. In light of everything, she thought it best to refresh his memory. "Sometimes things happen and—"

"Yeah, sometimes they do," he agreed, pulling her closer with a gentle tug as he murmured, "And it's a good reminder of what's truly important in life," before his lips brushed sweetly across hers, creating a riot of cascading sparks to shower her insides.

And suddenly, she forgot all the good reasons why she'd thought distance was best.

Chapter 17

Lucas hadn't planned on kissing Kenna. His intentions had been to explain his situation and alleviate any concerns she might have, but his heartbeat tripled when he saw her pulling back for all the wrong reasons. He knew she had something she didn't like to talk about in her past, but he wanted her to know he wasn't like whoever had hurt her, and he was willing to prove it.

But even as Kenna responded with the same hunger, he could sense that underlying fear pulling at her, dampening her response until she withdrew first. "Wait," she said, putting her hand against his chest. Her cheeks were flushed as she tried to catch her breath. "I can't do this here." She motioned to a closed door that he assumed was her son's room, and he understood.

"Can we go outside for a minute?" he asked.

Kenna hesitated but nodded and followed him to the porch. Should he apologize for kissing her? She didn't appear regretful but rather conflicted, and if that was the case, he understood.

"Tell me you only want to be friends," he said, "and I'll never push that boundary again. I never want you to feel uncomfortable around me, but I truly like you and I think you feel the same. Am I wrong?"

Kenna shook her head, admitting, "You're not wrong."

Relief flooded him. "Then tell me why I feel you pulling back."

"You don't know me well enough to make an informed decision," she said.

"We all have pasts, Kenna. I don't expect you to come to me as a nun who lived her whole life in a convent."

"Some pasts are more checkered than most," Kenna returned quietly. "Trust me when I say you deserve better than what I can give you."

"I think you should let me be the judge of that," he said. "I see an incredible woman who's been hurt in the past by a shithead ex, and I'm interested in showing that woman that not all men are monsters."

"I know you're a good man, Lucas—that's part of the reason why you deserve so much better. I come with baggage you can't even imagine, and it would kill me to watch your opinion of me change when my skeletons pop out of the closet."

"Who am I to judge? My skeleton popped from the closet and inserted herself in my life all over again. I can promise you, I'm not going to blink twice at anything you've got in your past."

"That's easy to say," she murmured, glancing away.

He doubled down, determined to ease her fears. "Sweetheart, there's literally nothing I can think of that would make me run in the opposite direction from you," he assured her, but she shook her head as if he couldn't possibly make that promise, so he called her bluff. "Okay, all cards on the table. Tell me what's hiding in your past that's got you so worked up. I can promise you, it's probably not as bad as you think."

Her dark eyes flashed as she bristled. "You have no idea, and I don't need to prove my trauma to you or anyone else."

Realizing his misstep, he immediately apologized. "Sometimes I'm a bungling idiot with words. Let me try again. I will not judge anything from your past. The past is called the past for a reason. Let me show you that my word is good."

"It's easy to make promises before the fact, and I can't take the chance that you might change your mind after I let you in. I have to think of Ty. He's been through things you can't even imagine, and it's all my fault. I'm not going to let him go through the wringer again because I couldn't stick to a single damn promise I made. Do you understand? It's about more than attraction or want, because you're right—if it was only about those things, I would give you a chance, but I have to be a better mother than I've been in the past."

His respect for her as a mother and a person with integrity swelled, but he could also sense that she would cut her nose off to spite her face in a desperate attempt to avoid making the same mistakes.

Kenna earnestly reached out to him, saying, "And honestly, with everything happening in your life now, don't you think it's bad timing to add more to your plate? I know you said that you're trying to distance yourself from Becca, but I don't know how you'll do that now that she's staying in your house."

"I'm working on finding new arrangements for Becca," he told her, refusing to let Becca's situation ruin his chances with Kenna. "I might not be willing to put her on the streets, but that doesn't mean I'm willing to let her take over my life again, and I told her that. Trust me, she knows exactly where I stand when it comes to her situation."

"I don't know, Lucas," she said, looking away with a subtle frown. "It seems like we're trying to force something that the universe is trying to pull apart before it's even formed. Seems like a sign we should stop while we're ahead."

He didn't believe in that but was careful not to insult her beliefs. He linked his fingers through hers, and when she didn't resist, he drew her closer. He pushed a thick lock of hair from her upturned face with his free hand, wondering how anyone could stand to hurt a single strand on her head. "I have an idea," he said. "At dinner I was going to ask if you wanted to go backpacking with me—a weekend trip, nothing too hard—so we could spend some time together without distractions. Given how much stress you've been under, I thought you might welcome the break. We could take Ty, too. He might even like it."

"I don't know, Lucas, don't you think that's moving a little fast given the situation?"

"I think we both need some fresh air and mountain doctoring, as I like to call it."

Kenna's uncertain expression cut at him. With one badly timed entrance, Becca had trashed what could've been a beautiful start with Kenna. "You and Ty can sleep in one tent. I'll take another. It'll be completely innocent," he assured her, adding, "Ty's gotta need a change of scenery with all that's been going on."

"I don't know. Ty isn't exactly the backpacking type. I'm not sure he'd enjoy it as much as you think."

Lucas wouldn't be deterred. "Maybe not, but I thought it might be worth a shot. And you never know—kids can surprise you."

A spark of hope burned in his chest when she didn't shut him down. He knew Kenna would enjoy the trip—the quick flash of interest in her eyes gave her away—but she still wavered. "I don't have the right gear…" Her voice trailed off with regret, and he swooped in with a solution.

"I have everything you'll need. I just splurged on a new pack, and I have my old one that's still in great condition. You can take the new one. I'll take my old one."

"I couldn't use your new one before you," she balked.

"I don't mind," he said.

"Really?"

"One hundred percent."

Kenna's shy smile was everything he needed. Hell, he'd give her the shirt off his back if she asked for it. Anything for that smile.

"Maybe," she finally answered.

Lucas leaned in to taste her lips again, and this time, she met him with a hunger that matched his. Their tongues danced, igniting a fire that could've burned the forest down. It was a long moment before they released each other, and even then, he wasn't ready.

"I'll get everything prepared," he promised. "All you need to do is be ready to get picked up."

"I said maybe," she reminded him with her tone's mild tease of caution. "I have to talk to Ty first."

But Lucas knew she'd already decided to go, and he'd take the win without pushing his luck.

He pressed a tender kiss to the back of her hand and then said goodbye before he couldn't make himself leave.

Lucas wouldn't let anything stand in his way of that trip. Nothing.

Not even Becca.

Kenna watched from the window as Lucas drove away. Her lips still tingled from his kiss, and a giddiness she hadn't felt in forever threatened to chase away all her good sense.

Had she just agreed to go backpacking with Lucas even though she knew she shouldn't?

Yes.

Should she come to her senses and back out?

Also yes.

Was she going to do that?

God help her, no.

The truth was, she wanted to go with him more than anything. Their recent hiking trip with the cadets had reminded her how much she'd missed doing simple things like walking through nature. She'd always found comfort in the woods when she'd been younger, listening to the birds or watching the clouds chase each other across the sky.

Before life had gotten in the way, she'd dreamed of becoming a ranger or possibly a wilderness tour guide so she could work with nature, but the universe had had different plans.

Luna used to tease her by saying her true name was probably She Who Walks a Thousand Miles, because she'd always found ways to take the longer route to get a little extra time with the dirt and sky.

Since moving back home, parts of her that'd been dormant for so long were awakening, reminding her of who she'd once been.

And she was hungry for more.

But what about this Becca character? She wanted to believe Lucas was being honest about his past with her, but she had precious little experience with men who told the truth, and she didn't know what to believe right now.

Kenna ran her fingers lightly over her lips, closing her eyes as she replayed their kiss repeatedly in her head. A small sigh escaped her as she reluctantly planted her feet back on the ground. She had to talk to Ty and see if he was interested in going along and, if not, would he mind if she went with Lucas.

Since their big talk, things had been better between them, and she was averse to doing anything that might tip the apple cart.

She was taking a gamble, but Ty deserved honesty, even if she didn't like his reaction or response.

Rebuilding a life wasn't easy, especially when you didn't know all the broken parts. Sometimes the broken pieces hid behind what appeared to be solid support beams, and you only figured out your mistake when everything crashed down.

That's how it felt watching Ty disintegrate and act out. She couldn't take chances with his mental health and assume he was okay with whatever she did.

But maybe he'd be okay with her going backpacking with Lucas. Hard to say and could go either way.

Once again, she double-checked the doors and windows, making sure the house was locked up tight, and turned off the lights before heading to bed. There was enough to think about to drive her crazy, but for once, the thoughts in her head didn't create terror, and that was an improvement she'd gratefully take.

Maybe tonight she wouldn't have nightmares.

That would be a nice change, she thought with a smile.

But the fracture in her skull zinged with phantom pain, reminding her how close Leon had come to ending her story, and she smothered a shudder at the memory.

What she needed right now was to climb into bed and sleep. Tomorrow would be here before she knew it, and the day would start again.

Kenna started to undress, but as she pulled her shirt over her head, prickles of awareness danced along her skin as if she'd caught someone staring at her. She hastily donned her sleep shirt and clicked off her bedroom light, going to the dark window to peer outside but only seeing pitch black.

You're being paranoid again, she told herself with annoyance.

It was unlikely someone was lurking in the forest, peeping through her window. For one, her parents' house was a mile off the road, and she would've seen any cars pulling up like she saw Lucas's headlights when he drove up. The forest was also full of wildlife at night. Cougars, bears, coyotes—things with sharp teeth and claws.

Someone would have to be an idiot to be out there right now.

She chuckled, but her disquiet remained even as she climbed into bed and pulled the light blanket over her. It was too hot for blankets, but the thought of leaving her feet open to grabbing made her feel like a little kid all over again, afraid of the monster under her bed.

Except Kenna knew now that monsters didn't hide under the bed—they hid in plain sight.

And whispered terrible things when no one was looking.

Chapter 18

"Ty, can I talk to you for a minute?" Kenna ventured as her son climbed into the car after summer day camp. Sweat dripped down his temples, and his face was flushed. A jump in the pool was probably the first and only thing on his mind, but he nodded warily as he waited for her to continue. She didn't blame him for being apprehensive, but she tried not to chicken out. "I want to be honest with you from here on out, but that means taking a chance on telling you something you might not like, okay?"

"Yeah, okay," Ty said, waiting for the shoe to drop. "Is this about Lucas?"

Damn, that boy was way too smart for his own good. She blushed and nodded. "He's invited us to go backpacking with him this weekend. I really want to go, but I want you to feel good about the invitation."

"Backpacking? You mean, like camping?" he asked, confused.

"Yeah, but in the backcountry, so it would really be roughing it."

His expression screwed into a disinterested scowl. "Sounds worse than hiking."

"You had fun when we went hiking," she reminded him. "Remember? You and Arrow really hit it off."

"I don't want to spend all weekend doing that," he said. "I mean, one day is fine, but a whole weekend? No, thanks. You think it's fun to sleep on the ground with the bugs and snakes? Pass."

"We'd have a tent to sleep in," she said, realizing with a sinking feeling that she hadn't passed on her love for nature to her son. He'd much rather play his video games or watch television, which made her wince. Somehow, when she'd been off screwing up her life, she'd inadvertently created a couch potato, but she had to believe that the situation was fixable.

"Can I spend the weekend with a friend instead?"

That surprised her. "You've made a friend?" she asked, tentatively optimistic. Ty had always been a little shy when it came to meeting new people and had often kept to himself, probably from moving as much as they had. She'd love to see him making actual connections here in Cottonwood. "Who is your friend?"

"Just a kid I met at day camp. It's no big deal, but he likes the same stuff I do. His name is Sam."

"Does Sam have a last name? Maybe I know his parents."

Ty shrugged as if that detail hadn't interested him. "So can I?"

"Well, I'd like some more information before I send my kid off to a stranger's house," she said, but Ty's immediate scowl made her curl with guilt for being a hypocrite. She'd introduced men into Ty's life way before she'd really gotten to know them, and it'd bitten them in the butt more than once, but she was trying to be a better parent. "I'm sure it's fine, but I'd like to know your friends."

Ty lost some of his bristles, saying, "Yeah, I can find out."

"Good." She drew a deep breath. "So, if you don't want to go hiking with us, do you mind if I go?"

Ty pursed his lips, considering her question. "You said you weren't going to date Lucas," he reminded her.

"I know. It's not a date, it's—" But she stopped short, realizing she was about to lie again and corrected course. "I like him, Ty. A lot. I tried not to, but I do. I don't know if it will work out, but I know he's a good man and nothing like the men I've dated before. Plus, Auntie Luna really likes him, and you know she's hard to impress."

Ty couldn't argue that point, but he still didn't look happy. "I don't think you should go."

"Why not?" she asked.

He shrugged, staring down at his hands. "I don't know, seems like a bad idea."

Her enthusiasm dimmed, hating the idea of turning Lucas down but knowing that she would if Ty couldn't find his way to being okay with it. "I won't go if you don't want me to," she said quietly.

Ty took a long moment to answer. She understood it was a big thing, asking him to give his stamp of approval. They were still healing from her last big mistake. She didn't know how to communicate to Ty that she genuinely believed Lucas was different, so she had to give him the space to come to his own conclusion.

"You really want to go?" he asked.

"Yeah," she admitted, adding, "and I'd really like if you came, too."

"Why?"

"Because I think you will enjoy yourself, for one, but two, I think if you spent more time with Lucas you'd see what I see, and it absolutely matters to me that you like Lucas."

Ty chewed his cheek, considering her answer. Some people might disapprove of her treating him as more mature than he was, but Ty wasn't like your typical ten-year-old. He'd been forced to grow up because of the circumstances she'd put him through. She wanted him to be free to be a kid, but she also needed him to understand that he had to be willing to take a chance on someone new if they ever hoped to move on from the past.

"I'll go with you," he said, heaving a sigh as if he'd agreed to climb Mount Everest with her. "But if after doing this backpacking thing with you guys I get the slightest weird vibe from him, I'm not giving him another chance."

"That's fair," Kenna said, nodding. "But you have to promise me you'll give him a real shot, okay? None of this setting him up to fail stuff."

Ty grinned as if she'd caught him at his own game. "Fine. Clean slate."

"Clean slate," she agreed, smiling. Her excitement was building. "Now, we need to get you your own backpack. This is going to be fun!"

Ty grumbled something about getting poked in the eye, but she'd take the win. She knew her son. Once they hit the trail, he'd see what she loved most about the open air, beautiful vistas and peaceful country.

And peace was something they all sorely needed.

"Thanks, buddy," she said, using her free hand to ruffle his hair. "You have no idea what this means to me."

"Yeah, whatever," he said, rolling his eyes. "Can we get ice cream?"

How could she say no? "Of course." She was on cloud nine. The boy could have whatever he wanted.

Lucas clicked off with Kenna, grinning from ear to ear. It looked like Ty was coming along for the trip, and he was eager to spend time with them. Ty was a good kid, but he'd been through some things. It was essential to Lucas that Ty saw that he was a trustworthy man, and the only way to do that was to put words into action.

Even though Kenna insisted she could share a pack with Ty, Lucas immediately put a rush order on a kid-size pack so that it would be here by Friday. It felt good to help, and who knows, maybe this trip would ignite a new love for the outdoors for Ty. He was impatient for Friday to get here, but he had personal business to handle in the meantime, which wasn't as pleasant.

He walked into his house and immediately smelled something burning. He sprinted to the kitchen to find Becca staring in dismay at some kind of ruined casserole, waving away the smoke from the charbroiled lump.

"What happened?" he asked.

"I fell asleep and didn't hear the timer. I was trying to have it ready by the time you came home. I thought it would be nice to have a home-cooked meal instead of a frozen burrito."

He saw what she was trying to do, and it wasn't going to work, but he wasn't in the mood to get into it. Besides, since Becca looked genuinely miserable and embarrassed, there was no need to make it worse.

"It was my grandmother's recipe. Brock used to love

it," she shared, staring morosely at the casserole. He moved past her to open up all the windows as she murmured, "Sorry."

"Don't worry about it. We need to talk," he said, gesturing to the living room where the air wasn't smoky.

Becca followed him into the living room and dropped into the chair with a petulant expression. "How was your day at work, dear?" she asked.

He cut her a sharp look to indicate he wasn't playing. "I've done some asking around, and I may have found a place for you. It's a group home for women in your position, and they offer in-house substance abuse treatment. You need to come down to the Behavioral Health Center and fill out the paperwork to get your application started."

Becca's eyes widened as if surprised and disappointed he'd found a place so quickly. "You really can't wait to be rid of me, huh?"

"Becca, if you're really serious about turning your life around, this is how it's done," he said firmly, refusing to be swayed by anything she threw at him. He wanted to believe Becca could be a good person, but his faith was hanging on by a thread. "It's not just for you—it's for your baby, too."

At the mention of the pregnancy, Becca looked away, her hand resting on her still-flat stomach. "Hard to believe there's anything in there," she admitted. "It feels surreal to think that a baby is growing in my guts."

Yeah, he felt the same and was still processing this new reality.

Becca drew a deep breath and met his gaze. "I'll fill out the application," she said, surprising him when she didn't push back with some excuse like he expected. "Can you take me tomorrow?"

He nodded. Now that the first hurdle was managed, he moved on to the next. "I'm going away for the weekend. You think you'll be okay while I'm gone?"

"You're going with *her*, aren't you?" she guessed, unable to hide her chagrin. She seemed jealous, which at one time he would've gobbled up as hope that maybe she was finally seeing him as more than Brock's older brother. Now, he couldn't believe he'd ever been secretly crazy in love with the woman.

"Her name is Kenna, and yes."

"What's she like?" Becca asked.

"Kind, gentle, a good mother," he said, leaving out the part where he thought Kenna shone with a light that nearly blinded him each time he looked at her. No sense in rubbing salt in the wound. "And an overall amazing person."

"Sounds like a saint," Becca quipped. "Is she even human?" Then, at his sharp look, she said quickly, "I'm just kidding. She sounds great."

"She is," he agreed, wondering if Becca had ever had feelings for him that she'd never shared. At this point, he hoped not. "Have you thought about what it's going to be like to be a mother?"

"Not really," she admitted, removing her hand from her stomach and folding her arms across her chest. "Right now I'd like to stop throwing up at random moments. That'd be fantastic. Honestly, this time around is totally different than the last time, and I'm kinda overwhelmed by the difference."

Her quiet admission caused him to look her way sharply. "What do you mean? Last time?"

Becca became reflective, sharing, "I got pregnant right before Brock died, but I miscarried. I should've known the baby wasn't going to make it. I was never sick and I never felt any different. Then, as suddenly as I discovered I was pregnant, I wasn't anymore."

His shock couldn't have been more profound. "Brock never told me," he said against the unexpected sharp spasm in his chest. "But then, Brock and I weren't exactly on speaking terms when he died."

"Which was my fault," Becca admitted with a frown. "I'm sorry. I didn't understand how much I was taking from the both of you by creating a wedge between brothers. I was being so selfish. I'm so ashamed of how I acted when you and Brock were literally my only family."

In all the years he'd known Becca, he'd never known her to apologize or humble herself. He wasn't sure how to handle this new version of her, but it was heartening to see the change.

Could he believe it, though?

He glanced toward the kitchen, where tendrils of smoke still curled from the ruined casserole. "I appreciate the gesture, even if it didn't quite work out the way you'd hoped," he said. "How about we head into town and grab a burger? You think your stomach can handle that?"

"It's worth a shot," she said with a tentative smile, accepting his help from the chair. "Thank you, Lucas."

Maybe it was wishful thinking, but Lucas felt something shift between them. Maybe Becca was truly trying to change for her baby, and if that was the case, he'd do what he could to help.

Only time would tell.

Chapter 19

Friday came, and with it, butterflies rioting in Kenna's stomach. She'd taken the day off so they could get an early start, and she was still blown away by Lucas's generosity when he'd insisted on buying Ty his own pack.

When men seemed overly generous, they usually wanted something from her, but Lucas didn't have that kind of energy, and his generosity felt genuine, which was a different experience altogether.

Was she naive to believe Lucas wasn't like all the rest? Of course, taking a chance on Lucas was risky, but it seemed like the right thing, so she was living on the edge of hope that, for once, her gut wasn't wrong.

Please don't be wrong.

Lucas came to pick them up in his truck. Ty rode in the back with Noble. Kenna was secretly glad Lucas had brought his K-9 along. Ty loved animals and had always wanted a dog, but that'd never been possible with their living situations. For one, apartments rarely allowed animals. When she moved in with Leon, she thought that might change, but Leon despised dogs and shut her down quickly when she broached the subject.

Ty tried not to show his delight when he saw the police dog, but it was hard to miss the way his eyes lit up when he realized his traveling partner was the sharp-eyed German shepherd.

The four-hour drive went relatively fast with entertaining conversation and music. By the time they reached the trailhead, they were ready to eat a quick sandwich at the truck before loading up their packs and heading out on the trail.

Immediately, the landscape took her breath away. Brilliant wildflowers dotted the terrain along the winding path as the Beartooth Range punctured the blue skies with glistening white caps of snow at the highest elevation.

"It's beautiful," she breathed, taken in by the view. Her heart swelled with appreciation as she inhaled a deep breath of the clean mountain air. The light scent of wildflowers mixed with the alpine spice created a heady mixture that immediately calmed her soul. God, she'd missed this. She cast a quick look Lucas's way to share her quiet gratitude, and he seemed to understand exactly how she felt.

They pressed on, determined to make the camping spot by late afternoon, trudging along the well-marked trail, making jokes and light conversation as they went. Noble was in dog heaven, stopping and sniffing everything he could put his snout on until his inquisitive nose found a bee, and Lucas had to intervene before Noble discovered bees weren't good playmates.

They reached their first campsite in good time and pitched their tents. Lucas and Noble had their tent, and

Kenna would share her tent with Ty. Lucas took the time to show Ty how to secure their tents and how to properly handle the bathroom situation, though Kenna had to bite back a laugh at Ty's expression when he learned he had to do his business behind a bush.

Ty cast Kenna a sour look, saying, "You never said anything about going to the bathroom outside."

She laughed. "It builds character."

"Yeah, right. What if a snake bites my butt?" he asked.

"Watch where you squat and that won't happen," Lucas answered with a grin, setting him on a task. "Go gather some firewood so we have something to cook our dinner on. Look for small, dry branches for kindling and bigger pieces, too. That ought to keep you busy for a little bit."

Ty started to grumble, but Noble distracted him with a playful, deep-throated woof as he ran to a tree with a disgruntled squirrel chittering from his lofty perch, and Ty followed.

"Aside from the bathroom inconvenience, I think he's actually having fun," Kenna whispered to Lucas, watching her son pick up sticks along the trail. "This was a great idea. Thank you."

"I've wanted to hike this trail since getting the job and relocating to Montana. Don't get me wrong, there were beautiful parts of Kansas, but the landscape never spoke to me the way Montana does."

"My mom used to say that the land has a voice and only those who are open to listening will hear it speak," she shared, smiling at the memory.

"I like that. Sounds like powerful wisdom," he said.

Kenna nodded shyly. She rarely shared personal things with anyone, but Lucas felt like a safe place to share such things. "My adoptive mother, Nancy, was Macawi, the same as my biological mom, but she wasn't raised on the reservation. However, her heritage was still very important to her, and she tried to share that love with us. Luna was never really into her indigenous background, and Sayeh wasn't interested until recently, but I always felt a connection to my Native American roots. I always thought it was something special—even if I lost touch for a while. It feels good to reconnect, like coming home was necessary to heal some broken part of me."

"You're not broken," he disagreed gently. "Maybe a little bruised, but who isn't nowadays?"

Kenna tried to stop the butterflies, but they were hard to control when Lucas was exceedingly kind when she needed it the most. "Well, my bruises go pretty deep," she said with a chagrined chuckle. "But I'm determined to heal."

"I think you're right—coming home for you was a good call. This is a special place. I have such deep respect for the indigenous people of any land. I always thought we could learn a lot from those who came before us, and I never understood why others didn't feel the same. Back in Kansas, I responded to a hit-and-run accident involving a pedestrian. The victim was an old man from the Kickapoo Reservation named Frank. Frank didn't have any family in the area, and I felt bad that he was all alone, so I'd go and visit him in the hospital while he recovered. He'd tell me stories about growing up on the reservation, traditions his family had and how it was all pretty much gone now because the young folk didn't want to carry on the way their ancestors had. Cell phones, modern technology and the pressures of society had crushed their way of life."

Kenna nodded, thinking of the Macawi Reservation, where her and her sisters' lives had begun and how different their lives would've been if they hadn't been adopted by Bill and Nancy. "Life is hard on the reservation," she murmured. "They don't have enough resources to grow and thrive. For many, it's a dead-end street. My sister was good friends with the woman who was killed a few months ago, Charlotte Leicki. Charlotte was working with the Macawi clinic to get updated medical equipment donated. Most tribes have to operate without even the bare minimum, and it's not fair."

"No argument here," he said gravely. "We need to do better."

Lucas met Kenna's gaze, and she was momentarily mesmerized by the kindness she saw in his eyes. Was it possible that men like Lucas actually existed? That they genuinely cared about others above and beyond what someone could do for them? Leon had tricked her into believing he was kind and generous by throwing his money around in situations where everyone could see how magnanimous he was, but she'd learned too late that it'd been an act.

Leon's true talent was a private show of abject cruelty.

Kenna pulled back as if slapped by the memory, saying, "Yep. We all need to do better," and rose with the excuse she was going to check on Ty's progress, but she really needed a minute to collect herself.

She'd spent her adult life placing the bar on the literal floor for every man she ever spent time with—and now she didn't know what to do with a man who insisted she set the bar high for herself.

It made her want to laugh—or cry.

Maybe both.

* * *

Had he said something wrong? Lucas sensed the minute her energy changed. Kenna's mercurial moods were like a tropical storm—appearing without warning, and then the clouds would clear and it would be as if it never happened.

Hiding emotions was a trauma response. If he could get his hands on the person who'd hurt Kenna so grievously, he'd probably commit a felony. Lucas didn't understand anyone who would put his hands on a woman, but to hurt a woman like Kenna baffled him even more.

He couldn't imagine a sweeter, more genuine person, yet someone had put the fear of God into that woman.

Just as he expected, when Kenna reappeared with Ty and Noble, her smile had returned as she helped Ty carry the firewood for their evening dinner. If she wasn't ready to talk, he wasn't going to push and would follow her lead.

"Noble found a dead raccoon," Ty exclaimed with ten-year-old boy enthusiasm around something gross. "I thought he was going to eat it, but he just sniffed at it and left it alone."

"Thank God for that. Sometimes dogs love to roll in smelly things," Lucas said, relieved, as he took the wood from Ty. *Time for another wilderness lesson.* "All right, let's get this fire started."

"I'll get water to boil," Kenna volunteered, gesturing to the gurgling creek that ran along the campsite.

Lucas had brought water purification tablets, so they could drink the creek water without picking up a nasty stomach bug, and it also enabled them to pack in fewer water jugs to carry—they could replenish their water supply directly from the trail.

Lucas showed Ty how to efficiently get a fire started,

and seeing the kid actually smile about his accomplishment when the fire began to crackle made him feel good.

But Kenna's warm smile, as she watched them, made him feel like a kid again, hoping his crush would look his way. In all his adult life, he'd never felt the way he did with Kenna. Was this what falling in love felt like?

Looking back, he knew he'd never actually loved Becca in the way that mattered—not the way Brock had. He'd once asked Brock why he loved Becca the way he did. Brock had replied, with stars in his eyes, "She's everything, man. I can't explain it. She's my world," and Lucas had rolled his eyes with annoyance, chalking Brock's answer up to being an idiot.

But maybe that's what love did to people—it turned them into willing, lovesick idiots.

Suddenly, it made sense.

"So what's for dinner?" Ty asked, curious.

"Rehydrated beans and rice," he answered with a grin, expecting the grimace that followed—and he wasn't disappointed.

"That sounds disgusting," Ty said.

"Give it a chance. You might be surprised."

"Not likely," Ty grumbled. "Man, I thought we were going to have hamburgers or something good."

"Not this trip. I rely on quality rehydrated foods and maybe fresh fish if we're lucky, but we can definitely schedule a different camping trip another time with hamburgers and s'mores on the menu if you end up willing to give me another shot." He winked at Ty, then at Kenna, who watched and listened keenly to their exchange. Maybe this was a test—he didn't know, but he felt good about his odds.

Kenna chuckled, saying to Ty, "Lucky for you, I anticipated your reluctance to try the rehydrated foods, and I brought a small package of hot dogs you can grill over the fire. Go find a small stick you can skewer your dog with."

Ty jumped up with relief. "Thanks, Mom," he said and ran off to find the right stick.

"No fair," Lucas said with a grin. "Did you bring enough for everyone?"

She smiled. "I did. So you're welcome to your beans and rice, but we're having hot dogs with a chocolate protein bar for dessert."

"Sounds good to me."

With Ty and Noble searching for the perfect cooking stick, Lucas took the private moment to pull Kenna into his arms, folding her against him for a kiss. His mouth sealed over hers, and she melted. He smiled against her mouth, admitting, "I've wanted to do that all day."

"Me, too," she said but quickly stepped away as the sound of Ty and Noble returning ended their stolen moment. The taste was a painful tease, but he'd take what he could get for now.

He couldn't imagine anything better than how he felt right now.

Time spent with Kenna was worth any potential obstacle.

"Found the perfect stick!" Ty announced with a triumphant grin. "Let's get started. I'm starved!"

You and me both, kid. You and me both.

Chapter 20

Kenna couldn't remember the last time she'd laughed so hard. Lucas was an incredible storyteller and a joker. He had Ty giggling at his stories of dealing with stupid criminals over the years, but Ty's favorite so far were ones involving a bad guy getting bitten by the K-9 officer.

"Noble is actually my second K-9 partner," Lucas shared around the campfire. "Back in Kansas, I had a Malinois named Bullet. He was the fastest thing on four legs I'd ever seen. He could take down a perp like a lioness chasing down a gazelle for dinner. He was great. No offense to Noble, but Bullet was as fast as his namesake."

Noble licked his chops as if to say, *whatever*, and stretched out beside Ty, who was stroking his fur. "What happened to Bullet?" Ty asked.

Lucas frowned at the memory. "Unfortunately, Bullet got a rare, aggressive form of cancer, and we had to put him down. But there's a plaque in his memory back at my old station. He was very much loved by everyone in the department." He pulled his cell phone free from his pocket, showing Ty. "This is Bullet. Forever in my heart, no matter where I go."

"He looks mean," Ty admitted, but his eyes widened with admiration. "I'd be scared of him if I were a criminal."

Lucas chuckled, putting his phone away. "Yeah, he made an impression, that's for sure."

"Is that how you knew you wanted to continue to be a K-9 officer, because of Bullet?" Kenna asked, curious.

"Yeah," he answered, nodding. "I really enjoyed having a K-9 partner. They're loyal, smart and they don't have an opinion on the music for road trips."

"Hey!" Kenna laughed, nudging his foot with her own. "I pick good music."

Lucas and Ty shared a look as if they agreed Kenna's tastes were suspect, and she faked outrage. "Well, too bad, I guess. Passenger always gets to pick the music, so you're just going to have to deal with it."

Lucas chuckled. "Fair enough."

Ty yawned, surprising himself as he rubbed bleary eyes, and Kenna suggested it was time to hit the bed.

"I'm not tired," he protested, but another yawn popped from his mouth, and Kenna laughed. Ty grumbled, "Okay, fine. Maybe I'm a *little* tired."

Kenna helped Ty into the tiny tent they would share and got him settled before rejoining Lucas by the fire. "I'll bet he's asleep the minute his head hits the pillow," she said.

"Fresh air will do that for you. Best sleep of my life is always right under the stars."

"It's been a long time, but something tells me I'll

sleep like a baby," she said. "My parents used to take us camping. Me and Sayeh loved it, but Luna was more content to stay in her room with a book in an air-conditioned house."

Lucas chuckled. "Are you and your sisters close?"

Kenna took her time considering how to answer. "We're getting there," she decided. "After losing our dad the way we did, it brought us together, which is really sad, because it shouldn't have taken something so awful, but that's what happened. For the first time, I think we're learning to trust each other and get to know one another on a different level. It's good and I'm glad, though it feels weird at first." She cast a questioning look his way. "Were you and your brother close before he died?"

He sighed, admitting, "That's a loaded question with a complicated answer. I loved my little brother, but it always felt like I was more of a father to him than a brother, because I was always looking out for him. When he got into drugs, I felt so helpless to stop what was happening, and also I felt it was my fault somehow. I wanted him to be happy, but he couldn't find his way out of the hole he'd fallen into. It also didn't help that his girlfriend was more interested in keeping her party buddy than helping Brock get clean."

"That's Becca, right?" Kenna surmised. "The one living with you?"

"Yes, but not for long. I've found a treatment program for pregnant addicts that will take her. The paperwork is already in motion."

"It's kind of you to help, given your past with her. Complicated connections are hard to untangle. You're a good man, Lucas."

He ducked her praise, blushing a little in the dim,

flickering light. "I don't know, just trying to be a decent human. Seems like the world needs more of those than ever before." He sighed. "I mean, Becca isn't a bad person. She's just got her demons. Like Brock did. To be honest, I hope I'm not being played, but I think Becca actually wants to change this time."

"Change is hard, even when we want to," she said quietly, understanding the struggle. How many times had she staunchly declared that she would stop making stupid decisions when it came to men, and yet she still seemed to fall for every sweet talker that came her way? And each one was progressively worse than the last. "I read somewhere that statistically, it takes seven failed attempts to change your environment before it happens. It's not that you don't want to change, but sometimes it feels impossible and you fall into old patterns."

"Kenna, you're nothing like Becca," he said, the authority, the conviction in his voice making her wince. He had no idea who she was or what she'd been through to make that determination.

"Please don't make that assumption," she said, shifting against the discomfort rioting along her skin. "I might be just like Becca—and then how would you feel about me?"

She held his stare, her heart hammering hard inside her chest. This was a moment of truth. Clearly, Lucas had his issues with Becca, which was his business, but what if her struggles were too similar? Would he eventually stop looking at her with such kind eyes? She couldn't bear to lose that grace from Lucas. She needed to know if he wasn't in it for the good, the bad and the ugly, because her past was a war zone of bad decisions.

Lucas felt Kenna's pain and fear radiating outward, and he knew this was a deciding moment for her. She was testing the waters to see how deep the river went. "Everyone has a story, which means there will always be a chapter they don't like to read aloud. I'm not scared by what might be in your pages, Kenna."

"Famous last words," she murmured. "What if it's not a chapter but an entire section of the book that's problematic?"

"Give me a chance to show you that I can be the person you need by your side," he said. "I can't rise to the occasion if you won't let me try."

"What if you deserve better than someone like me?" she asked.

"I think you're pretty great," he returned, refusing to let her talk about herself that way. "The question is, why don't you see what everyone else does? Do you realize I haven't come across a single person with a bad word to say about you?"

"You've asked about me?"

He admitted, "Yeah. I had to know more about the stunning vet tech. From the moment I saw you, I was transfixed, and I don't use that word lightly. To be truthful, I'm hard to impress, but you snagged me with a glance and I've been mesmerized ever since." He was being painfully honest, and being this vulnerable wasn't within his comfort zone, but he was willing to show her this side of him if it helped her feel more secure. "I know you've been hurt, but I can promise you, whatever that guy did, I won't. And if I ever do something that makes you uncomfortable, or triggers you, just let me know and I'll take note so it doesn't happen again."

Kenna blinked back sudden tears, as if she couldn't believe anyone would be that serious about her health and welfare, and it made him more determined to show her that she deserved the world, not the scraps she'd been given. "You don't know what you're trying to promise," she said, her voice clogged as she hugged herself, trying to make herself smaller. "There are things you don't know."

"So, tell me," he said. "I'm willing to listen."

Kenna bit her trembling lip. "What if I scare you away?"

"All cards on the table is the only way to find out if you're qualified to play," he said. "I'm putting what I got out there. It's your turn."

She drew a deep breath and released it slowly, as if gathering strength, and he waited for her to go at her own pace. An owl hooted overhead, joining the chorus of frogs along the creek bed and the snap from the fire. "I've told you my ex was abusive," she started, and he nodded. "But it was so much more than that. There are things not even Ty knows, and I'm trying to keep that stuff in the past. I'm ashamed of what he made me do, and I just want to forget it ever happened."

"What kind of things?" he asked.

She shook her head, not ready to go there. "I don't want to talk about it. All I can say is, I was never that person, but he turned me into someone I no longer recognized, and I swear I'm never going back. That's the promise I've made to myself, and I'll die before I go back on it."

The conviction in her voice gave him goose bumps.

"I know you're not like him," she said, "but I don't know how deep the damage goes from what he did to me, and I don't want to put you through my mess to find out. That's what I mean by *you deserve better than me*. I'm not a bad person, but I'm a hot mess that you didn't create, so why should you have to deal with the fallout?"

"It's not a factor of *dealing* with anything," he returned as he reached for her hand and held it firmly. "It's being there for someone you care for who's been hurt. That's all. I'm willing to do that. Whatever it takes."

She shuddered, her eyes glistening. "But you don't know what you're promising," she insisted.

He answered with his mouth brushing against hers. She trembled as she sank into his kiss. Lucas would do anything to wash away the fear living in her heart but was determined to go at her pace. She clung to him as a tear slid down her cheek. "Lucas," she cried softly. He drank in her tears, replacing her fear with wonder as he coaxed sweetness from her lips until she was breathing heavy and her touch became bold.

Kenna was an enigma he was desperate to solve. She was a contradiction that drew him ever deeper into the mystery. She was afraid for him—not of him—which made him want to protect her with every last breath in his body.

His heart was beating fast enough to break through his chest. He wanted nothing more than to make love to her on the forest floor, but Lucas wasn't about to create a core memory for Ty that might scar him for life should he wake up and see some guy with his mom.

It took Herculean effort to peel himself away from Kenna's lush body, but he slowed their passion to a final lingering kiss before stopping and pulling her into the cove of his arms to hold her tightly. She snuggled against him like a lost koala bear, and he knew at that moment that he'd go to war for this woman.

He wasn't sure how long they sat like that, watching the fire crackle, listening to the forest sounds, drinking in the simple comfort of one another, but he knew it would never be enough.

"I should turn in," Kenna said with a small yawn.

"Probably a good idea," he agreed. "Morning comes

early in the mountains." He wished more than anything she was following him into his tent. Their situation was a great opportunity to cultivate patience. He told himself this as he said good night and watched her disappear into the tent.

Although it was good advice he should've taken, Lucas stayed up a bit longer to ensure the fire was tended properly. This was his favorite time when camping—when night blanketed all around him and a sense of peace calmed any storm raging in his life.

He truly believed nature had the power to heal whatever ailed you—at least, that'd been his experience. If it hadn't been for his love of hiking, what he went through with Brock would've broken him.

Noble, snoozing like a lazy lug without a care in the world, suddenly bolted up in full alert mode, his sharp gaze piercing the unending pitch-black forest around them.

"What is it, boy?" Lucas asked, staring in the same direction, listening for the sounds of a bear shuffling around in the dark, but unnerving silence bounced back, giving no clue why Noble was tensed and ready to go on full offensive if Lucas gave the command.

Lucas climbed to his feet, moving stealthily to his pack to get his hunting knife, just in case.

They were surrounded by uninhabited forest—bears, coyotes, wolves, even cougars prowled this wilderness, but they were usually averse to approaching humans.

Noble looked to Lucas, whining as he licked his chops, eager for the command, but Lucas didn't want Noble tangling with a wild animal. "Settle," he told Noble quietly. Noble sat on his haunches, but his gaze never left a spot in the dark. "It's probably a hungry critter. If we leave them alone, they'll do the same."

But it took a long while for Noble to lose his tense posture, which seemed odd if it were an animal snuffling around too close for comfort.

Lucas waited until Noble huffed and relaxed once again before he felt comfortable putting out the fire and climbing into his tent.

Never in his life had he felt in danger in all the times he'd hiked alone in various locations around the world.

Tonight, he couldn't shake the odd feeling of being watched—and he didn't like that at all.

Chapter 21

Morning broke, and they awoke to find their food stores thrown around and dumped onto the ground.

"What happened?" Kenna asked, alarmed at the destruction, watching as Lucas tried to salvage some of their breakfast. "I didn't even hear anything rummaging around in the camp, and usually bears are loud snufflers."

Lucas's disconcerted frown worried her, but he calmed her anxiety with a plausible explanation. "Well, bears are loud, but raccoons are bandits. It's my fault. I should've known better than to not secure the food in a bearproof container."

"But you just said it probably wasn't a bear," Ty said, glancing around as if worried a bear was going to jump from behind a bush and eat his leg like a Thanksgiving turkey.

"Bearproof works for all critters," Lucas explained

with a brief smile. "Well, luckily, I have some oatmeal in my tent that didn't get tossed around."

"Oatmeal?" Ty's grimace wasn't complimentary, but after some convincing—and the promise of a pizza when they returned home—Kenna convinced Ty to try the strawberry-banana oatmeal. When he finally agreed to take a tentative bite, his expression of surprise was followed by eating the entire package with a noncommittal "Not bad."

"I'll take the win," Kenna said, laughing as she finished her breakfast and helped Lucas strike the camp and clean up their space for the next camper. But Kenna noticed Lucas was unusually quiet and kept scanning the forest around them.

When she was sure Ty wouldn't overhear them, she asked, "Is everything okay?"

"Yeah, it's just odd that I didn't find any animal tracks around the food. In fact, there were no tracks at all, which is even odder. I know our food didn't just launch itself from the packs by itself, but a lack of tracks makes it look like that."

Kenna's easy smile faded; she seemed to share Lucas's confusion. "But if someone entered the camp, which is unlikely out here in the middle of nowhere, wouldn't Noble have alerted us to an intruder?"

"Yeah, it's not making much sense. It had to be a critter of some sort," he finished, bracketing his hips with his hands as he puzzled out the situation. He blew out a short breath, shaking his head. "Well, some mysteries don't require solving. We lost a bit of our food, but I was thinking fresh fish would be better for dinner tonight anyway. Ready to hit the trail?"

Kenna relaxed at Lucas's calm assurance and nodded, excited about the next trek. "Ready when you are."

They planned to get a few miles in to reach the next spot, which promised a beautiful swimming hole and a place to enjoy lunch, but they had to move if they wanted to make the schedule work.

Kenna felt decidedly lighter after last night's conversation with Lucas. She'd forgotten how buoyant hope made the soul, and her smile came more quickly and less guarded.

She couldn't stop thinking of how wonderful Lucas's lips felt against hers. Kenna was happy Ty was there to experience the weekend with them, but she wasn't above wishing for some actual alone time with Lucas to continue what they'd started last night.

Right about now, Lucas's earlier offer of dinner sounded great. When they returned to Cottonwood, maybe she'd be the one to make the invite to cook him dinner at his place.

Lucas caught her privately silly grin and called her out playfully. "You look like you're up to no good," he teased. "What are you thinking about?"

She smiled, shaking her head. "Mind your business and focus on the trail."

But he must have read her thoughts and saw the heated memory flash across her face, because his grin turned knowing and his responding wink almost made her trip and eat dirt.

Oh, that man is trouble, girl.

Kenna giggled to herself, tentatively ready for whatever trouble Lucas could bring.

They reached the swimming hole in perfect timing. After a few hours of walking in the hot summer sun, the calm waters of the swimming hole were a glorious sight. A waterfall poured from the rock shelf, creating a foam bubble bath below in the crisp water. "Okay, this was worth the hike," Ty admitted, dropping his pack and immediately shedding his shirt. He didn't wait for them as he stripped down to his underwear and ran full tilt for the water, jumping in with a squeal. Noble barked at the water's edge until he also jumped in, dog-paddling after Ty as if trying to save him. The sound of Ty's laughter was music to her ears.

"Ty's got the right idea," Lucas said with a grin, following Ty's lead. He stripped down to his boxers, and Kenna's mouth dried at the sight of his ripped abs, strong shoulders and lean hips. She blushed and tried to look away, but her eyeballs were glued to the man. Lucas dived into the water and resurfaced, shaking the water free from his hair, his eyes dancing as he gestured. "Your turn."

"I didn't bring a bathing suit," she said, grinning, but Lucas wasn't taking no for an answer.

"A sports bra and panties are the same as a bathing suit, just different marketing," he said. "C'mon, the water is perfect."

"Yeah! C'mon, Mom!" Ty yelled, flipping on his back to float as Noble climbed from the water to shake, sending droplets flying in every direction.

Kenna had good intentions to wait by the shore, but that water was too tempting. Sweat dribbled down her back, reminding her that she'd just humped a heavy pack several miles, the same as the boys, and she desperately wanted to feel that cool relief. "Fine," she said, smiling, carefully folding her clothes and placing them on her pack before gingerly stepping into the water.

Lucas and Ty rushed her and dragged her squealing into the water, dunking her. She came up laughing and sputtering and somehow ended up in Lucas's arms.

"See? Isn't that better?" he murmured, whispering

in her ear, "You couldn't look sexier in a string bikini than you do right now."

Kenna blushed, but her heart smiled. "You're a sweet talker, Lucas Merritt. Keep it up, because it's working," she advised with a lighthearted grin, pushing off him to swim over to Ty and repay him for dunking her by pushing him underwater.

They played in the water until they were ready to eat and then climbed onto the rocky shore to dry off and dig into their salvaged lunch of peanut butter and jelly sandwiches.

Afterward, Kenna climbed onto a warm rock to sun herself like a lizard. Lucas was teaching Ty the different kinds of knots used in rock climbing, and Ty was trying his hand at the newfound skill with Lucas as his patient teacher. She smiled, happier than she'd been in forever, wondering how she'd gotten so lucky in finding a man like Lucas when she'd all but given up on men entirely.

Ty's laughter was sunshine on her soul. Her sweet boy was slowly returning to her, and she felt hopeful for the life she'd feared was forever out of reach.

"Time to hit the trail again," Lucas announced, shouldering his pack and helping Ty secure his properly. Kenna sighed and rose from her perch, dusting off her behind before climbing down from the rock.

Lucas lifted her pack, and she slid her arms through, buckling the straps in the front and cinching it tight. Kenna cast one last look at the achingly beautiful swimming spot and fell in step behind Ty with Lucas in the lead.

"Do you think—"

But Ty's question was cut short as a sharp *crack* split the air and something embedded in the tree bark beside Lucas's head. Noble tensed and growled as Lucas exclaimed, "What the hell?" stopping abruptly to investigate the tree. A small, perfectly round hole punctured the bark, and Lucas's expression filled her with dread.

"What is it?" she asked.

But before he could answer, another shot rang out, another round of lead burying itself in a tree, narrowly missing Noble, and Lucas yelled, "Get cover! Someone is shooting at us!"

Lucas's first and only thought was getting Kenna and Ty to safety as he herded them deeper down the trail, away from the open line of sight, making them less easy targets. Kenna's frightened eyes were wide with confusion as she took cover behind the thickest tree with Ty crouched behind her. "What's happening? Do you think it's a hunter or something? Why would someone be shooting in this area?"

"I don't know," he said, keeping Noble behind him as he scanned the rock ridge, looking for signs of someone standing there, irresponsibly taking shots or purposefully aiming for them. There was only one way to determine if the shot had been accidental or on purpose. To Kenna, he said, "Stay hidden—don't reveal your location, okay?"

"What are you going to do?" she asked in a panic.

"I need to find out what's going on. Hopefully, it's just an idiot who didn't see us."

"And if it's not an idiot?"

"Then we have a different problem, but let's not build bridges for rivers we don't have to cross yet."

Kenna didn't want him to put himself at risk, but he didn't see any other way to find the answer they needed. The odds were on their side that it was a dangerous oversight on the part of a novice hunter.

Lucas came out slowly, his hands up in a nonthreatening manner. "I'm coming out with my hands up. Don't shoot. I'm unarmed," he called out, walking slowly into the open. "My name is Lucas Merritt. I'm an officer with the Cottonwood Police Department. Are you aware you nearly hit me and my dog?"

Silence rebounded in the canyon. Sweat dotted his forehead as a growing apprehension made him feel dangerously unprotected in his current position.

Before Lucas could try again, a voice rang out from a hidden location along the ridge. "I don't miss. If I wanted you dead, you'd be dead."

A chill washed over him. "Do I know you?"

The shooter ignored his question. "Send Kenna and the boy out into the open. Do it now."

Lucas was taken aback, immediately confused. "How do you know Kenna?"

"I know her very well. The question is, how well do *you* know Kenna, lover boy?"

Lucas knew with fatal certainty that whoever was on that ridge was who Noble had been growling at last night, which meant this guy had been following them. Suddenly, their trashed camp made more sense. An entirely different emotion crept up his spine in warning.

"You have ten seconds to send her out."

That wasn't going to happen. "Let's talk this out. Whatever your beef with Kenna is, maybe I can help work it out with you."

"Don't waste my time, *Officer Lucas Merritt*," the shooter drawled with disdain. "Send her out or I'll put a bullet in your brain."

A man with a gun who didn't care about shooting cops was a different kind of dangerous. Lucas narrowed his gaze, trying to discern the shooter's position. "You know I can't do that."

"That's too bad for you."

Lucas wasn't a professional negotiator, but he could sense there was no deal to be made with the shooter. Mentally, he calculated the closest cover. He didn't wait for the shooter to start counting down to zero and bolted, diving for a small boulder jutting out from the trail. Granite exploded as the bullet buried inside the rock. Lucas bolted to his feet, returning to Kenna, Ty and Noble, pushing them deeper down the trail where the tree canopy blocked the shooter's view.

"Mom, what's going on?" Ty asked, fear in his young voice as they ran. "Who's shooting at us?"

Kenna didn't answer, and Lucas kept them moving as far and fast as they could deeper down the trail.

But Lucas knew the well-traveled route was practically a bread-crumb trail that led straight to them, and he gestured for them to follow his lead as he left the trail and melted into the heavily forested area until he found a giant rock formation with decent coverage.

Kenna wrapped her arms around Ty as the boy started to shake. "It's going to be okay," she whispered, casting a desperate look Lucas's way. "Everything's going to be fine. We just need to get back to the truck and call for help."

Except the truck was parked directly in the path of the shooter. The hiking trail was a clearly marked loop to accommodate experienced and amateur hikers alike—but that also made it a convenient trap for someone looking to cause trouble.

"It sounded like Leon," Ty whispered to his mom fearfully, and she tightened her grip around him, shaking her head, but the blood had drained from her face.

Lucas looked to Kenna. "Who is Leon?"

"No one," she answered quickly.

Ty scowled, reminding her, "No more secrets, remember?"

Kenna licked her lips, reminding Lucas of Noble when he was anxious, and he knew Kenna was terrified. After a long, tense moment, Kenna relented, her voice strained. "His name is Leon Petticott. I don't understand what he's doing here or how he found us, but maybe if I talk to him, he'll back down before someone gets hurt."

"Mom, you can't," Ty said, shaking his head, his eyes wide. "He'll kill you."

"He couldn't have come all this way to kill me," she said, but the quiver in her voice belied her statement. "I don't want anyone getting hurt over this."

Lucas shook his head, agreeing with Ty. "I'm not letting you walk into the arms of a gun-toting lunatic. We'll find a different way off the mountain."

"What different way?" Kenna asked fearfully. "The trail is the only way around, and he's likely well aware of the trail's route."

"What's this guy's background?"

Kenna swallowed. "Former Army Ranger. Dishonorably discharged. He's an excellent marksman with a flair for cruelty. I don't doubt that if he's here, he's done his homework. He could even have traps set. I don't put anything past him, but I never imagined he would follow me from Kentucky."

Lucas digested the information. Former special ops military meant he had specialized training, above and beyond the average soldier. It took a certain kind of person to excel in special ops—it was possible the guy had narcissistic tendencies or even sociopathic borderline personality disorder. Given the fact the shooter had taken two shots with the intent to intimidate a cop, he clearly didn't fear any consequence from authority, which also meant he thought himself above the law.

And given the fact that he'd followed them here, he'd already scoped out the terrain.

"He's going to anticipate every move we make toward the parked truck unless we throw him off by going in the opposite direction."

"Which is where?" Kenna asked, looking around bewildered. "There's nothing but dense trees everywhere."

Lucas said, "There's an old abandoned covered bridge scheduled for demolition next week farther up the river. If we can get to it, we can get to the other side and come up the back side to the truck. Hopefully, he won't expect us to come that way."

Lucas rose from his crouched position, but Kenna stopped him with a fearful "An abandoned bridge sounds really dangerous."

He agreed but said, "I'd rather take my chances with the bridge than the bad guy with a gun," and Kenna reluctantly conceded. "Okay, then. Stick to the trees and follow me."

Chapter 22

"Where are we going?" Ty asked as he kept checking over his shoulder, his voice shaking. "Why don't we just call the cops and wait for them to show up? He can't take on everyone at once."

"My cell doesn't have service here," Lucas said, his mouth set in a grim line. "That was part of the allure. I wanted to be able to disconnect."

"I bet you're wishing you weren't in the middle of a stupid forest with no service now," Ty grumbled with a hint of his smart-ass personality, and Kenna didn't know if she should laugh hysterically or cry. Either reaction felt appropriate in the face of the terror curdling her insides.

"It has lost some of its appeal," Lucas admitted, stealthily moving forward, setting the pace while keeping a watchful eye.

They remained mostly silent as they navigated the forested terrain, climbing over rocks and pushing through brambles of brush that at any moment could've held the potential of a snake nest, but Kenna's head was a terrifying mess of even more fearful questions.

How had Leon found her? Hadn't she been careful enough? She'd always used cash, never put anything in her own name and avoided sharing personal details about herself. Cold sweat drenched her back as she followed Lucas, watching where she stepped and simultaneously looking out for Ty.

If Leon was here now, how long had he been watching her?

All those times she'd felt eyes on her—that night at the clinic, the dead cat, the prank call—it'd been Leon, playing with her like a cat with a mouse, waiting for the right moment to strike.

Creating the most terror had been his favorite game, and now he'd come to collect his favorite plaything.

Tears blinded her and she stumbled, going straight to the forest floor, banging her knee hard on a buried rock. She bit back a cry and tried to catch herself, but the weight of the pack, coupled with the pain, took her down. Immediately Lucas skidded to a stop and ran to her side to help her up while Ty watched anxiously.

"You okay, Mom?" Ty asked.

She wiped at her eyes, smiling as Lucas helped her stand. "Just clumsy. I'm okay," she assured them both, wincing as her knee protested, threatening to buckle again. She tried to step forward, but a painful zing took her breath away.

Lucas helped her to a fallen log to lean against it, taking the weight off her leg. "I think I just bruised it pretty good," she said, rubbing at her knee through her jeans. "I'll be okay in a minute," she promised, privately praying she was right. Lucas nodded but knelt beside her, taking her knee into his hands, gently manipulating the joint to check for injury. Aside from the soreness, it seemed to be okay. She breathed a sigh of relief, looking at Lucas. "I think I can walk now."

"Go slow," he said, helping her to her feet. "If we can keep this pace, we'll reach the bridge in about an hour. There's an unoccupied ranger station near the bridge that might have a radio. If we can get there, we might be able to radio for help."

Kenna nodded, trying not to let fear get the better of her. She knew Lucas would do anything to keep them safe, but Leon had a gun, and all they had was their wits.

Would it be enough?

"I'm sorry," she blurted through a sheen of tears. "I don't know what else to say."

"This isn't your fault," he said, knuckling her cheek. "I'm not going to let you blame yourself for the actions of an obsessed lunatic."

Fresh tears threatened to fall, but she sniffed them back. Now wasn't the time to disintegrate into a sobbing mess. Maybe if they managed to get out alive, she'd have a much-needed mental breakdown, but until then, they had to keep moving.

They reached the bridge, and immediately Kenna balked at the idea of trying to cross a structure that looked older than Noah's ark and condemned for good reason. "We can't cross that," she protested, gesturing toward the structure. "It's literally falling down. I can see the rotten timbers from here. We'll have to find another way."

"There's no other way," Lucas returned with a solid shake of his head, but he shared her concerns as he surveyed the bridge with a critical eye. "It's definitely worse than I hoped, but we don't have a choice."

"If that thing disintegrates, we'll fall to our death in the river canyon," Kenna said, more afraid for Ty than her own life. "There has to be another way."

"The one saving grace we might have is the shooter not knowing about this bridge. It's purposefully not on any of the newer trail guides because they didn't want people taking the chance and crossing it. The only reason I know about it is because I found an old trail guide from the 1970s that still had it listed, but it's been scheduled for demolition for years and now it's finally getting the attention it needs because of a federal grant. It's likely the shooter is anticipating we'll cross at the newer bridge and he's waiting there to ambush us. This is the only element of surprise we have."

Lucas was right, it was the only play, but their odds were terrible.

Ty gave his mom courage as he showed his own. "We got this, Mom. We walk spaced apart so our weight doesn't crush the wood, and if we go slow and careful, we should make it."

How had her son become so brave? He was just a kid, yet he was still managing to prop her up when she wanted to collapse. If he could find the courage to move forward, so could she. Kenna readjusted her pack and gave Ty a resolute nod. "You're right. We can do this."

Lucas's approving smile gave her the extra boost she needed to shore up her insides and push forward with a fervent prayer that this wasn't the way they all ended up dead.

Lucas didn't want to let Kenna know how deeply he shared her fears about crossing the bridge. It didn't matter how apprehensive he was—they didn't have a choice—but they could better their chances by lightening the load. He unhooked his pack and gestured for them to do the same.

"What are you doing?" Kenna asked.

"Improving our odds," he answered, helping her take her pack off and dropping it to the ground as he did the same. Ty followed his lead. "We need to be as light as possible, and these packs add forty pounds apiece."

"We can't leave them here," Kenna said.

"If we survive, we'll come back for them," he said. "Right now, our lives matter more than the cost of new packs." Lucas pulled his hunting knife free and tucked it into his waistband, stuffing his truck keys in his pocket. "Let's go."

Kenna and Ty followed his lead and left their packs behind. With a quick check to ensure the shooter hadn't found them, Lucas approached the bridge, ducking under the bright yellow caution tape and assessing the best place to step. The rotten wood was brittle and crumbling to dust, with whole sections missing in the middle as the old structure slowly sagged, broken down by the elements and poor maintenance over the years. Walking along the frame supports seemed the best option, with equal spacing, as Ty suggested. "I'll go first. Walk where I walk, stay away from the center where the wood is the weakest and keep a slow and steady pace. Here we go." He gestured for Noble to fall behind him, and the police dog, as if sensing the danger, too, walked gingerly into the darkened structure.

Shafts of sunlight punctured the covered ceiling, casting cascading rays filled with swirling dust motes, but pockets of shadow felt ominous as the wood creaked beneath their boots, as if moaning a warning to trespassers.

They were halfway across when Noble stiffened and

bolted ahead to a shadowy corner, anxiously barking at something they couldn't see, but the sharp sound of his bark bounced off the walls, creating an echo that might as well be a beacon to their location.

"Noble, heel!" Lucas hissed, but the dog was in a defensive posture, growling at something that he sensed was dangerous.

And the danger was right in their path.

"Heel!" Lucas commanded in a harsh whisper, and Noble whined but slowly backed off. Lucas inched his way closer, pulling his knife from his waistband. As he approached, above the sound of the rushing river below, the ominous warning of a rattlesnake echoed in the dark. As his eyesight adjusted to the low lighting, he saw a giant snake coiled and ready to strike, two beady eyes trained on him, waiting for Lucas to come close enough to sink his fangs into.

"You're in our way, buddy," Lucas said, moving slowly forward, knife at the ready. "You can either move on or you can meet your maker, your choice."

He hoped the snake chose to move on, but the glitter of his slitted eye gave away his intention. Quick as lightning, the snake lunged, narrowly missing Lucas's leg as he danced out of the strike zone and rebounded quickly to launch the snake through a broken plank, sending it spiraling to a watery death.

Before he could breathe a sigh of relief and gesture to Kenna and Ty that it was all clear, his foot went through a rotten plank beneath him, and he nearly followed the snake down to the river below.

"Lucas!" Kenna gasped and grabbed Ty, holding him tightly. "Are you okay?"

"I'm fine," he assured her, carefully pulling his foot free to find a firmer footing. His heart was beating like a wild thing as he tried not to fixate on how narrowly he'd cheated death—because, for all he knew, the Grim Reaper could be waiting around the corner for another try.

They inched their way across the bridge, finally reaching the other end without another incident. An overgrown footpath wound its way away from the bridge to the ranger station. He could see the faded green top of the station from where they stood. "There's the station," he pointed, hoping it would still have a radio even though it was uncrewed. Sometimes ranger stations were kept in working order and stocked with nonperishables on the off chance it could save someone's life if they were lost, thirsty and starving after losing their way.

They started running for the station, but just when they thought they'd made it, a man in full camo gear stepped into view with a nine millimeter pointed straight at them.

"That was a bold choice to take the abandoned bridge. I almost didn't think you'd take that option. Imagine how differently this might've played out if I'd underestimated my quarry."

Lucas stared at the man, realizing with a start he recognized his cut jaw and well-defined facial features, but his energy was completely different from the first time they met.

Lucas narrowed his gaze, mentally calculating whether or not he could get to his knife before the man pulled the trigger and sent him into the hereafter, but he had to do what he could to keep the man focused on him and not Kenna and Ty.

"Something tells me you were never interested in getting a dog," he said coolly. "*Ambrose.*"

The man grinned as if caught, admitting, "You got me. I hate dogs."

Noble growled, but Lucas kept him still. Ambrose looked past Lucas to slide a hard smile Kenna's way. "Hello, sweetheart. I've missed you."

"Don't call me sweetheart," Kenna said in a low tone, clutching Ty to her.

"But you are my sweetheart," he said with an indulgent frown. "It seems you've forgotten who you belong to, and you've created a whole mess that I've had to clean up. Very naughty of you. But that's part of your charm—so unpredictable. Keeps me on my toes, that's for sure."

"What do you want, Leon?" Kenna asked, lifting her chin, braving the man's stare.

His smile curved as if delighted she would ask. "I came for my property. I've missed my best girl. *Everyone* has missed you, darling. You were our favorite girl."

"Shut your mouth," Kenna hissed, but Lucas saw her curling in on herself with shame, and he wanted to bury his knife in the man's forehead.

"Come with me and I'll let your boyfriend live. Make things difficult and I'll leave his body for the vultures to pick apart. Your choice, sweetheart."

"I'm not your sweetheart."

"You are what I say you are…or have you forgotten?"

"I haven't forgotten a goddamn thing about being with you," Kenna shot back, her eyes brimming with tears.

"Good. Then you know what I'm capable of—and how I have no problem putting your boyfriend in the dirt without blinking an eye. You don't want his blood on your hands, do you?"

A dribble of sweat crept down Lucas's face. The tension between them was thick as molasses. "Don't listen to him, Kenna," he warned.

But Leon knew exactly how to press Kenna's buttons. "Such a shame—his only crime was falling for a no-good whore like yourself. Does he even know the things you've done? You play the innocent so well, but then, that's part of your charm, isn't it? You don't really want to make him pay for your lack of judgment, do you?"

"Stop, please stop," Kenna whispered painfully, tears still brimming in her eyes. "You promise not to hurt him?" she asked.

Lucas shook his head. Ambrose would kill him no matter what he promised, and he was playing on Kenna's soft heart.

Ambrose nodded. "I only want my family back. You and Ty, that's all I care about. We can make this work, darling, and forget all about this ugliness. Be a good girl."

"I..." Kenna looked to Lucas, her eyes wide with fear as she started to step forward, even as he vehemently shook his head. "This is my problem, not yours. I'm sorry," she whispered, the anguish in her tone nearly breaking his heart in two.

But there was no way he was letting that happen.

He'd die first.

Chapter 23

It was as if she'd suddenly stepped outside her body and was watching the scene unfold, removed from the situation. She didn't feel her heart beating painfully or the sweat dribbling down her back. She didn't realize she'd pushed Ty behind her until she'd already started taking her first steps toward Leon.

For all the times she'd seen that exact smug expression stamped on his hateful face, as he'd humiliated, abused and forced her to his will, she wanted him to die.

The part of her that'd always backed down in fear, cowered in the shadow of his influence and cringed at the sound of his raised voice was eerily silent and still.

Maybe she'd finally snapped.

She would've put a bullet in his brain without hesitation if she'd had a gun. She knew that she'd be damned before she let Leon hurt Lucas.

Lucas was a good man and didn't deserve any of

this. He'd taken a chance on Kenna only to run head-long into her psychopath ex.

But before she could take another step, Noble burst from his spot beside Lucas, springing into action like vengeance on steroids, launching at Leon with snapping jaws and malicious intent, as if the dog somehow knew Leon was evil without needing a command to execute.

The shot rang out, echoing in the canyon. Noble yelped in pain, dropping to the ground, the fine dirt curling in a soft puff with the impact of his body. Kenna and Ty screamed in horror, and Lucas charged Leon with a bloodcurdling roar. "You son of a bitch!" He ran full tilt, without thought to his own safety.

They went down hard, both rolling and fighting for possession of the gun. The gun discharged into the air as Lucas prevented Leon from getting the advantage, but they were equally matched in strength even though Lucas was younger. Leon spent hours in the gym per-fecting his physique, building muscle to compensate for his age. Lucas landed a good punch, sending the gun flying, but Leon recovered with barely a grunt, driv-ing his knee straight into Lucas's groin for the insult of making him drop the gun.

"You're a wily bastard, aren't you?" Leon said, breathing hard. "I'm going to make you wish you never dared to touch my woman."

"Leon, no!"

Kenna wanted to vomit, watching in horror as Leon got the upper hand while Lucas writhed on the ground. Before Lucas could get away, Leon's boot came down hard on Lucas's throat, smiling as he put pressure on his windpipe. Lucas kicked and tried to push Leon's boot away from his neck, but Leon had the advantage.

Noooo, she wanted to scream, frantic with terror. She couldn't stand by and watch Leon kill Lucas. She'd rather die than have Lucas's death on her shoulders. Confident in his assumed victory, Leon didn't see Kenna sneak up behind him. "Leave him alone!" she screeched, bringing the granite piece clutched in her hand down hard on his skull, desperately hoping to impale his brains on the hard rock. Leon spun away, stunned but still very much alive, and Kenna knew he would kill her if she didn't hit him again.

Distracted by the blow, Leon blinked as blood gushed from the gash in his head, wiping the blood away with a snarled "You bitch," as he lurched toward her, but she saw Lucas roll to his feet, coughing and gasping for breath.

Leon lunged for her, his grasping fingers scraping her skin, but she danced out of his reach in time for Ty to toss her the gun.

"Mom! Catch," he yelled.

Kenna caught the gun, and everything moved in slow motion. For the first time in her life, she wasn't afraid or timid. She knew exactly what she needed to do—and she didn't hesitate.

Safety off, she aimed and fired.

The irony? Leon had been the one who'd insisted she take a firearms safety course when he'd still been playing the part of the generous suitor concerned with her welfare.

Leon stopped short, his eyes wide with surprise as a smoking hole in his forehead sizzled around the edges. Shock froze his features into a frightful grimace. Leon raised shaking fingers, as if to touch the entrance wound, but his legs crumpled beneath him and he went down hard like a puppet with his strings cut.

"Good shot, Mom," Ty said in a shaky but awed voice, and Kenna realized what she'd done.

"Damn good shot," Lucas agreed, his voice a painful rasp from the damage done by Leon's boot.

She looked to Lucas, her hand beginning to shake. Kenna dropped the gun from her nerveless fingers. Leon was dead. No more looking over her shoulder, fearful of what might lurk in the shadows. She felt no remorse, only relief.

But that relief was short-lived as Lucas ran to his fallen partner.

Oh my God, Noble. "Is he dead?" she asked, afraid to know the answer.

Lucas gently checked for a pulse. Noble whined softly, and Kenna moved quickly into action. Blood seeped from the gunshot wound onto the dirt as Noble clung to life. Kenna ripped a piece of her T-shirt free and pressed it to Noble's wound. "We need to get him to an emergency vet," she said, switching gears to focus solely on Noble. "I'll stay with him. Go call for help."

"I can't leave you," he said.

"It'll be okay. Leon is dead. Noble needs us."

Lucas blinked back tears and nodded, pausing for the briefest moment to ensure Leon was truly gone, and then took off at a sprint down to the ranger station. Kenna prayed the radio worked. She couldn't imagine Lucas losing his partner because of her.

"Hold on, boy," she said to Noble, gently keeping pressure on the wound. "Help is coming."

Everything happened in a blur. Lucas burst through the door of the defunct ranger station, sending dust flying as he entered the building that appeared forgotten by time. He went straight to the radio and flicked the switch, overcome with relief when the radio came to life, crackling with static. He found the frequency for the operational Beartooth Range Ranger Station and quickly shared his location and the situation as well as his credentials.

"This is K-9 Officer Lucas Merritt with the Cottonwood Police Department. I need immediate assistance at the defunct ranger station at the old covered bridge off the hiking trail. My K-9 partner has been shot by an unknown assailant. I repeat, immediate assistance is required. Over."

"Copy that, Officer Merritt. Sending rangers to your location now. Is the scene secure?"

"Yes," he answered, his voice still raspy. "The aggressor is dead."

"Copy that. Sit tight—we'll get you handled."

Lucas released a deep exhale, biting back a wave of pain at the thought of losing Noble. No, he wouldn't lose him. He was a strong boy—he'd make it. Shaking off his fear, he sprinted back to where he'd left them, relieved to see Kenna still talking to Noble softly, keeping him with her.

He knelt beside Noble. "Help is coming," he said, stroking his coarse fur with pride. "You were so brave." He looked at Kenna, so many questions going through his head, but now wasn't the time to ask them.

The rangers showed up with Search and Rescue to load Noble into the vehicle and take care of the body. The Beartooth Range was a national park, making Leon Petticott's death a federal issue. There would be an investigation, but Lucas knew it was self-defense, and he'd make sure the investigators knew the facts. At the moment, he was more focused on getting Noble the help he needed.

But he needed answers to things that made him question everything he thought he knew about Kenna, and that made him sick to his stomach.

Lucas went with Noble as he was transported to an emergency vet clinic. At the same time, Kenna and Ty stayed behind to give a statement about Leon Petticott's death.

While Kenna answered questions about Leon and how she happened to put a bullet in his head, Lucas was anxiously waiting for Noble to come out of surgery. His cell phone was still in his abandoned pack, but he placed a quick call to Luna from the vet clinic, letting her know what happened and why.

"Where are Kenna and Ty?" she asked.

"They're with the park rangers, giving a statement. It was self-defense," he said, rubbing the grit from his eyes. "It'll be a while to process the paperwork."

"I'm on my way," she said. "And Noble?"

"Still waiting. Crossing my fingers he didn't lose too much blood, but I don't know."

"He's a tough boy. He'll come through," Luna said with conviction. "He deserves a medal for his bravery."

Lucas nodded, choking up. "So does your sister," he said, leaving it at that. "We had to leave our packs behind, but the rangers said they'd send someone to pick them up. Hopefully, my phone is still in the pack. I'll let you know as soon as I know more. I just wanted to let you know what's happening so you can let the chief know for me."

"Will do."

Lucas clicked off and walked back to the hard seat in the lobby. The emergency vet hospital was mainly empty, which was probably a good thing, but the empty room only magnified the turmoil in his head.

He wasn't blaming Kenna for a psychopath coming after her—but some of the things Leon, or Ambrose, had said raised questions that he couldn't entirely dismiss as the crazy ramblings of an obsessed ex.

He'd always felt Kenna was holding something back, and now, he knew parts of her past needed explaining.

Was it his business? A part of him said it wasn't. Her past was her own to keep private, but he wanted Kenna to be a part of his life, and how could he do that if he didn't know what lurked in her past? What other kind of secrets was she keeping from him? Hell, did her own sister know about Kenna's past?

Leon was gone, but Lucas had to know what secrets she was keeping, or else he'd always wonder and it would eat at his mind and heart.

He rubbed his aggrieved throat, playing the events over in his head. From Noble's lunge that distracted Leon to the final moment when Kenna, without hesitation, put a bullet in the man's brain.

Kenna had told him that her ex had been cruel, but the level of cruelty had to be on par with a sociopath for Kenna to kill the man without blinking.

Sweet, kind and gentle Kenna had turned into a savage right before his eyes.

For good reason, a voice reminded him, but he couldn't escape that disquieted feeling nagging at him. And what had Leon meant by saying Kenna was good at playing the innocent? What the hell did that mean?

Clearly, the man had been crazy and obsessed with Kenna—he would've said anything, right? But something about Kenna's reaction—almost sheer terror—at Leon's taunt kept sticking in his head. Was there more to the story than she was sharing? He'd promised her that there wasn't anything he couldn't forgive from her past, but he couldn't shake the last vision of her, when he'd felt he was looking at a stranger.

Stop it, he told himself. It felt weak and cowardly to judge Kenna for her past when she'd tried so hard to get beyond it.

If it weren't for Kenna, they'd all be dead.

Remember that.

Chapter 24

Hours after Kenna finished with her statement, Luna walk into the ranger station, a look of anxious concern etched on her face. They connected, and Luna ignored the ranger watching her every move to pull her sister straight into a tight embrace. "Are you okay?" she asked.

Kenna nodded as she withdrew. "Still in shock, I think," she admitted. "Any news on Noble?"

"Nothing yet. Lucas said he was still in surgery when I talked to him, but he said he'd let me know if anything changed."

Kenna tried not to break down and cry. "He has to make it," she told Luna, her heart breaking. "I can't take it if Noble dies because of something I did."

Luna shook her head vehemently. "*You* didn't do this. Some psychopath did this, okay? I won't listen to you take this on yourself. Not on my watch, you hear?"

"You don't understand. Leon came here because of

me. I should've known he would follow me, but I stupidly thought he'd let me go if I just disappeared. How could I be so wrong?"

"We can't predict how another human being is going to react, and to try is a recipe for disaster," Luna said firmly. To the ranger, she showed her credentials and said, "My sister has been through a significant trauma. Is she free to go?"

"I'm sorry, but we'll have to take your sister into custody for now."

"I'm being arrested?" Kenna asked in disbelief. "It was self-defense. Leon was going to kill us all."

"And if the witness statements corroborate your account of the situation, we'll go from there. For now, all we have is your account of the incident and a dead man who can't exactly tell us anything."

Luna looked hot under the collar, but she also knew tangling with a federal agency wouldn't land them anywhere, either. "Fine, I'll wait," she announced. "I'm not leaving until my sister can leave with me. Lucas said his phone was still in his pack. Have your rangers picked up their packs on the trail?"

"We're still looking," the investigating ranger said. "Chances are they were picked up by other hikers. Especially if they were high-quality packs."

Misery crashed down around Kenna for many reasons—and while the packs were seemingly small in light of the murder she'd just committed, the loss of Lucas's packs felt the heaviest.

"I told him I was bad news, but he didn't listen," Kenna said, fighting back the tears. "I tried to warn him."

"You're not bad news, Kenna," Luna disagreed, frustration lacing her tone. "But I wish you would've told me you were running from a man like this. I could've helped protect you."

Kenna wiped at her eyes, overwhelmed by everything. "I didn't think I needed your protection. I was handling the situation on my own, but I had no idea Leon was that obsessed. If I'd known…" But Kenna wasn't sure if even then she would've told anyone and couldn't finish her sentence. Right now, she didn't know anything. In her mind's eye, she could see Leon's boot on Lucas's throat, crushing him, and she wanted to scream.

"Where's Ty?" Kenna asked, sniffing back the tears, keeping from losing her composure.

"He's in the other room, talking to a ranger." Luna assured her he was okay, but Kenna wanted her son. Only Ty knew how terrible Leon was, and even though killing him might've been justified, she couldn't imagine how all this would affect her son.

The investigating ranger spoke up, gesturing to Luna. "Your sister is welcome to take your son with her. We've taken his statement and he's free to go."

But Luna shook her head. "I'm not leaving without my family. Kenna was defending herself against a madman. My nephew has already given his statement that his mother acted in self-defense. I'm not sure why you can't release my sister into my care. I mean, look at her—she's clearly not a violent criminal."

The investigator wasn't moved. "That's not how we do things, Detective Griffin. The federal government moves at a different pace than a small-town department."

That last part felt condescending, but Kenna didn't want her sister to get into trouble on her account. "It's okay, I'll be fine. Just take Ty home, please," Kenna said, ready to put this entire situation behind her. "And please, let me know if Noble is okay."

Luna looked ready to make waves, but she backed down at Kenna's quiet request. What mattered right now was Ty and Noble. Everything else could wait its turn.

"I need to know everything about Leon Petticott," Luna instructed. "I'm going to have Sayeh look into his background."

"Detective, that's not necessary—we'll handle it," the investigator said with a frown.

"I'm sure you'll do a thorough job, but when you have a sister in the FBI, you take advantage of the resource," Luna said with a short smile that didn't reach her eyes. "I'm sure you can appreciate that."

The investigator heaved an annoyed sigh and shook his head, rising from his seat and gesturing for the officers waiting. "Officers, please prepare Miss Griffin for transport."

Luna protested, "Is that necessary?" as the officers put the handcuffs on Kenna, but the wheels were already turning.

Kenna said, "Tell Ty everything will be okay." Her voice trembled as she was led out of the room. She could only pray her assurance was true.

There was one thing she'd kept to herself during questioning, and given the treatment she was receiving, it seemed a blessing.

Killing Leon had been the right and only choice—but she didn't regret pulling that trigger.

Not for one minute.

In fact, watching him go down had given her indescribable joy.

Try explaining that without sounding like a psycho.

Taking a life was wrong, she knew that, but she

couldn't muster even an ounce of remorse for snuffing out his light.

Because Leon had been comprised of darkness, his soul rotten to the core.

Taking him out felt like a blessing to the world at large.

At least in her world.

And she wouldn't apologize for wanting to live.

"Officer Merritt?"

Lucas looked up sharply, his heart leaping in his chest at the on-call veterinarian. He nodded, holding his breath. "Yeah?"

"Noble is in recovery. He's going to be just fine. He's a strong boy. He'll need a course of antibiotics while recouping, and he's going to need six weeks of light duty, but he should heal up real nice. Of course, you're going to want to follow up with your regular veterinarian for the aftercare."

Lucas rose, relief sapping the strength from his legs, to shake the doctor's hand. "Thank you! That's the best news. Thank you so much."

"That's one lucky dog," the veterinarian said, shaking his head. "The bullet narrowly missed a main artery. I heard he was shot on duty?"

"Not exactly, but he saved my life," Lucas said. "He's a brave boy. When can I see him?"

"He's still knocked out. It'll be a while. You might want to grab a hotel room for a few hours while you wait. I can't say our lobby is all that great for long waits."

But Lucas wasn't leaving his partner behind, not even for the comfort of a shower and a bite to eat. No, he couldn't fathom leaving Noble's side even for a second. "I'll wait. I want to know as soon as he's awake," he said.

"Suit yourself," the veterinarian said, but he seemed to understand and instructed the vet tech before disappearing behind the double doors.

Remembering that he told Luna he'd share the news as soon as he heard, he asked to borrow the landline again.

He dialed Luna's cell—thankful he'd taken the time to memorize phone numbers instead of simply relying on his phone—and got her voice mail. He quickly rattled off the news and wondered why Luna wasn't picking up.

Worry for Kenna pricked at him. She had to be a wreck right now. Even seasoned officers were required to have their mental health checked after an officer-involved shooting, but Kenna was a civilian.

A civilian who'd handled that gun like a pro.

She'd shot Leon without blinking an eye.

How did he feel about that?

Before this trip, he'd been consumed by thoughts of Kenna. For the first time in his life, he'd understood that starry-eyed gaze he'd seen his brother give Becca. Lucas had actually contemplated what life with Kenna might look like.

Was he wrong to promise Kenna there was nothing he couldn't get over when it came to her past? He hadn't thought a psychopathic ex was in her closet of skeletons, much less the threat of Kenna having to shoot the guy between the eyes.

Maybe he'd bitten off more than he could chew. Even his damn dog got hurt in the mix. He couldn't have imagined that Kenna had something in her past as dangerous as a special ops killer.

He'd wasted a lot of time and energy trying to be the hero to Becca when he should've walked away. Was he making the same mistake with Kenna?

The phone rang, and the receptionist called him over. "It's for you," she said, handing over the receiver.

It was Luna. "Sorry I missed your call. I was in a bad cell-service area. I'm so happy to hear Noble is going to be okay. I know Kenna will be so relieved."

"Is Kenna with you?" he asked.

"No, they wouldn't let me take her into my custody. The feds will need your official statement ASAP. They're being real pricks about this, but I guess it's understandable given a man died, even if that man deserved it."

"I'll call the rangers after I hang up," he promised, hating the idea of Kenna sitting in jail, even for a short time. "They're just following protocol."

"I know that, but it hits different when it's your family," she grumbled. "I'm going to have Sayeh pull some background intel on this Leon character, see what she can dig up."

Lucas felt foolish for being duped. "He'd been stalking her the whole time. The bastard had the balls to approach me at the station under a fake name with some bullshit story about wanting a dog like Noble."

"I wish Kenna had told me she was in danger. I would've done everything I could to prevent this from happening."

"Yeah, I wish she'd been honest, too."

Luna must have heard the odd note in his voice. "I can't imagine what you're feeling right now, but please don't judge Kenna for trying to handle this on her own. She did what she thought was best. Kenna has the best heart—"

"I know," he cut in, not wanting to hear more. He already felt like a jerk for pulling back, but he couldn't stop the way he felt, and he respected Kenna too much to be fake with her. "I'll give the rangers my statement and let them know in no certain terms that Kenna acted in self-defense."

"Thank you," Luna said, seeming to sense the change, but she stopped pressing. "I have Ty with me. The rangers are still looking for your packs, but they said it's unlikely they'll find them."

Lucas figured as much. "The only saving grace I might have is no one was supposed to be on that section of the trail because it was closed for demolition, but you never know."

He thanked Luna for the return call, and he clicked off, breathing against the sudden tightening in his chest.

How would he handle this situation without creating more damage between them? He didn't have an answer, but he could handle one crisis at a time, and top of the list was giving his statement.

Lucas dialed the ranger station and made arrangements to give his official statement when Noble was free to go home.

He hated that he couldn't do more to get Kenna home immediately, but arguing with the federal authorities was about as effective as yelling at a brick wall—and just as unmovable.

Better to focus on the problems he could solve rather than the unfixable ones.

Were his feelings about Kenna unfixable?

So that guy wins? Kenna loses no matter what?

Lucas groaned at his internal dialogue, hating how he was arguing with himself.

He cleared his bruised throat, wincing at the tenderness that would take a while to heal. He was lucky his windpipe was only bruised and not crushed.

Things could've ended so differently.

But was this the kind of thing that could happen again? Did Kenna have more than one Leon Petticott in her past? And what exactly did Leon do to Kenna that'd terrified her into silence? He hated the questions badgering him, but was he ready for the answers?

Chapter 25

It took a few days, but Kenna was able to come home, finally released from federal authority after Lucas corroborated her account of the incident and Sayeh came through with some unsavory background information on Leon Petticott—Leon Ambrose Elliott Petticott, to be exact.

Dr. Mallory gave Kenna the option of taking a few more days off from work, but Kenna needed the comfort of routine to put her mind at ease—not to mention she couldn't fathom sitting at home with nothing but her thoughts to keep her company after everything that had happened.

Except when she got to work, she'd underestimated the toll on her mental health Isabel's chatter would take as she pressed her for juicy details.

"You live such an exciting life," Isabel said, shaking her head in awe as if seeing Kenna in a different light than before. "You actually shot him dead, like in the movies? You're such a badass, Kenna. I wish I had a story like that in my life."

"No, you don't," Kenna disagreed quietly, hating the misplaced hero worship. She'd taken a life, not won an Olympic medal. "Do you have that file on Mr. Whiskers ready?"

"Oh yeah, right here," Isabel said, grabbing the file and handing it over but completely missing Kenna's attempt at swerving more conversation away from the unsavory topic. "I can't believe a man was so obsessed with you that he followed you to Cottonwood. It's kinda romantic if you think about it—"

That was all Kenna could take. "It's the opposite of romantic, Isabel. Grow up. It's not like in the movies. There was nothing cool about taking someone's life. My son is scarred by the incident and has once again retreated into video games when he'd finally started making some progress, and Lucas hasn't spoken to me since giving his statement, so even though I'm safe from Leon, I lost more than you can possibly imagine." She drew a deep breath, squaring her shoulders as Isabel stared in stunned silence. "Now, if you don't mind, I'd like to never speak of this again. I'm taking my break."

Kenna didn't wait for Isabel and walked outside, fighting the urge to cry. Everyone was looking at her weirdly since the incident. She was now labeled That Griffin Woman Who Shot that Guy, and no one thought to ask if she was okay or if that guy deserved it. Not that she wanted to talk about the shooting—she'd much rather everyone mind their own business—but if they couldn't do that, they could at least give her the benefit of the doubt.

She wasn't a bad person.

But Lucas's silence had her questioning herself. It didn't matter that she'd been exonerated by Lucas's statement—the embarrassment and trauma of being arrested and taken into custody for defending herself and saving Lucas's and her son's lives was something she couldn't quite get past.

She desperately wanted to talk to Lucas, but she wasn't about to risk rejection by calling him without some kind of indication he was open to listening.

It was better if she left him alone. That saying, "If he wanted to, he would," was loud and clear in her head, and it made sense, so why push it?

Even from beyond the grave, Leon had managed to steal happiness from her grasp. *That bastard.*

Taking a moment to compose herself, she returned to the office to a contrite Isabel. "I'm so sorry. It was insensitive of me to babble on about that stuff when clearly it was terrible. I've never had anything serious happen to me, and I guess I didn't know how to react."

Kenna accepted the apology. She didn't hold a grudge against the young woman, and it wasn't in her nature to be mean for no reason. "I understand. I'm just trying to move on, and it's hard when people aren't truly interested in knowing my side of things. They want to make assumptions and they are, more times than not, totally wrong."

"I can relate to that," Isabel admitted, sharing sheepishly, "You know that older guy I was seeing?"

"Yeah?"

"He turned out to be married," Isabel said, embarrassed. "I found his social media profile and did a deep dive. Found out he's married with *five* freaking kids. In fact, he celebrated his thirtieth wedding anniversary with 'the love of his life, Melinda' at some fancy restaurant."

"I'm sorry, that's terrible," Kenna commiserated. "How did you confront him?"

"I was shocked at first because I felt so stupid, but then I got mad and I let him have it. He tried to deny it until I showed him the screenshot of his anniversary picture. Then I sent his wife screenshots of all our conversations as well as a naked picture he'd sent me. He might've celebrated his thirtieth, but he likely won't be celebrating any more anniversaries with her after that."

Kenna smothered a chuckle at Isabel's savagery. "That was pretty good. Sounds like he deserves to get kicked to the curb."

"Definitely." Isabel fell silent, admitting, "It hurt to know how easily I'd been fooled, though."

That was something she understood. Leon had charmed her blind. "Sometimes the worst people are the best at hiding their red flags until it's too late. Be thankful that you thought to dig a little into his background. I didn't think to do that, and look what happened to me."

Isabel shuddered, realizing, "Do you think it was that guy stalking you here at the clinic?"

"I do," Kenna answered without a doubt. "He was trying to keep me on edge, and it worked. I started looking over my shoulder constantly, second-guessing everything. He was a master manipulator and very dangerous."

"How did he find you?"

Kenna sighed, shaking her head, still trying to wrap her head around the details. "I was naive to think he wouldn't look for me. I thought I was being so careful by using cash for everything but I should've reestablished myself by my birth name, not Griffin. All he had to do was call up one of his military buddies with a background in intelligence and do a background check on my name, which found my adoption paperwork. Then he just followed me right to Cottonwood because he knew I had nowhere else to go with no money."

"You know, people are always saying privacy is an illusion in today's world, but I never really took it seriously until now," Isabel said, her eyes wide. "Kinda makes you paranoid, huh?"

Kenna didn't want her experience to crush Isabel's innocent verve for life, but Kenna wouldn't be remiss if she hoped Isabel was a little more cautious, especially when dating. "Most people are decent human beings, but it doesn't hurt to be careful," she told Isabel.

Isabel nodded, seeming humbled by Kenna's experience, but frowned, asking, "But wait, why hasn't Lucas wanted to talk to you?"

Kenna fought the tears that sprang to her eyes. "Um, I'm not sure," she admitted. "But whatever is keeping him away must be a good reason."

"Like what?" Isabel scowled. "You literally saved his ass. Seems kinda weak, if you ask me. Maybe you're better off without him if he's going to be a big baby."

Kenna chuckled, shaking her head. "Be that as it may, I'm respecting his decision. No one likes to go where they're unwanted."

"A little awkward, though," Isabel said. "You're being way more cool about this than I would be. I'd have left a few nastygrams on his phone. Did you at least bitch him out for leaving you high and dry when you needed him the most?"

"No," she answered, knowing she wasn't the kind of person to do that, but then something pricked at her—

why wasn't she willing to stand up for herself? She'd done nothing wrong. Sure, on the surface, it was terrible, but seeing as she'd saved their lives, it seemed that bad was leveled out by the good.

Maybe she was trying to find a justification, but the more she thought about it, the more she wanted to yell at Lucas for backing off when he promised he'd never do that to her, for any reason.

Was he no better than every man who'd broken a promise to her?

She didn't have an answer, but maybe it was time to get one.

It'd been a week since Lucas had seen Kenna, and his mood was getting progressively worse, despite the blessing that Noble was home and recovering, no worse for the wear for being plugged with a bullet. Noble didn't seem particularly pressed that he wasn't in the field chasing bad guys as long as he was getting treats.

Given that Noble had attacked without command, he was going to have to go through a training refresh, which Lucas thought was a bunch of bullshit and punishment for a job well done, but he didn't make the rules, so he made the appointment for six weeks out at the K-9 training facility.

But that's not what was eating at Lucas.

Each day seemed gloomier than the last, and he couldn't shake the feeling that he had walked away from the best thing in his life.

Luna remained in her lane, but he felt her judgment—and he didn't blame her. He almost welcomed an ass-chewing by Kenna's sister, but Luna remained professional, if not aloof, and that was more than he deserved.

But what was he supposed to do? He believed in being honest and genuine, and he couldn't go to Kenna with these misgivings, because what if they bloomed into something more malignant? It wasn't fair to Kenna to string her along when he was uncertain.

Yeah, he kept telling himself that, but it didn't work.

Sitting on his porch with a beer, morosely going over all the ways he had failed as a man and as a friend to Kenna, he was surprised to see Becca join him.

Becca approached him with tentative energy, and when he didn't immediately send her back into the house, she sat beside him. "I know you feel I'm not the one qualified to give advice on life decisions, but I feel I can talk a little bit about making decisions that are wrong."

Lucas wasn't in the mood, but maybe a different perspective was what he needed. Since coming to Cottonwood, Becca had seemed to really be taking seriously the chance to change her life, and he would be a jerk not to give her credit for the work she was doing.

Becca took a deep breath—she must realize what a rare occasion this was. "Look, I don't know Kenna, but I do know you. You were always a good brother to Brock, and for a long time, you were really good to me, even when I didn't deserve it. But in all the time you were busy taking care of me and Brock, I never saw you doing things for yourself. I never saw that look of happiness on your face like I saw when you talked about her. That means something. If I'm being honest, I have to admit I was jealous. Not because I thought you and I had a future together, but because it made me miss Brock all the more. I think that I never really dealt with my grief, and now that I'm having this baby, I have to figure out what truly makes me happy and what's still making me sad."

Lucas was stunned. In all the years he'd known Becca, he'd never seen her so vulnerable. Not even when Brock died did she open herself up and share her raw feelings with anyone, turning instead to drugs to numb everything away.

"I don't know how to talk to Kenna about what I'm feeling," he admitted. "There's a lot going on beneath the surface."

"Yeah, like what?"

"You wouldn't understand."

"Try me," she said. "We may have drifted apart, but I still know you pretty well."

Lucas couldn't argue that fact. Like it or not, Becca was the only family he had left, and he'd tried to cut all ties for reasons that seem pretty selfish right now. Hell, maybe he wasn't as great a guy as he'd thought.

"Is it because she killed someone in self-defense?"

"No, it's not that. What she did was incredibly brave, but having a secret like Leon Petticott in her past is pretty big to get your head around. Most people's secrets don't show up and try to murder you. What if there's more guys like that Petticott in her past?"

"Let's be honest, it's highly unlikely. Going off first impressions, the woman doesn't seem like a superspy or something. She got mixed up with a bad guy. It happens. Only she was damn lucky to walk away—and save your ass in the process."

"Okay, okay, I get it," he grumbled, chasing the thought with the rest of his beer.

But Becca had more. "Do you really think she is the kind of person who could just kill someone without it taking a toll? She probably really needs you right now because she's dealing with some big stuff. Probably a lot of guilt, too. I mean, her kid saw her *kill* a man. And that poor kid has already been through a lot, according to what you told me. So I can only imagine how abandoned she must feel right now."

Lucas groaned, hating the feelings curdling his gut. "Yeah, I've been thinking about that. I promised her I wouldn't abandon her, that there was nothing she could say that would make me walk away, and yet here I am keeping my distance. How can I not feel like an asshole?"

Becca didn't pull any punches. "Well, you feel that way because you *are* being an asshole. But the good thing is that you can change that. Call her. Tell her how you feel. Let her know that you were struggling, too, but that your feelings haven't changed."

"But that's just it—I don't know what I'm feeling right now. All I know is that I thought a hiking trip was going to be great, and it turned out to be a nightmare for all of us. My dog almost died and the girl I was falling in love with had to kill a man in self-defense while her son watched. I don't know how to get past that. Maybe we don't."

Becca snorted. "Everyone has issues. Everyone has baggage. You think your baggage is any less heavy for her to carry? Stop being such a baby—man up and figure it out. You can't let a woman like her get away. She's probably the love of your life, and if you're gonna let something like this tear you apart, then you don't deserve a girl like her."

Lucas scowled. "That's pretty judgy coming from you."

Becca shrugged off his comment. "Yeah, but it's no less true. Sometimes the screwups have the best advice because they have lived through their mistakes. Look, you're a good man and you always have been. Don't let this ruin your life."

"That's a little dramatic. It's not going to ruin my life if I don't end up with Kenna." But just saying the words made him feel sick to his stomach. "It's not like we were actually seeing each other yet."

Becca chuckled. "If you could see the way that you looked at her, you would know that what you're doing right now is stupid and something you'll regret for the rest of your life. You're in love with her. I don't care if you've never done anything more than peck each other on the cheek, your heart is with her. You just have to get your brain onboard."

Becca was spitting facts that he couldn't dispute. He didn't know how she was the voice of reason, but it was no less accurate. He was in love with Kenna but ashamed that he had kept his distance. He'd done the very thing he promised he wouldn't. How could he make it up to her? Would she forgive him? Now there were different problems to solve. *Where to start?* Becca understood and promptly offered solutions.

"First, don't show up empty-handed. You better have a beautiful bouquet of flowers and an apology in your mouth and then just lay it on the line. Something tells me she will forgive you."

"How can you be so sure?"

"Because there's nothing I wouldn't forgive Brock for, no matter what he had done, because I loved him. That's how it works. Love is forgiving. Love is supposed to be kind. And sometimes when we need that kindness the most is when we feel we deserve it the least."

Lucas sat in stunned silence, watching as Becca left him to think about what she'd shared. Of all people to humble him, Becca was at the top of that most-unlikely list. He never expected to learn an important life lesson from someone he'd distanced himself from to lessen the stress in his life. Becca was a handful, sure, but they'd been through a lot together, and he never should've bailed on her like he did.

Hell, he was starting to see a distressing pattern in his own behavior that wasn't so attractive. Becca was right; life was messy and sometimes the last thing you wanted to do was the cleanup, but it had to be done.

But as much as he missed Kenna and wanted her in his life, questions still remained that needed answering, and he was more afraid of what Kenna might tell him than he wanted to admit.

Could he forgive her past, no matter what, and move on, or would it always be something stuck in his craw, choking him until he couldn't breathe?

That was the question he couldn't answer.

And it was the question that kept him from picking up the phone to beg for a second chance.

Chapter 26

Luna must've noticed how quiet and withdrawn Kenna was, but to her credit, she didn't press Kenna to talk. It was no great secret why she was depressed. Kenna was trying to process her feelings on her own, but it didn't help that she'd been sleeping poorly. Every night since the incident, she'd been plagued with nightmares, and the fatigue had become a physical thing with cold, spindly fingers that dragged on her reserve of strength, leaving her running on fumes.

But as a single mom, life went on. She didn't have the luxury of marinating in her own misery when she had to make sure Ty was okay. In a sense, having a purpose and focusing on her son made the pain easier to bear, because she was too busy to spend time on the hurt inside her heart.

Kenna went to work, got Ty to day camp and encouraged him to talk in therapy about what'd happened, but she mostly felt like she was walking in a fog.

Maybe she needed therapy, too. *Not a terrible idea*, considering everything she'd been through, but she couldn't bring herself to take that step yet. So much pain simmered beneath that lid that she was afraid if she gave it one stir, it might bubble over.

Add it to the bucket list.

Damn you, Lucas, for bailing on me when I needed you the most.

Lucas hadn't tried to contact her since she was released from federal custody, and it hurt more than she wanted to admit. Even though she was trying desperately to take the high road, possibly for Ty's benefit, there were times when she couldn't escape the bone-deep pain of his leaving.

Can you blame him? You nearly got him killed.

Anyone in their right mind would have run away after going through what they did, but a part of her—the hopeful part of her—had hoped that he would stick to his word and not run away. *But it is what it is*, she reminded herself when the hurt became too much.

But she wasn't prepared for Ty's questions one night after dinner—mostly because she didn't have the answers to her own questions, either.

"Why is Lucas mad at you?" Ty asked, helping Kenna put the dinner dishes away.

Kenna faltered, unsure of how to answer. She didn't want to put words in Lucas's mouth, but how the hell should she know how Lucas felt when he hadn't picked up a damn phone to tell her? "I don't think Lucas is mad. I think he just realized we weren't a good match."

But that was a bald-faced lie, and Kenna swore beneath her breath and tried again, because she'd promised to always be honest with her son going forward. "Actually, Ty, I don't know, but I am not going to chase after someone who has shown me with his actions that he's not interested. Being rejected is a part of life that we have to deal with, and it's no one's fault when situations happen to change the feelings involved."

But Ty wasn't accepting that answer. "If it weren't for you, we might all be dead. Doesn't he understand that Leon was a bad man?"

"I'm sure he knows that," she assured Ty, searching for a better way to explain something she didn't understand, either. "Maybe it was too traumatizing, what happened with Leon. I mean, Noble almost died. We all could've died that day. It's a lot to process. Most people don't have to think about how they might react to a situation like that, but it happened, and well, I don't know, if Lucas isn't interested in sharing his feelings about it, I can't make him."

Ty scowled, declaring, "No. I don't accept that. Lucas was supposed to be better than that."

I know, buddy. Kenna wanted to cry. "Sometimes people disappoint us."

"You need to call him up and tell him what a jerk he is for not being who he pretended to be."

Kenna was stunned by her son's feelings. "I thought you didn't want me dating Lucas," she reminded him. "I would've thought that you would be fine with me and Lucas not being together."

"I don't, but like, you're never going to date again? C'mon, Mom. I'm not that dumb."

"I would never accuse you of being dumb," she assured him. Sometimes Ty was too smart for his own good. "But I understand why you wouldn't want me dating anymore. Seems I'm not so good at it."

"Yeah, not really," he agreed, not cutting her any slack. "But I thought Lucas might be good for you.

He seemed like a decent guy, even if he did like hiking too much."

Kenna winced, hating that Leon had not only stolen Lucas from her but also her son's burgeoning enjoyment of the great outdoors. But she couldn't argue her son's perspective, because she felt the same. "Maybe everything happens for a reason," she murmured, trying to make sense of it all. "We have to focus on the positive—Leon is gone and he can never hurt us again."

"Kill shot, right to the dome," Ty said, horrifying Kenna. He shrugged. "He deserved it."

"Tyler, I'm struggling to hang on to the hope that I haven't permanently scarred you for life with everything you've gone through, but when you make comments like that... I think I might be deluding myself."

He had to know she was being serious, but Ty waved off her worry. "Mom, I'm already in therapy—what more can you do but laugh about it, right? I don't feel bad about Leon. He was going to hurt all of us. He was lying about letting Lucas go. I could tell. You did the right thing, and I'll always think of that moment when my mom was the bravest woman alive."

Tears burned beneath her lids, but she asked, "How'd you know?"

He shrugged. "I just knew."

Kenna digested her son's admission, wondering how her son had become so wise when she was still struggling to make sense of everyday life. "I guess Grandma Nancy was right about you."

Ty cracked a grin. "About me being an old man or something like that?"

"An old soul," she corrected him with a small chuckle.

Ty looked at Kenna, his expression sobering. "So what are you going to do about Lucas? I saw the way you two were looking at each other—all goofy-eyed and gooey. I know what that means. But now you're sad all the time, and that's not right. You deserve to be happy for once, Mom."

Kenna bit back the urge to bawl. She was supposed to be the strong one with all the advice, not her ten-year-old son. *What am I going to do with you, kid?* She sniffed back the tears and nodded. "I will be," she promised, though she had no idea how. "It'll take time, that's all."

"Just call him, Mom," Ty said, as if she was dancing around the most obvious solution. "I bet he's just as sad as you are, and you're both being stubborn."

"Ty, it's not that simple," she said, wishing it were. "It's honestly better this way—a clean break without hard feelings. Someday, when you're older, you'll realize that letting something end naturally is the best way to prevent it from turning sour later."

Ty rolled his eyes at her wisdom. "Sure, Mom." And he left the kitchen to play his video games.

Was Ty right? Was she being stubborn when she ought to pin Lucas down for a simple conversation, if only to put everything on the table?

Maybe, but the truth was, she wasn't sure she could stomach watching Lucas walk away from her twice, and better to heal from his rejection now than let herself fall a little harder for a man who didn't have what it took to stick around.

It was time for Noble's checkup. Lucas had successfully avoided Kenna, but Noble's care took precedence over his feelings. "You had to go and be the hero, didn't you?" he said to Noble, ruffling his fur gently. "Now,

I have no choice but to face the one person I can't stop thinking about."

Noble huffed as if Lucas were being stupid. He felt judged by his dog.

"You're supposed to be on my side, remember?" he said.

Noble licked his chops and looked away.

Solid show of support, bud. Thanks.

But the reality was that it was a small town, and they were bound to run into each other. It was a miracle it hadn't happened yet. "Guess it's time to face the music," he murmured, gesturing for Noble to follow and load up into the vehicle.

Becca had suggested he show up with flowers, but that seemed inappropriate, given he was coming to the vet clinic on official business for Noble's care.

His stomach was in knots, but his expression remained neutral as they walked into the clinic. Then, before Lucas could even say hello, Kenna got up and walked out of the room, disappearing into the back, leaving him with the younger receptionist, Isabel.

Isabel pursed her lips, as if he should've expected that reaction and said, "Checking in Noble?"

"Yes," he answered, hurt that Kenna had bailed the second he walked in. He couldn't have felt more like he had a communicable disease than if he'd walked in dropping bits of flesh from leprosy.

"Great. Exam room two," she said, showing him to the room. "Dr. Mallory will be in shortly."

While Lucas and Noble waited, he couldn't help remembering the first time he'd seen Kenna and how his world had flipped upside down with a glance from those lush, dark brown eyes. He'd been thunderstruck in ways he didn't think were real. Now she couldn't bear to be in the same room with him—and it was his fault.

Dr. Mallory came in, smiling as she saw Noble. "Here's our hero," she said. "How's his wound healing?"

"Seems pretty good to me, but you're the expert," he said. "I know he's enjoying his time off. Lots of treats and fun time."

"That's what I enjoy about vacation, too," the doctor said with a grin before approaching Noble to check the surgical spot. She took a minute to examine Noble carefully but confidently announced, "Healing perfectly. Very good. All right, we'll stick to the antibiotic regime until he's finished with the prescription, and then I'll see you in another two weeks." To Noble, she said, "No chasing bad guys just yet, young man."

Lucas chuckled, and Dr. Mallory left to attend to her next patient. Lucas and Noble exited the exam room, and Lucas found himself hoping Kenna had returned, but it was still only Isabel. Resigned and sharply disappointed, he and Noble left the clinic to head to the station, but his head was elsewhere.

Maybe Becca was right—he needed to show up and make a concentrated effort to resolve this black cloud hanging over them.

But how?

He should've known to never ask the universe openended questions, because sometimes the solution came sidewise.

Before reaching the station, he saw the road blocked by two vehicles smashed into each other. It'd clearly just happened, as emergency services hadn't arrived yet. He flipped on his lights and rolled up on the scene, calling it in as he went.

His heart sank as he recognized Kenna's car. He

jumped from the car and ran to Kenna's vehicle, finding Kenna with a gash on her forehead from slamming into the steering wheel. He gentled his voice, knowing she was going to be disoriented when she opened her eyes. "Kenna, help is coming. Stay with me. You're all right. The ambulance is coming."

Kenna moaned and tried to touch her forehead in confusion. "Did someone hit me?"

Relief flooded Lucas. The fact she was talking and seemed lucid was a good sign. The ambulance siren split the air, and paramedics were there within minutes. The other driver, an elderly man, had run the stoplight and plowed his car into Kenna's, but luckily, his front bumper had missed the driver's side door and instead smashed into the passenger side behind her, and she'd been traveling alone.

Paramedics helped Kenna from her vehicle and checked her out. By this point, she was completely aware of what'd happened, and she groaned when she saw the state of her car. "There's no fixing that," she said with a distressed frown but asked, "Is the other driver okay?"

Lucas wanted to kiss her right then and there, and his reaction shook him to his core. Kenna was the kindest, most gentle and loving person he'd ever known. Even though the other driver had been at fault and totaled her car, her first question was to inquire if they were okay.

How could he be so stupid and think his feelings for her had changed because of what'd happened?

Leon Petticott had abused Kenna and then tried to kill them all. She'd saved their lives—and he'd responded by bailing.

"I'm sorry," he blurted even with the paramedic still there, putting a butterfly bandage on her forehead gash.

Kenna looked at him with confusion. "Sorry for what?"

"For being a jerk." There was no prettying up what needed to be said. Even though this wasn't how he'd envisioned his meal of humble pie, the universe was serving it up hot and ready. "I never should've run the way I did. I was stupid and—"

The paramedic, who seemed intensely uncomfortable, interrupted with a "Can this wait? I'm not done assessing her injuries."

"No, it can't wait," he answered, shaking his head. "I'm sorry, this has to be said now."

Kenna blushed, assuring him, "It's fine. We can talk about this later."

"Nope." He wasn't going to let it go. He'd waited too long as it was. "I should've been there by your side instead of running away. There's no excuse. I pride myself on being a certain kind of person, and I failed myself and you by acting in a way that was shameful. I'm owning my mistake right here and now. I don't want you to ever feel the need to avoid me because things are weird between us."

"I think they're weird between *all* of us now," the paramedic muttered, shooting him a look. "Lucky for you, she's okay." The EMT climbed out of the rig and left them alone, adding to Kenna, "You should follow up with your doctor if you have any persistent pain. Otherwise, if you don't want to go to the hospital, you're free to go."

"Thank you," she murmured, meeting Lucas's gaze. Her expression was guarded, but he could see the hurt lurking in those beautiful eyes and knew that he'd do whatever it took to make sure he was never the cause of that pain ever again. "What are you doing?" she asked.

"Apologizing for the biggest mistake of my life," he answered gravely.

"You didn't make a mistake. I understand why—"

"No, don't let me off the hook so easily. I was a coward. Plain and simple. I own when I screw up, and that's what I did. I screwed up, big-time. I should've been there for you like I said I would be, but I got spooked."

"Almost dying will do that to a person," Kenna replied with a small, wry smile. "I don't hold it against you."

"You should."

"Lucas—"

"No." He held out his hand and helped her from the rig. Her hand in his felt right, as if she were born to be his other half. "I thought I came to Montana for a fresh start, but I'd really run away from my situation with Becca, something I didn't realize was a pattern until I did the same thing to you. That's not the man I want to be. I want to show you that I'm not the running kind anymore. I once told you that there was nothing you could tell me that would change my opinion of you, and now I want to prove it."

"What do you mean?" she asked, suddenly seeming nervous.

Lucas gestured for her to wait for a minute while he cleared leaving the scene with the investigating officer and then helped Kenna to his car.

"You don't have to do this. I can call Luna," she said, distressed. "Seriously, Lucas, I understand why it was too much. I would've probably done the same."

In the privacy of his vehicle, he said, "There's no excuse for why I freaked out, but I can tell you right now, it won't happen again."

The light in her eyes dimmed. "You don't know that,

and my heart can't take the risk. I appreciate that you wanted to make things right between us, but I'm not holding anything against you. Eventually, we can be friends, but I need time for now."

He shook his head, resolute. "I can't be your friend."

She frowned in hurt confusion. "Why not?"

Time to put everything on the line.

"Because I'm in love with you, and that's not going to change, so we're going to sit in this car and figure shit out—even if it takes all day."

Chapter 27

Kenna couldn't stop staring, unable to trust what her ears had heard. "Excuse me? What?" she asked, shocked.

But Lucas wasn't backing down, not for a minute. "I'm in love with you," he repeated without blinking an eye, holding her gaze. "And I know we haven't known each other for that long and all we've done is kiss, but I can't explain it. I just know you're the one for me."

Kenna groaned. "You don't know me—you can't love someone that you don't know."

"Fair enough, so let's put it all on the table. You and me both. Right here, right now."

She stared. "What?"

"Okay, I'll start." He drew a deep breath before launching into a confessional. "My younger brother, Brock, and I were raised by a shitty, abusive father. Becca's father was cut from the same mold. The three of us became tight friends, promising through thick and thin to always have each other's back. I'm not going to lie—for years I thought I was in love with Becca, but she never had eyes for anyone but Brock. Still, we were as close as any family, because as far as we were concerned, we were all the family we needed. But Brock and Becca started partying hard, and I didn't realize how bad the situation was until it was practically too late. I blame myself for not making a bigger effort to help them both."

"You can't help an addict that doesn't want help," she said. "All you can do is love them until they learn to love themselves."

"Yeah, well, by the time I realized how bad things were, Brock was gone. Becca spiraled after that, and it was everything I could do to keep her alive. I couldn't take it anymore. It wasn't just that I was exhausted—I was angry. I was pissed at Becca for enabling and feeding Brock's addiction instead of siding with me to get him clean, but she was struggling, too. I think I placed all my anger on her shoulders because it made it easier to walk away."

"I'm so sorry," she murmured, her heart breaking for him.

"There's only two years between me and Brock, and I wasn't prepared to be a father. I wasn't as present as I should've been. By the time I realized he was in trouble, he was deep in his addiction, and I couldn't seem to reach him. I put myself through the police academy while Brock continued to spiral. I still didn't know how to reach him, and I was angry that he was bringing me down. I gave him ultimatums, which he refused, and we didn't speak off and on—until the night I got the call that he'd OD'd."

Kenna winced, feeling the pain and guilt radiating

from Lucas's body. She wanted to reach out to him but held back. She appreciated his sharing, but he wasn't at fault for his brother's choices. She couldn't blame anyone but herself for the choices she'd made. It was apples to oranges. But she would listen, because it seemed Lucas needed to purge whatever was eating him.

"It's taken me a long time to admit that I was angry at Brock and Becca for throwing their lives away when I spent so much of my life trying to keep them both safe and alive. I wasn't willing to see that they had an addiction that needed treatment, and I blamed Becca for a lot of it, too. It wasn't their fault. I could've been more understanding, more willing to listen—maybe that might've given them the courage they needed to actually seek help. Instead, I just hounded them with constant judgment and disgust, which only made them withdraw more. I was a shitty brother." He hung his head low, bowing beneath the weight of his admission. "And when I came to Cottonwood, I swore I wasn't going to let anyone get close who was determined to drown, because I wasn't going down with them."

"And then you met me."

"Yeah, but I didn't see a woman trying to drown, I saw a woman trying to stay alive. It was the opposite of what I was scared of. You're such an incredible person—you are everything I wish I was—kind, gentle and compassionate, in spite of everything you've been through. That's true strength. What I did was run away from the pain of Brock's death and the hand I had in what happened to him. I couldn't deal with the truth. You slowly made me see where I was wrong."

"How?" she asked, bewildered. "I nearly got you killed."

"It was probably the best thing that ever happened to me."

"Lucas," she said, shaking her head. "I can't believe that."

"On the surface, I know it sounds bonkers. Trust me, I can hear myself saying it and I get your disbelief, but sometimes we have to get shook hard to realize what we've been ignoring for way too long."

As impassioned as Lucas was, she couldn't wrap her brain around what he shared. How could he possibly think he'd been to blame for his brother's addiction and conversely thankful for almost dying on a hiking trip that should've ended with laughter and a few bug bites?

"I've bared my deep, dark secrets in the hopes that you'll feel safe enough to trust me with yours. I want to start a life with you that's a clean slate moving forward. I'm ready to listen to whatever you've got from your past."

Easy to say. Harder to follow through. "I know you have good intentions, but I can't take the risk that you might change your mind." Not to put too fine a point on it, but it was something he'd already done. "We should part as friends. That's probably for the best."

"Do you love me?"

His blunt question took her by surprise. Her heart threatened to stop. She couldn't lie. Her eyes watered. "It doesn't matter how I feel," she answered in a choked whisper, hating that she'd fallen so hard for Lucas when she'd known it was a bad idea from the start. "You're going to end up just another bad decision on my part because I ignored the red flags."

"Fair enough. From your perspective, what are my red flags?"

"I don't want to hurt your feelings," she said.

"This is the time and the place to put it all out there. I can't fix what I don't realize needs fixing if you don't tell me."

She'd never had anyone so openly ready to dive into a deep conversation. Most guys in her life were like, *eww, feelings, run away!* But Lucas wasn't afraid to get his hands dirty. Kenna didn't want to be impressed, but she felt herself slipping.

Was it possible Lucas was the real deal? The man she'd always dreamed of? Strong, compassionate, kind, intelligent—genuinely good—everything all the other men had turned out not to be?

Did she dare give him another chance?

Could her heart take another fall?

Lucas felt Kenna's reluctance to share, but he was honest when he said he was willing to listen. He never wanted Kenna to question his integrity again, and the only way to do that was to put his money where his mouth was.

"Tell me about Ty's father," he prompted, trying to be helpful.

"He's not part of our lives. He signed away his custody rights when Ty was a baby. I haven't seen him since Ty was about six weeks old."

"Okay, that's probably a blessing," he said. "So, if it's not Ty's father that's the skeleton you're trying to hide, what is it? I mean, I already know about Leon Petticott. Is there more to know?"

Kenna's eyes watered. "But that's just it—you don't know everything about Leon. He made me do things I can't even say without wanting to vomit. I don't want anyone to know about that part of my life, much less someone I care about."

"Why not?" he asked, hurting at the open shame in her expression. He softened his voice. "Your secret will be safe with me. I promise to hold whatever darkness you're carrying so you don't have to carry it alone."

"Stop it," she pleaded, her eyes watering. "You say that now, but what happens when you know the full story and you realize how tainted I am?"

"You could never be tainted, but if what you mean is that I'm witness to how deeply you were hurt, then I'll make it my life's work to make sure we heal those wounds together. All I ask is that you let me in."

"It's not that simple," she cried, hiccuping as the tears started to flow unchecked down her cheeks. He gently knuckled the tears away, waiting for her to come to him. "I—I—he made me do things that I didn't want to do, but I didn't have a choice. He threatened to hurt Ty if I didn't do what he told me to."

"You did what you had to in order to protect your son. I would never judge you for that."

"Lucas, you don't know…."

Lucas flashed to something Leon had insinuated on that mountain trail, and he suddenly understood. "Did he make you prostitute yourself?"

Kenna squeezed her eyes shut with shame, jerking a short nod as another wave of mortification rolled off her, shaking her body with silent sobs. She covered her face and refused to look at him. His heart hurt for her pain, but new rage at a dead man made him hunger for the pleasure of watching him die again.

"How can you ever look at me the same?" she asked fearfully, peering at him with red-rimmed eyes.

But Lucas only saw a fearless beauty who somehow managed to remain soft when the world had tried to harden every edge—and he knew how much strength it took to resist that urge to let circumstances change you.

If anything, Kenna had humbled him with her resilience, and he felt nothing but admiration. Kenna mistook his silence for judgment, and she pulled away with a subdued request. "Please, take me home. I have to deal with the insurance paperwork and find a new way to work."

But Lucas wouldn't let another misunderstanding come between them. He purposefully snagged her chin and held her gaze. "You're a blessing in my life, Kenna Proudfoot Griffin, and I stand by my previous promise—nothing about your past could change how I feel about you. *Nothing.*"

She opened her mouth to protest, but he sealed his mouth to hers, their tongues seeking and dancing as he drank in the essence of the woman he wanted to make his wife.

When he came to Cottonwood expecting a fresh start, he hadn't anticipated finding the love of his life, but Kenna had showed up and changed everything he thought he knew about love and how to grow in the face of a challenge rather than run away from anything that made him uncomfortable.

This time, he wasn't shying away from potential challenges but instead agreeing to meet halfway toward a solution. He wanted a partner to grow with, which meant being willing to admit when he was wrong.

Kenna and Ty were his future, and he was ready to embrace whatever that might entail.

He could spend a lifetime kissing her, but making out like wild teens in his squad car wasn't an option. Lucas reluctantly pulled away, falling ever more deeply for this incredible woman, and he wanted to make sure there was no confusion about where he stood.

"Kenna, when the time is right for both of us, I want to marry you. I want to build a life together that includes psycho-free hiking trips, long weekend beach vacations and quiet nights cooking together. I want to be there for Ty as he grows into a man, and I want to show him that his mom means the world to me."

Kenna wiped her eyes. "You're sure? That's a tall order."

"That's going to be the easy part."

"Yeah? And what do you think will be the hard part?"

Lucas cracked a rueful grin. "Convincing Ty to try another hike."

Kenna laughed, agreeing with his dark humor. "That's going to be a struggle, but I'll help you try."

Lucas couldn't resist and brushed a tender kiss across her lips, murmuring, "Is that a yes? Does that sound like something you could get on board with?"

She met his gaze, smiling through the sheen of happy tears. "Yes," she answered with a nod. "I think it all sounds just about perfect."

Lucas's heart threatened to burst, but his giddy smile stretched from ear to ear. "All right then, how about you and Ty come over for dinner tonight and we'll break the news?"

"Actually," she said with a slow, seductive curve of a smile, "I think you and I need to enjoy a little quality time first. I want to know what I'm getting as the future Mrs. Lucas Merritt."

The subtle purr in her tone was like a shot of adrenaline straight to his groin, and suddenly, he wasn't thinking about food at all.

"You hungry now?" he asked, his voice strained.

"Starved."

And that's all Lucas needed as he shoved the car into Drive and maneuvered onto the road as he radioed dispatch with a quick, lusty look at Kenna in his passenger seat, announcing, "Officer Lucas Merritt, clocking out for a long lunch."

"Copy that."

Kenna's throaty laughter tickled him in places he hadn't known existed—but he was eager to find out all the places that made her laugh and moan, until the end of their days together.

Epilogue

"Be careful with that box, Ty," she called out as her son grabbed another box marked Fragile to load into the moving truck. Today she was moving out of her parents' house and moving in with Lucas.

The chill air of late autumn promised a storm later in the day, and clouds moved across the darkening sky as if trying to soak her things before they could get everything safely in the house, but Kenna smiled, unperturbed by the potential storm.

Her sister Sayeh had come home for the weekend to help, seeing as Luna was with Benjamin for a few weeks.

"So you're really doing this?" Sayeh asked, pausing to wipe a bead of sweat from her brow as she took a short break. "You're ready to live with a cop and his dog?"

"I love animals," Kenna responded with a chuckle, "and so does Ty. Yes, I'm definitely doing this." She

couldn't help the smile that followed at the life she had
with Lucas. She couldn't wait to marry him and possibly have more babies. She'd love to give Ty a sibling.
Possibly a sister. She couldn't imagine not having her
sisters with her, and she was determined to make up
for the lost time.

After spilling her awful secret to Lucas, she found
the courage to talk to Luna and Sayeh about what Leon
had forced her to do and how he'd threatened Ty's life
to keep her compliant. Everything she'd been terrified
of happening with her sisters hadn't happened.

Luna had cried, so brokenhearted that Kenna had
been trapped by a monster and she'd had no clue, and
Sayeh had wanted the privilege of murdering Leon herself but settled with setting the FBI's forensic account-
ing department on all his assets. Even though he was
dead, it gave her pleasure to know that his dirty money
had been confiscated.

Luna was all for the future Lucas-and-Kenna wedding and had been pestering her for a date, even though
she and Benjamin had been dating longer and still
hadn't set a date. They were too busy jetting off on
Benjamin's motorcycle, playing weekend warriors in a
new location and enjoying every minute to bother with
wedding stuff.

In truth, Kenna knew Luna just wanted more nieces
and nephews to spoil, and Kenna was okay with that
because, secretly, she was ready to have more kids.

Sayeh, on the other hand, was more reserved but still
supportive. Then again, Sayeh had a lot on her plate.

"I heard the investigation ruled in your favor," Kenna
said while rolling up a glass in newspaper. "How's everyone treating you around the office?"

"Like a pariah. No one likes a snitch," Sayeh said but

shrugged. "I don't care. I'm actually thinking of maybe getting out of the FBI."

That was a shock. "Really? And doing what?"

Sayeh answered, "I don't know, maybe put in for a position with the Bureau of Indian Affairs."

"You would leave New York?"

"For the right job, sure. Besides, I think I've outgrown my interest in what I was doing. I don't get the same thrill from chasing drug dealers across the city that I once did. Seems pointless sometimes. It's like playing whack-a-mole. You take down one, and two more pop up in its place. I want to do something that actually makes a difference."

"And you think working with the BIA would satisfy that itch?" she asked.

"Maybe? Since digging into our parents' deaths, I've discovered a whole world that's operating in the shadows without anyone paying attention to what's going down."

"Like what?" Kenna asked, concerned.

"Indigenous women are disappearing at an alarming rate. Plucked right from the streets and found murdered hours or days later. No one is talking about it—not the media, not law enforcement. Someone needs to be a voice for those who can't speak."

Kenna shuddered. "How awful. Have there been any disappearances from the Macawi Reservation?"

Sayeh nodded with somber sadness. "Yes. It's happening on all the reservations. Got me to thinking… I'd rather chase down traffickers than drug dealers. I think that's how I can make a difference."

Kenna was supportive of anything her sister wanted to do, but she couldn't help but worry. "Sounds really dangerous, though."

Sayeh quipped with a grin, "Everything I do is dangerous. That's the way I like it."

"Good Lord, girl, your adrenaline-junkie ways will be the death of you—or me from a heart attack. Please be careful, whatever you do."

"Don't worry about me, you silly goose. Worry about how Lucas's small house is going to fit all your crap," Sayeh teased, hefting another box. "I hope he knows you have a shopping habit and a Pinterest addiction."

"Oh, he knows," Kenna laughed, watching Sayeh take the box to the truck. Sayeh would never be satisfied with a regular life. She would never find happiness in a quiet evening spent cooking dinner with her partner. Her little sister needed adventure, danger and purpose to feel alive.

And Kenna would do whatever she could to make sure Sayeh knew she always had her support, even if what Sayeh did terrified her.

Thankfully, Sayeh was pretty good at taking care of herself.

In short, her baby sister was a badass and tough as nails, but bullets had a way of leveling the playing field. Kenna would have to trust that Sayeh would always find a way to keep herself safe, otherwise Kenna would never sleep again.

Lucas pulled up, and she instantly smiled. That man did things to her heart that she didn't even know were possible—and she loved every inch of him.

"How's the packing going?" he asked, still dressed in his uniform. Noble hung his head out of the squad car window, interested in everything going on.

"Excellent. Just about finished," Kenna said, accepting a kiss before gesturing to Ty. "My little helper has been an efficient packer since realizing his new room would be bigger than the one here at Grandpa and Auntie Luna's place."

"To be fair, you put him in Mom's old sewing room, and that's no bigger than a glorified closet," Sayeh said, returning for another box like she was born to move freight. The woman was a machine in action. "But hey, glad it was him and not me."

True, they'd had to make do with what was available, but Kenna wouldn't trade her decision to come home for the world.

Everything had worked out perfectly.

Well, maybe not perfectly, but she'd definitely come out on top.

For the first time in her life, Kenna wasn't fearful of the future but excited to see what came next.

Lucas wrapped his arms around her waist and pulled her tight to kiss her neck, murmuring, "You sure you're ready for this next step?"

She answered with a dreamy smile. "I've been waiting my whole life for you, Lucas Merritt—and I can't wait."

For the first time in a long time, the truth didn't hurt, wasn't something she had to hide or be ashamed of— it just felt right.

And she was ready for it all.

* * * * *

*Be sure to look for the next book in
Kimberly Van Meter's Big Sky Justice series,
available soon from Harlequin Romantic Suspense!*

#2227 COLTON'S UNDERCOVER SEDUCTION
The Coltons of New York • by Beth Cornelison

To investigate the Westmore family, rookie cop Eva Colton goes undercover as ladies' man detective Carmine DiRico's wife on a marriage-retreat cruise. As the "marriage" starts feeling alarmingly real, Eva becomes the lone witness to a shipboard murder and the target of a killer determined to silence her...permanently.

#2228 SAVED BY THE TEXAS COWBOY
by Karen Whiddon

When Marissa Noll's former high school sweetheart and now-injured rodeo star Jared Miller returns to Anniversary, Texas, and needs her help with physical therapy, she vows to be professional. After all, she's moved on with her life. But when she starts receiving threats, the coincidental timing makes her wonder if Jared might have something to do with it.

#2229 THE BOUNTY HUNTER'S BABY SEARCH
Sierra's Web • by Tara Taylor Quinn

Haley Carmichael discovers her recently deceased sister had a baby—a baby who's currently missing—and she knows her ex-husband, Paul Wright, is the only one who can help. Reuniting with his ex is the last thing the expert bounty hunter wants, but he isn't willing to risk a child's life, either—and a second chance might help both of them put past demons to rest.

#2230 HUNTED ON THE BAY
by Amber Leigh Williams

Desiree Gardet will change her address, her name, her hair—anything—to leave her past behind, but when fate brings her to sweet and sexy barkeep William Leighton and the small town he calls home, she longs for somewhere to belong more than ever before. Unfortunately, her past has a way of catching up with her no matter what she does, only this time Desiree finds that she isn't alone in the crosshairs.

HARLEQUIN
PLUS

Try the best multimedia subscription service for romance readers like you!

Read, Watch and Play.

Experience the easiest way to get the romance content you crave.

Start your **FREE TRIAL** at
www.harlequinplus.com/freetrial.